HER MAJESTY'S NECROMANCER

MINISTRY OF CURIOSITIES, BOOK #2

C.J. ARCHER

To all my readers, thank you for spending a few hours with my characters. I hope you enjoy my stories as much as I enjoy writing them.

CHAPTER 1

London, autumn 1889

"Put your arm around me," I told Lincoln Fitzroy.

He did, and as with every other time he touched me, my blood responded with a throb and my skin tightened. Imagine how I would react if he touched me with desire and not violence.

I hooked my fingers onto his forearm, dropped so that he suddenly held most of my weight, and spun toward his elbow, uncurling myself from the headlock he contained me in. I stepped away and beamed at him. He scowled in return.

It was the first defensive move he'd taught me, and after two months of daily practice, I'd finally succeeded in getting free from his grip. I probably could have managed it a month ago if my opponent had been an unsuspecting thug and not Lincoln. The element of surprise would work in my favor. It might even be my best weapon. Despite fattening up a little since moving permanently to Lichfield Towers, I was still on the small side. Any man would expect to defeat me if he attacked, but I was better equipped to defend myself now, thanks to Lincoln's training.

"That was adequate." Lincoln—I no longer referred to him as Fitzroy in my head—signaled that the session had ended.

He snatched up his waistcoat from the shrub he'd cast it across and marched off toward the house. As usual, his mood had darkened during my training. No matter how even-tempered he was at the beginning of the three-hour sessions, he always ended them by either snapping at me or not speaking at all, then storming away to his private chambers. It wasn't fair. I hadn't done anything to deserve his terseness. Buoyed by my success, I wasn't going to stand for it any longer.

"Adequate?" I called after him. "I got away from you for the first time, and the only thing you can say is 'adequate?'"

"You left yourself open to another attack. You should have run off."

"Or pulled out the knife hidden up my sleeve, but we weren't practicing combat, only getting free from your headlock."

"Weren't we?" He stopped and I almost ran into him. His face wasn't the least flushed from our exercise, whereas my skin felt damp and hot, despite the cool autumn air. Dusk had settled quickly, but there was enough light left for me to see that his features were set hard. "You have a knife strapped to your forearm?"

"Not at the moment, but I would if I were wandering about the city alone."

He walked off again and I trotted beside him to keep up with his long strides.

"'Well done, Charlie' would have sufficed," I said. "Even a simple 'good' is better than 'adequate.'"

He took the front steps two at a time and reached the door before me. He held it open even though he was entitled to enter first, being my employer. I didn't enter, but stopped in the doorway, blocking his entrance. We stood so close that we were almost touching. I tilted my head to peer up at him. He took a step back, crossed his arms, and watched me through thick black lashes.

"You require praise." He didn't pose it as a question, but I nodded anyway. "Very well. You have improved. You were always fast, but now you understand how to apply what strength you possess to greatest effect, and how to use your size to your advantage."

I smiled.

"Yet your skills are merely adequate. You might be able to escape from the average man who attacks you precisely in the manner we've employed in your training, but that's all. There is much to be done, if you want to fight off an opponent who is smart and strong, or one who uses dirtier tactics."

He waited as I thought through my response. In the end, I decided to focus on the positive. He'd not told me anything I didn't already know anyway. "Thank you. Your praise means a lot to me. However, you have a great deal to learn about being a good teacher. Indeed, I'd say you're merely adequate. For one thing, you need to learn when a student requires praise, and when they need to be told their deficiencies. This was a time for praise." I patted his arm. "Don't worry. You'll learn with time and practice."

His eyes tightened. "You're mocking me."

"I wouldn't dare, sir."

The eyes tightened more as they usually did when I called him sir. It was the only sign he gave that he hated me referring to him in the formal manner, even though he'd told me it was one of two acceptable ways to address him. The other was Mr. Fitzroy, which I usually used. I only said sir when I did indeed want to tease him, something I rarely did. We had few opportunities outside of training to speak. I was always too busy with my maid's duties, and he seemed to go out of his way to avoid me. I never called him Lincoln to his face.

"Same time tomorrow, then," I said, walking ahead of him into the house.

"Charlie."

I stopped, and so did my heart. The uncertainty in his voice intrigued me as much as worried me. He was not usually a hesitant man. "Yes?" I asked, sounding a little breathless.

Several beats passed, in which he continued to watch me from beneath his hooded lids. "Have Seth or Gus bring up tea," he eventually said, before striding across the tiled entrance hall to the stairs. He took those two at a time too and was quickly gone from sight.

I remained at the foot of the staircase, blinking stupidly. Had I said something wrong? He was such a difficult man to read that I wasn't entirely sure if I'd heard uncertainty in his voice at all now. I wish I had the courage to ask him what he'd really wanted, but it felt too awkward between us. Ever since he'd noticed my infatuation with him, as he'd called it, we'd grown more distant. Our only communication involved him giving me orders.

"You look like you've seen a ghost," said Seth, approaching from the service area at the back of the house.

"Oh, I...no. Not today."

He winced. "Apologies. I spoke without thinking."

I smiled. "No ghosts, just a master whom I suspect stops himself from saying the things he really means."

"Death?" He glanced up the staircase. "Are you sure? He always seems to say exactly what he means to me. Then again, I'm not a pretty young woman living under his roof." He winked and grinned.

"Ha! I hardly think that's the problem." On the few occasions when I'd thought Lincoln did see me as a woman, and one he would want to know intimately, he would do or say something that made it clear I was mistaken.

"Perhaps he needs his undergarments mended and is too embarrassed to ask you," Seth said.

"That's more likely. Perhaps it's best not to tell him that you pass on all needlework to me."

Whereas I performed the housekeeping duties, Seth and Gus took care of Lincoln's personal needs—except the mending. They even took turns cleaning his rooms. He'd refused to allow me in them, these last two months, even to deliver his meals. The only other employee at Lichfield was Cook, and between the four of us, we managed to keep the house organized, if not perfectly clean. If Lincoln ever decided to host a dinner party, however, we would be in all sorts of trouble. Fortunately, he disliked company. Our only guests were Ministry of Curiosities committee members, who paid calls from time to time. Mostly it was either General Eastbrooke or Lady Harcourt, and once Lord Marchbank had dinner with Lincoln. Lord Gillingham hadn't come at all in the last two months, thank goodness. I might have been tempted to tip the gravy in his lap if he had.

"Come into the kitchen." Seth beckoned me with a jerk of his head, sending his fair hair tumbling over his forehead. The tousled locks made him look even more boyishly handsome. "We've got a surprise for you."

"For me? Why?"

He didn't answer so I dutifully followed him. Cook and Gus stopped what they were doing and all three men broke into applause.

"What's this for?" I asked, laughing.

"For beating the master, fair 'n' square," said Gus. His broken-toothed grin was so broad that the deep crows' feet wrinkles swallowed the scar at the corner of his right eye.

"You saw?"

"We sometimes watch from a window," Seth said, with a shrug of his broad shoulders.

Cook had disappeared into the adjoining pantry and now emerged with a small round cake. He handed it to me. "Sponge," he announced. "Your favorite."

"You didn't have to bake me something special."

"Didn't. Baked 'em to have tomorrow, but you can eat that one now." He winked one of his lashless eyes at me. "It's only small, so won't spoil dinner."

Gus snorted. "Probably fill her up, the way she eats."

"I eat well now, thank you." Far better than when I first came to Lichfield from the slums. That didn't stop the men

5

from always encouraging me to eat more, however. I suspected I would never eat enough to satisfy them.

Cook returned to the range where his face and bald head soon became shiny from the heat, and I sat at the central table and ate my cake. Gus sat alongside me, mending a broken garden tool, while Seth prepared plates and cutlery for the meal. Doing chores didn't seem to bother them, even though they weren't actually footmen. Perhaps they were bored and the jobs gave them something to do. No one at Lichfield liked to be idle, not even Seth, a gentleman born and bred who must be used to servants doing everything for him. If he resented his lowered position here, he didn't show it. I wasn't yet certain what had led him to work for the ministry. He'd been living in reduced circumstances before Lincoln employed him, and was grateful to have a roof over his head and food in his belly. I understood how he felt. Lichfield Towers was a vast improvement over my previous living quarters of a damp, stinking basement shared with a dozen boys.

A loud knock on the back door echoed through the house. We all stopped what we were doing, but for a moment, no one moved. Who would be making deliveries now?

"I'll get it," Seth said. Gus and I followed him out of curiosity.

We met Lincoln striding along the service corridor. Ragged twists of damp hair framed his face, softening the hard planes but not the sharp gaze that locked with mine. For a moment I thought he was going to order me to remain hidden. My necromancy had made me a target for a madman two months ago, but he was dead now, and few outside the ministry knew what I could do. Nevertheless, I still felt vulnerable, and Lincoln was perhaps aware of it. He did not ask me to leave, however, as Seth opened the door.

The Highgate Cemetery head groundsman stood on the courtyard stoop. The crooked-backed fellow with bulging forearms and long black beard eyed each of us in turn then quickly removed his hat when he spotted Lincoln.

"Good evenin', sir." He bobbed his head and screwed his hat in his hands. "Sorry to bother you, sir."

"You have news, Mr. Tucker?" Lincoln asked.

"Aye, sir. I been keepin' an eye out for them filthy robbers, ever since you reported seein' 'em, sir." Tucker sniffed and wiped his nose on his sleeve. "Ain't seen hide nor hair of 'em until just now."

Seth fell back to allow Lincoln to face the grounds man. "They stole another body?" Lincoln asked.

"Aye, sir, real late this afternoon it were. They took a corpse from the East Cemetery."

"Was it a recent burial?"

"Aye, sir."

"Did you get a look at them?"

"No, sir. I was doin' the rounds, as I do every day since you reported the last robbery, and saw the dug up grave. I came here directly, sir, as you asked."

"Had it definitely been dug up today?"

"Aye, sir. In the last two hours."

Lincoln suddenly walked off and headed back along the corridor. We all stood and watched, as if we expected him to return any moment, but he didn't.

"Thank you, Mr. Tucker," I said to the groundsman. "Mr. Fitzroy is very grateful to you for notifying him immediately. If you'll wait here, Gus will fetch you something to show our employer's appreciation.

Gus didn't move until I elbowed him in the ribs, then he scuttled off, back toward the kitchen.

"Is there anything else you can tell us about the body snatchers?" I asked Mr. Tucker. "Any clues as to their identity?"

"None, miss." He shrugged an apology.

"Who do you think would do such a thing?"

"Doctors. Ungodly fellows, if you ask me." He hawked up a glob of saliva and spat it on the stoop. It would be my job to clear it away. *Ugh.*

"Amen," Seth muttered.

"Most doctors are good men," I said to them both. Just because Dr. Frankenstein, my real father, had proven to be a madman, it didn't mean they all were.

"Ain't nothin' good about a man who wants to chop up a dead body, miss, and they all want to do that, if you ask me."

I shivered. Frankenstein had chopped up bodies, only he hadn't been doing it to understand anatomy. "It's for the advancement of science," I said, shoving aside the awful memories of Frankenstein's monsters. "Their intentions are good, mostly."

Gus returned with something wrapped in a cloth. "Ham," he said as he handed it to Tucker. "That do?" he asked me.

Tucker's face lit up as he accepted it. "I think it will," I said. "Thank you again, Mr. Tucker. Take care."

He bobbed his head as he backed away. I sighed at his glob of spit before closing the door.

"Why do you think Fitzroy walked off like that?" Seth asked.

"He's going to the cemetery." I didn't return to the kitchen, but headed up the service stairs to the second floor. I emerged from the hidden doorway in the corridor and knocked on Lincoln's door.

He opened it and pushed past me. He was dressed in long black coat, boots and gloves but no hat. With his dark hair, he wouldn't need one to blend into the night, and it would only hinder him if he needed to give chase.

"You're going to investigate," I said, trotting after him since he'd not stopped to speak to me. When he didn't respond, I added, "I'd like to come with you."

"No." At least he spoke to me.

"Why not?"

"There's no need."

"I could try to raise a spirit who can help identify—"

He rounded on me. "You are not to use your necromancy, Charlie."

"It's dark now. No one will see."

"No." He strode off again, with more determination in

his step than ever. It was as if he were trying to get far away from me as quickly as possible. "Besides, unless the spirit was present at the time of the robbery, they couldn't have seen anything. They would need to be very recently dead, and not yet crossed to their afterlife, to be of use to us."

I followed at a rapid pace behind him down the stairs. "You would think a cemetery would have a few new ghosts floating about, ones who haven't yet crossed for one reason or another."

"Ghosts that remain to haunt are confined to the place where they died, not where they were buried."

"Yes, thank you, I have read the books in your library on the subject. I only thought..." I sighed. "Never mind. It would seem my necromancy will be of no use to you. How about my keen powers of observation, instead?"

"Stay here. It's warm and there's food."

I pulled a face at his back, only to have to quickly school my features when he glanced over his shoulder. He speared me with that dark gaze of his and then looked forward once more. The man had an uncanny intuition sometimes, which made his lack of empathy all the more baffling.

"There'll also be warmth and food upon my return," I told him, as he opened the front door.

"Do not make me you lock you in your room again." He shut the door before I even had a chance to gasp at his response.

I marched back to the kitchen. "Of all the ill-advised things to say!" I waved away Seth's questioning look and accepted a plate from Gus.

"Did I hear the front door?" Seth asked.

"He's gone out." I spooned peas onto my plate. "To investigate the robbery."

Gus accepted the bowl of peas from me. "What's he expect to find in the dark?"

"P'haps he's expectin' another robbery tonight," Cook said as he placed slices of beef on our plates.

"It's been two months since the last one," I said. "I doubt there'll be two in one night."

We ate and waited patiently for Lincoln to return. Or rather, I ate little and my heart leapt at every noise. The men finished their meals, and mine, then collected the plates.

"Told you the cake would ruin her appetite," Gus said, heading toward the scullery.

I helped with the washing up, then tried to play cards but couldn't concentrate. I lost my share of the dried broad beans we were wagering with and removed myself to the library to wait for Lincoln. From there, I could see the drive and front lawn. The moon glowed faintly behind a bank of clouds and haze, providing little light to see by. I didn't bother with candles or lamps; I knew I wouldn't be able to concentrate on a book. I wasn't sure why I felt anxious. Lincoln was more than capable of taking care of himself. Perhaps it was simply because Lichfield had been so quiet and calm of late that a part of me hadn't expected it to last.

Despite my worry, I must have fallen asleep. I awoke to the sensation of something brushing my cheek. When I opened my eyes, Lincoln crouched in front of me.

"You're awake." He stood and placed his hands behind his back. Someone had lit candles and the light flickered across his cheeks only to be swallowed by his eyes. They seemed blacker than ever.

"What time is it?" I smothered a yawn and uncurled my feet from beneath me.

"Early hours of the morning. You should be in bed."

"So should you. Did you see anything at the cemetery?"

"The robbers didn't return, and it was too dark to look for clues."

"You mean you can't see in the dark? And here I thought you were capable of anything." When he didn't respond, I mumbled an apology. It would seem he didn't like my teasing and I needed to remember that my position at Lichfield was a precarious one. The committee members had wanted me removed from the country altogether. Only Lincoln had wanted me to stay and only then because he thought the nation was safer where he could keep a close eye on me. He could change his mind and have me sent away at any moment. No one would gainsay him.

"Can I get you anything?" I asked, rising. "You must be hungry."

He dismissed my offer with a wave of his hand. I bobbed an awkward curtsy—something I didn't usually do but felt I ought to every now and again—and was about to walk away when his hand on my arm stopped me.

"Charlie." He let me go and resumed his military stance. "I want to apologize for my joke earlier."

"You made a joke? Was I present at the time?"

His jaw hardened. "About locking you up again."

"That was a joke?"

"I can see now that it might not have been taken as such, considering the circumstances under which you were first brought here."

"I see. Thank you. I appreciate you seeking me out to say so."

Without another word, he strode past me and disappeared in the direction of the service area. I sighed and extinguished one of the candles. I grabbed the other to light my way upstairs. I thought about going to him in the kitchen, but since I wasn't sure what to say, perhaps it was best to avoid him. Every conversation we had of late just widened the gap between us. I wished I'd never let him see how much I desired him.

* * *

I WAITED for the rain to stop before heading to the cemetery. It was Saturday, my morning off, and I wanted to visit my adopted mother's grave.

"You haven't been there in two months," Lincoln said when I informed him. He liked to know when I was heading out, and I had no objection to telling him. I had no secrets, and he was simply worried, after what had happened with Frankenstein.

"Then it's high time I go." I fastened the glove at my wrist and pulled on the other. "I do think of her as my mother still, and she did care for me."

He rested his hand on the doorknob then after a brief hesitation, he opened it for me. "Of course."

I half expected him to announce he was coming with me, but he didn't. He seemed to believe that my calling upon my mother was entirely innocent and had nothing to do with looking for clues as to the grave robbers' identities. I was able to fool him easily when I put my mind to it.

The damp air curled the ends of my hair before I'd even reached the estate's gates. My hair had grown a little but it was still short at the back, skimming my collar. I wished it would grow faster.

I quickened my pace and reached the cemetery's grand stone entrance a few minutes later. I headed for my mother's grave and spent a few moments thinking of her as I stared down at her headstone. She might not be my birth mother, but she'd loved me—and I her—when she was alive. She'd been the first spirit I'd raised, and her death had sparked my banishment by the man I'd thought was my father, Anselm Holloway. Yet I couldn't be angry with him—or her. I would never have ended up at Lichfield Towers if my necromancy hadn't been reviled and feared by Holloway. Lichfield was where I belonged. I knew that to my core.

I muttered an apology to Mama about seeking out my real mother, even though I knew I had no reason to feel guilty. I'd made little headway, anyway. None of the orphanages I'd visited so far had records of an adoption by a couple named Holloway. But there were still more orphanages to visit, and I'd not given up hopes of finding something. All I had to go on was my mother's first name—Ellen—and that she was a necromancer like me.

I removed one of my gloves, kissed my fingertips and

touched the headstone. With a sigh, I turned away and went in search of the robbed grave. It was easy to find, as a pile of soil marked the empty hole. I half expected to see Lincoln there, having anticipated my real motive for going to the cemetery, but there was no one about.

The ground near the grave was scuffed up and boot prints headed away from the site. There was nothing special about them. They were of average size and could have belonged to Tucker or one of the other groundsmen.

There were several other graves nearby, all of them quite new. Lincoln was probably right about the spirits not knowing anything. They needed to be present to have seen anything, and according to the books and what I'd already observed, spirits parted from their bodies at the time of death, not at their burial. Besides, the thought of raising the dead chilled me to the bone. I only wanted to do it as a last resort and preferably when I wasn't alone.

But I wasn't alone. A man watched me from beneath a tree, where he leaned on a rake. When he saw that I'd noticed him, he quickly continued to rake up leaves.

"Excuse me," I said as I approached. "Do you work here?"

He turned his back to me and continued raking a patch of earth that was already clear. Well, that was rude.

"My name is Charlotte," I said. "They told me my uncle's grave was robbed last night. Do you know anything about it?"

He nodded.

Since he made no effort to look at me, I skirted his pile of leaves to face him. He was a young man with a port wine birthmark covering one cheek and a squint that made his eyes all but disappear. He removed his cap and scrunched it in his hand.

"Is it your job to tidy this area?"

He nodded into his chest.

"But you weren't here last night when the grave was robbed."

"I was, miss," he mumbled. Thank goodness the man

could talk. I was beginning to think he'd have to write his answers in the dirt.

"But Mr. Tucker didn't mention a witness."

"I didn't see anything, miss."

"That's a shame. I hoped you could tell me something about the men who took the body of my uncle."

He glanced at me then down at the ground again. His hand tightened around the rake handle while the other continued to scrunch the cap. He seemed quite agitated.

"Is there something you want to tell me?"

He nodded.

"Let me see if I understand you. You were here, you know something, but you didn't see anything." I gasped. "Did you *hear* them?"

He nodded again. Finally, I was getting somewhere. Shyness was one thing, but I didn't have all day to coax the answers from him.

"What did you hear?" I prompted.

"One was called Jimmy."

"Anything else?"

He shrugged. "Jimmy said the body was heavy. I mean, your uncle was heavy. Pardon, miss." What little I could see of his face colored. He placed his cap on his head again, pulled the brim down, and resumed raking.

I suspected he had more to say, but his sudden flare of embarrassment had caught his tongue. If I wanted answers, I had to make him feel comfortable. I fetched the empty wheelbarrow from beneath a tree and wheeled it over to him. He stopped raking and actually met my gaze with his own. I smiled gently.

"Did you learn the other man's name?" I asked.

He shook his head.

"Did they say where they were going?"

This time he gave a half-shake before he stopped and frowned. I encouraged him with a broader smile. "They mentioned The Red Lion," he said.

"The one in Kentish Town?"

He shrugged.

"In what context did they speak about it?"

"They had to be there by nine to meet someone for a game of dice."

I tapped my finger on the wheelbarrow handle. The Red Lion tavern in Kentish Town wasn't too far. I knew the area well, having lived in a gang there a few years ago.

"You going to tell the police?" he asked.

"Yes," I lied.

He looked relieved. "I thought about telling them..."

"There's no need for you to do so now," I assured him. "I'll pass on everything you told me."

He dipped his head and continued to rake.

"Thank you," I said. "You've been very helpful." I didn't admonish him for not speaking up to Tucker, Lincoln or the police. Being confronted by authority figures must have been daunting for such a shy man.

I thanked him again and headed out of the cemetery. The costermonger who often parked his cart near the entrance eyed me from beneath the brim of his wide hat. The man's scrutiny unnerved me. I'd been arrested because of him, and he'd told Anselm Holloway where I lived. Both incidents had almost ended badly for me. Those dangers had passed, so why was he taking such an interest in me now?

I hurried home to tell Lincoln about the link to The Red Lion, but decided to wait when I saw Lady Harcourt's carriage at the house. She mustn't be staying long, or the driver would have taken the horses and coach around to the back. Still, I didn't particularly want to see her. While I liked her on the whole, she'd been distant toward me since I'd become a housemaid at Lichfield. Perhaps she felt I'd snubbed her after she offered a similar position to me in her own household—before she'd agreed that banishment from London would be better. Or perhaps she didn't want to associate with a mere maid. I shouldn't be surprised. She ought not to even notice me now. I was privileged to get a nod in greeting from her whenever she visited.

I walked around to the servants' entrance and hung up my coat and hat on the hook inside, by the door. Cook and Gus looked up as I entered the kitchen. Gus greeted me by handing me a tray with teapot and cups.

"Now that you're back, you can serve 'em," he grumbled. "Your pretty face will be more 'preciated than mine."

"Is something wrong?" I asked. "Where's Seth?"

"Out. He gets to run errands and I get stuck here serving tea. It ain't fair."

"Tell that to Death," Cook said with a grunt of laughter.

I carried the tray to the parlor and was just about to enter when I overheard Lady Harcourt mention my name. An eavesdropper hears nothing good, so Mama once told me, but I couldn't help myself. I hugged the wall and inched closer to the doorway.

CHAPTER 2

"She shouldn't be given so much leeway," Lady Harcourt said in her perfect clipped tones.

There was no answer and I couldn't imagine how Lincoln reacted to her comment.

"Charlie's a maid now," Lady Harcourt continued, "and maids do not rearrange furniture."

"I don't care how the furniture is arranged," Lincoln intoned.

"That is not the point. The point is that you are the master, and you set this room up in a certain way. She shouldn't come along and move things as if she were mistress here."

"Lichfield has needed a woman's touch for some time. Charlie is the only woman here. If she wishes to move things, I don't mind."

Lady Harcourt sighed. "You're much too easy on her."

I almost choked on my tongue to stop myself bursting into laughter. If she'd seen the way he drilled me in our training sessions, she wouldn't claim he was easy on me. Indeed, the thought of Lincoln being easy about anything was absurd.

I should have taken advantage of the pause in the conversation to announce tea, but I needed a few moments to compose myself, and by the time I had, she was speaking again.

"You need a wife, Lincoln."

My lips parted in a silent gasp. I leaned forward, straining to hear Lincoln's response. But if he gave one, it wasn't audible from where I stood.

"You think you won't marry, but you will. Lichfield needs a mistress, for one thing."

"There are too many secrets here. A wife would only get in the way."

"Then you need the right wife." Was she offering herself? A woman who already knew ministry secrets? "Besides, you ought to have a companion." Her voice had become velvety thick, throaty.

I held my breath and tried not to picture her draping herself over Lincoln and he holding her, but the image wouldn't go away.

"I have all the company I need," he said.

I breathed again and relaxed my fingers. I didn't realize I'd been clutching the tray so tightly.

"Oh, Lincoln." A swish of silk skirts followed her deep sigh. "What about love?"

"You know I'm not capable of it."

I blinked slowly. This was obviously a conversation they'd had before, and I felt horrid for eavesdropping on their private moment, but I couldn't drag myself away now. I'd wanted to learn more about Lincoln and this seemed to be the only way to do it.

"You are capable," she said. "You simply don't know what it is. Since you've had no love in your life, you don't see it when it's staring you in the face."

"That's enough, Julia."

"No, it's not. You owe it to me to listen." She paused again, perhaps waiting for his response. "You *need* to love and be loved in return, just as much as anyone."

"Julia—"

"Don't deny it. I can see it in the way you protect your family."

His family! I knew Lincoln had parents, both of them still living, but he told me he'd never known them. He'd been raised by General Eastbrooke, to be the leader of the Ministry of Curiosities, since birth, so perhaps she was referring to the general's family. It was likely he thought of them as his own.

"I have no family," Lincoln said in that cool, bland voice of his.

"Oh, my darling—"

"Don't."

Silk rustled and swished. "But Lincoln—"

"It's time you left. There's nothing more to discuss."

I backed up a few steps then walked forward. I was several feet from the parlor door when Lincoln emerged. Our gazes locked and a spark of surprise burned in the depths of his eyes.

"You're back," he said to me.

"I brought tea." I held up the tray, feeling somewhat exposed and terribly guilty. Did he suspect I'd overheard their conversation? It was impossible to tell.

"Lady Harcourt was just leaving."

Lady Harcourt sailed past us as smoothly as a swan on a lake, her head high, her long white neck exposed above the low-cut gown. She didn't meet my gaze, or his, and if it weren't for the vein pulsing in her throat, I would have thought her unperturbed by his dismissal.

"Take the tea back to the kitchen," Lincoln told me. "Have one of the men bring a cup to my rooms."

One of the men, not me.

Lincoln followed Lady Harcourt to the front door, but it opened and shut before he reached it. I slipped back to the kitchen as her carriage drove off.

"Does Mr. Fitzroy have a family?" I asked as I set the tray down on the central table.

Seth had returned and he looked up along with the others

upon my entry. "None that we know of," he said. "He doesn't want tea?"

"Lady H just left."

He formed an O with his lips.

"He wants you to take tea up to his rooms." I removed the extra cup and saucer. "He has parents, I know that much."

"Does he?" Gus asked mildly. "Thought he was spawned by the devil."

"Or the Reaper." Cook grinned as he held out a plate with a scone on it. "That be why he's called Death."

Gus took the plate. "No it ain't. He's called Death because Seth and me saw him dressed in a dark hooded cloak one night, holding a bloody big knife."

"And because he killed a man with the knife," Seth added. "The fellow's head had been almost severed from his body."

I felt the color drain from my face. Seth took my elbow to steady me, but I waved him away. I knew Lincoln had killed people; there was no need for me to be shocked at hearing about another death he was responsible for.

"He knew the fellow," Gus said. He set the plate down gently on the tray yet the *clink* sounded loud in the silence. "Fitzroy called him Mr. Gurry."

"Who was he?" I whispered. Even Cook was listening intently now, the pot on the stove forgotten.

Seth shrugged. "We don't know. We didn't dare ask him."

"The fellow begged Fitzroy not to kill him," Gus said. "He pleaded for his life, but Fitzroy killed him anyway."

"I'll never forget the look on his face when he ordered us to remove the body," Seth went on. He and Gus exchanged bleak glances.

"Was he upset?" I asked, unable to imagine such an expression on Lincoln's face.

"No. He was satisfied."

Satisfied? After killing a man who begged for mercy? The notion left a sour taste in my mouth and set my mind reeling. Surely there had to be an explanation. Lincoln had a reason for everything he did. Didn't he?

Seth picked up the tray but I touched his arm. "I'll take it," I said.

"Are you sure?"

I nodded. "I need to tell him about something I learned at the cemetery."

"He'll probably be in a bad mood. He usually is after Lady H leaves.

I smirked. "He's always in a bad mood of late." I took the tray and steeled myself for an awkward meeting with my master. I had some questions that I wanted answered, and now was as good a time as any to ask them.

* * *

"I ASKED for one of the men to bring up tea." Lincoln blocked my entry to his rooms with his arms crossed over his chest. His shoulders and jaw were rigid. I was a fool to want to speak to him. I knew it, yet I couldn't help myself. I wanted to get a reaction from him. Anything was better than the way he'd been ignoring me of late.

"They're busy." I inched closer, and he had to step aside or risk touching me. He chose to step aside.

I set the tray down on one of the occasional tables near the deep armchair. There was no room to place it on his desk, between the papers, books and another tray laden with dirty dishes.

"Why haven't Seth or Gus collected these yet?" I asked, picking up the breakfast tray.

"They haven't been up."

The sunlight spearing through the window picked out the thin layer of dust on the sill. "They haven't dusted in some time either. And I see your bed hasn't been made."

He shut the door to his bedroom. "They've become lazier with their duties since you became maid. I'll have a word with them."

"Or you could allow me in here to clean."

"You already do enough."

"I don't mind the extra work."

"Seth and Gus will suffice."

"Clearly they don't want to do it. Let me clean for you, Linc—Mr. Fitzroy."

"No. Thank you for the tea. Send up Gus, when you see him."

I set the breakfast tray down again. "Why don't you want me in here? What are you afraid I'll find?"

His lips flattened. He crossed back to the exit and stood with his hand on the doorknob, waiting for me to leave.

I walked over to him and laid my hand over his. His nostrils flared then he quickly withdrew his hand, allowing me to shut the door. I stood in front of it, hands on hips, and regarded him. He stared levelly back.

"Why have you been ignoring me these last two months?" I asked.

"Ignoring you? Hardly."

"You've been pushing me away."

"I didn't want to overwhelm you. I thought it best if the men show you what needs to be done and you make the position your own. Your service has been admirable, Charlie."

His praise caught me off guard. "Thank you. Admirable is much better than adequate."

His eyes narrowed.

"Don't change the subject," I said. "You've been avoiding me for two months except during training, and even then we hardly talk."

"There's nothing to talk about."

"There is! And not only that, you don't join the men after dinner to play cards anymore."

"I rarely did before."

"Now you don't at all. Nor do you join them for tea, or breakfast, as you used to do on occasion. You're avoiding me, Mr. Fitzroy, and I want to know why."

I thought his jaw couldn't harden any more, but it seemed

it could. The muscle bunched tight. I resisted the urge to stroke it until he relaxed again.

He suddenly turned away and strode to the window. He leaned against the frame, crossed his arms again and stared up at the sky. He didn't ask me to leave, and after a moment, his jaw relaxed. I waited until he was ready, even though it stretched my nerves.

"I thought you wouldn't want to be near me after what I did."

I was about to ask him what he meant when it clicked into place. He was referring to paying that man to scare me beneath the bridge. The brute had almost raped me, and Lincoln had saved me by killing him, but that didn't change the fact that he'd set him on me in the first place. I'd been furious with him at the time, but my anger hadn't lasted. Perhaps a scare *had* been the only way to make me stay at Lichfield Towers. Nothing short of a severe fright would have succeeded. Now, I couldn't imagine living anywhere else, but then, I'd been scared of exposing my necromancy and unsure if I could trust Lincoln or the ministry.

"That doesn't make sense," I said, approaching. "I asked you to teach me to defend myself. Why would I do that if I wanted to get away from you?"

"Outside of those times," he said without looking at me. "I thought it best to give you space and time while you settle in, without my interference."

"Perhaps I want your interference." I touched his shoulder but withdrew my hand when he flinched.

The fingers on his right hand curled into the left shirt sleeve at his bicep. "You should hate me."

"I can't."

"You should!" He pushed off from the window frame and stalked past me, bumping my arm as he did so.

"I know I should," I snapped. "But I don't. You're not all bad, Lincoln, no matter what everyone thinks. Or what *you* think, for that matter."

He pulled open the door. "Is that all?"

"Actually, no. I came up here to tell you what I learned at the cemetery about the grave robbers."

Some of the tension left his shoulders. He blinked at me. "You told me you were visiting your mother's grave."

"I did. I just happened upon a helpful groundskeeper afterward. He was in the vicinity when the grave was robbed."

"The one with a birthmark on his face?"

I nodded.

"I spoke to him. He claimed not to have seen anything."

"Did you ask him if he *heard* something?"

"I thought that was implied in my first question."

"For most people, yes, but he was terribly shy and loathe to speak up. I had to be delicate with him. I expect you interrogated him in your usual brutal way."

"I didn't hit him."

"I meant your intimidating brusqueness."

"I find that method works well. As does using my fists."

"On some, but not this man. He was extremely anxious. I can only imagine how overwhelming it must have been for him to be confronted by you."

"You think speaking to you is less overwhelming?"

I held my hands out from my sides. "My physique is considerably less threatening than yours, wouldn't you say?"

"That depends on what you mean by threatening."

I rolled my eyes. "It would seem my technique worked better than yours, anyway."

"On this occasion."

"Do you want to find out what I learned or not?"

"Go on."

"It may not be much, but the robbers spoke about playing dice at The Red Lion. I only know of one Red Lion tavern. It's in Kentish Town."

He tapped his finger on the doorknob. "I know it."

"One of the robbers was named Jimmy. Unfortunately that was all the groundskeeper learned."

"It's more than I discovered."

I waited but he said nothing more. "A simple thank you will suffice. There's no need for any grand praise this time."

"Thank you, Charlie. But next time you plan on interrogating someone, take me with you."

"Since I don't plan on *interrogating* anyone, that won't be necessary."

The corner of his mouth twitched.

"Will you go to The Red Lion and look for Jimmy and his friend?"

He nodded. "I'll go tonight. I need to know for certain whether they're robbing the graves for medical reasons or... something else."

I supposed he would use *his* usual method of interrogation on the boozers. I doubted my methods would work in a tavern full of men anyway.

I crossed over the threshold into the corridor. I decided it was best not to ask him why he'd killed the man named Gurry, or about his family. Things were tense enough between us as it was.

"I'll see you soon for training," I said.

"Not today. I have too much work."

"Oh." I tried not to sound disappointed, but I wasn't successful. "Tomorrow, then."

He nodded. "Thank you, Charlie," he said as I turned to go.

"You've already thanked me."

"Once wasn't enough."

* * *

"Go to bed, Charlie," Gus said when I yawned into my hand of cards for the fourth time. "You've lost the last five rounds."

I tossed the eight of diamonds onto the table. "I'm not tired."

Cook snorted. "Are you waitin' up for Seth or Death?"

"Neither!" I threw another card down.

Gus slid it back to me. "It ain't your turn."

"Might not be back hours yet," Cook said as he added another card to the small pile.

"Do you know who he's seeing?" I asked. "Seth, not Fitzroy." Lincoln had gone to The Red Lion to see if he could learn something about Jimmy and his friend. Seth was visiting the same widow he'd called upon several times over the last few weeks. All he'd told me was that she was wealthy, attractive and restless. I wasn't entirely sure what restless meant, but from the smile he sported every morning after he visited her, I had an inkling.

Gus shrugged. "Lady Harcourt?"

I stared at him. "Surely not."

He shrugged again. "Maybe. Maybe not." He poked the back of my hand of cards, pushing them upright. "You ain't too good at gambling."

"I thought she was still in love with Fitzroy," I muttered.

Cook snorted. "Love ain't got nothin' to do with fu—"

Gus thumped the burly cook on the arm. "None of that talk around the girl."

"She be the one who mentioned love." Cook winked at me.

Gus's face flushed. "I wasn't talking about love. I meant the other…"

"Do you think she expected to marry Fitzroy?" I asked them.

"Fitzroy, marry?" Cook threw down a card and scooped up the pile. "Not him. He ain't the marryin' kind."

"All gentlemen must marry," Gus said in a falsetto toff voice as he shuffled the deck. "It's their duty."

"Does Fitzroy have a family line to continue?" Cook asked. "We don't know who his father be."

Gus shrugged. "Lady H wouldn't marry him anyway. He ain't important enough for the likes of her."

"But she can afford to do what she wants," I said. "She has money and position enough for both of them, surely."

"Those that got much always want more, Charlie." Cook

got up and placed the kettle on the cooking range. "There ain't no such thing as enough."

"Aye," Gus said. "Toffs only want one thing. Power. The more, the better."

"I think that's a little unfair," I said. "Fitzroy's a toff and I wouldn't say he desires power above all else."

"He ain't a real toff. Not like them committee members. He's different."

"He be that," Cook muttered.

I yawned again and Gus gently ordered me to go to bed. "Will you take up a jug of water for Death? Saves me doin' it later."

I waited as he filled a jug from the large pot that sat at the back of the range. It was warm now, but would likely cool by the time Lincoln returned. It was still early, and I doubted he would be back for hours.

With jug in one hand and candlestick in the other, I made my way upstairs. My rooms consisted of a bedroom and small sitting room down the hall from Lincoln's. He hadn't moved me into the servants' quarters in the attic, perhaps because the men slept there and I'd have little privacy. The informality of Lichfield's arrangements was one of the reasons I liked living there.

The door was unlocked so I entered. I was familiar with the layout of Lincoln's rooms, having been held prisoner in them for a few days. I set the jug beside the empty bowl on the washstand in his bedroom. I should cover it with a lid to keep the water as warm as possible. A book wouldn't do—the steam would damage the cover.

I looked over the surface of his desk for something to use, but could only find papers and writing materials. The top drawer contained a blotter, spare ink and quills, but the second drawer was more promising. Beneath some papers was a slate of the kind children used in school. It was just the right size to cover the jug. My fingers touched a thin chain at the back from which the slate could be hung. I couldn't imagine why anyone would want to hang a slab of slate on the wall, but I flipped it over to make sure it wasn't something that could be damaged by steam.

It wasn't a chain for hanging the slate, but a necklace that had been nailed to either side of the wooden frame. A flat, oval pendant dangled from the center. Something had been carved into the pendant and I held the candle closer to see. It was a blue eye, rather crudely rendered.

How curious. Why was it nailed to the back of the slate? Had Lincoln done it or someone else?

The soft click of the door made my heart leap into my throat. I dropped the slate back into the drawer and shut it with my hip, but it was too late. Lincoln stood in the doorway. He held no light and I couldn't see anything more than his silhouette, but I felt the force of his glare nevertheless.

"What are you doing in here?" he growled. "I haven't given you permission to enter."

CHAPTER 3

" *I* 'm not stealing anything!"

"I asked what you were doing." His sharp voice cut through me as savagely as a blade.

"I brought up a jug of warm water, and I didn't want it to cool before you returned so I came out here looking for something to cover it. The steam would damage a book or papers, so I searched through the drawers." I sounded like a rambling simpleton, but he was making me nervous. I swallowed heavily. "I know it looks like I was stealing or sneaking around your rooms, but I wasn't. Well, I *was* looking around, but not for valuables. Gus asked me to bring up the jug. Ask him if you don't believe me! The water will be still warm too, if you want to check."

He left the door open and strode toward me. I backed away and stumbled into a table, causing the lamp on it to wobble. His hand lashed out, reaching past me. He caught the lamp, but the action brought him closer. We were a mere inch apart. His breath fanned my hair. His pitch black eyes searched mine and instead of anger, I saw something else in their depths. Desire. I was certain of it. Almost.

My heart stopped dead in my chest. It didn't dare beat for

fear that any movement might frighten him away. I waited for his kiss.

It never came. He drew in a slow, deep breath then turned away. He pressed his hands to the surface of the desk and lowered his head. My eyes fluttered closed and I tried to will my chest to stop aching. I should have encouraged him instead of remaining still. If only I'd had enough courage to instigate a kiss instead of hoping.

"Lincoln—"

"Next time Gus asks you to do his chores, tell him no."

"Your knuckles," I muttered. "They're cut and bruised."

He crossed his arms, hiding his hands. "I had to interrogate some of the patrons."

I smiled a little, but my heart wasn't in it. "And did your interrogation reveal anything useful?"

"That people don't like to lose at dice," he said, not quite meeting my gaze.

"Let me see your knuckles."

"They're fine."

"You ought to rub a salve onto them. Let me fetch—"

"There's no need," he growled. "Goodnight, Charlie."

Well. So be it. I turned to go, but he called my name softly before I reached the door. I expected him to approach, but he remained near the desk, his arms still folded. He didn't look quite so fierce, however.

"I'm sorry for my temper," he said. "I mean no offence."

I sighed. "I know. I'm used to it now."

The corner of his mouth quirked to the side. "Take the day off tomorrow."

"Your apology was sufficient."

"You've been working hard and haven't had an entire day to yourself since you started."

"That's because I don't know what to do with all that spare time." Although Lincoln paid me a wage every month, I had nothing to spend it on. There was no need for clothing, since I wore a maid's uniform, and the Lichfield library housed enough books to keep me occupied for another year or so.

"Go to the theater," he said. "Or the museum."

"Alone?"

He lifted one shoulder. "You don't like to be alone?"

I'd spent five years feeling utterly alone in the world, despite always being in the company of boys, and ought to be used to it. But I disliked solitude now that I'd found friends. I craved company more than ever. "Not particularly."

He leaned back against the desk and clutched the edge with his hands. He looked down at the rug. "You'd better go."

I slipped out and shut the door. The conversation had been odd, but at least he hadn't remained angry with me. Nor did he seem to assume I was stealing. I would have hated for him to think that I was.

I undressed for bed and drew on my nightgown quickly, as it was a little chilly in my room. By the time I snuggled under the covers, I had three ideas for occupying myself on my day off, none of which involved museums or theaters. First thing in the morning, I would find out where Lady Harcourt lived.

* * *

LADY HARCOURT'S late husband had left her their London residence in his will, while his eldest son from his first marriage inherited the "crumbling country pile," as Seth called it. Seth seemed to know quite a lot about Lady Harcourt, but perhaps that was because he was from a noble family too. I still couldn't imagine she would risk losing Lincoln's respect by secretly dallying with his employee.

I caught an omnibus to Mayfair, where most of England's nobility lived when in London. The streets were lined with five story townhouses, strung together like pale jewels on a necklace. Their tall windows and smooth façades commanded attention. The view from the top floor of Lady Harcourt's residence must take in much of the city.

I wasn't sure whether to knock at the service entrance

below street level or the main front door. In the end, I decided I was calling on the mistress of the house and had every right to use the same door as her other callers. It was answered by a smooth faced butler of indeterminate age. He took in my drab housemaid's attire—minus the apron—and wrinkled his beaky nose.

"Go downstairs. Someone will let you in." He went to close the door, but I stuck my foot through the gap. Unfortunately he didn't notice and the door came down rather hard on it.

"Ow!" I cried. "Bloody hell."

"There'll be none of that language here," he whispered hoarsely. "Be off with you."

"I'm here to see Lady Harcourt and I won't be leaving until I do."

"She's not home."

I sighed. "We both know it's too early for her to be paying calls. Tell her that Miss Charlotte Holloway is here to speak with her about Mr. Fitzroy. She'll agree to see me."

Lincoln's name must have meant something to him. He let me in and indicated I should wait in the entrance hall. While the hall wasn't as grand as that at Lichfield, it was very impressive, with a white marble staircase sweeping up to a balconied second floor where Lady Harcourt appeared a few minutes later. She glanced down at me then dismissed her butler with a small nod.

"Good morning, Charlie," she said as she glided down the stairs. Her black hair hung loose around her shoulders, softening her features and making her look far lovelier than any of her fancy arrangements did. She clutched the edges of a lavender over-gown at her bosom. It was more like a feminine version of a smoking jacket than a dress, and a long white chemise was visible where it remained open below her hand.

"Good morning, my lady." I bobbed a curtsy as she'd shown me to do soon after joining the Lichfield household as a maid. "I'm sorry to have woken you."

"I wasn't asleep, although it is rather early. Is everything all right? Lincoln...?"

"He's well, my lady. I saw him last night." I was about to tell her that his knuckles were a little bruised, but decided that she didn't need to know every detail of ministry business. If she did, she could get the answers from Lincoln himself.

She smiled in relief. "I did think it odd that *you* would be sent if something was wrong."

I arched my brows, but she didn't elaborate.

"You told Millard that you wanted to speak to me about Lincoln," she prompted.

It would seem we were going to have our discussion in the entrance hall. Perhaps I wasn't fit to be invited into the drawing room. So be it. "I wanted to ask you about Mr. Gurry."

Her lips parted and she stared at me. "Gurry?"

"Yes."

"How do you know about him?"

"Seth and Gus."

"Oh. Of course. They were there." She pulled the gown tighter at her throat as if there was a draft. The entrance hall wasn't very warm, but it wasn't cold either and there were no drafts. "And why do you wish to know more about him?"

"They told me Mr. Fitzroy killed him," I said quietly, so that no servants who might be hovering in one of the adjoining rooms could overhear. "Is that true?"

"Yes." She didn't appear to notice my avoidance of her question by asking one of my own.

"But nothing ever came of the murder? Mr. Fitzroy wasn't arrested?"

"Of course not. He's a gentleman, and the matter was an internal ministry one. Lords Marchbank and Gillingham saw that nothing came of it."

It was more than I'd hoped she would say. I decided to press my luck. "How did Mr. Fitzroy know him?"

She adjusted her over-gown again, this time letting the edges part, revealing her lush bosom through the nightgown laces. "Gurry was one of Lincoln's tutors as a child. He taught international politics and relations, I believe."

"Why did Mr. Fitzroy kill him? It would have been some years later, long after Mr. Gurry stopped tutoring him."

"I don't know, and if you want my advice, Charlie, you won't ask him. I did once and he...made it clear to me that he didn't like that I knew about Gurry's death. He'd be furious with us both if he knew you'd come here seeking answers and I'd told you this much."

It begged the question then, why had she told me anything at all? Getting answers from her had seemed rather too easy; although, to be fair, she knew very little. At least I now knew Mr. Gurry had been Lincoln's tutor.

"Thank you, my lady. I appreciate you speaking to me."

She smiled. "I know things haven't been comfortable between us lately. But I hope you understand that I was quite upset when you didn't take up my offer to work for me."

"I'm sorry I offended you. It wasn't my intention." Considering she'd recanted the offer when Lord Marchbank suggested exile was better for me, I didn't feel all that sorry.

"How is Lincoln?" she asked. "I thought he seemed a little distracted yesterday. Does he get enough exercise, do you think?"

"I suspect so." In addition to training me, he also continued with his own exercise routine in the evenings, according to Seth and Gus.

"Good. I do worry about him there, all alone in that big house. I know he has your company, and Seth's," she added quickly, "but I'm not sure it's enough for a man like Lincoln."

From what I could see, Lincoln didn't require much company at all. He seemed content to spend time alone and work. Then again, I didn't know him as well as Lady Harcourt. Perhaps she was right and he ought to get out into society more and befriend his peers.

"I can't picture him attending a ball or soiree," I said, trying hard not to laugh at the image of Lincoln dancing or making idle conversation with toffs.

"What a grand idea!" She beamed, dazzling me with her perfectly white teeth. "A ball would be just the thing."

"Are you sure?"

"Very. He needs to get out of that macabre old house of an evening. It's stifling. I'll see that he's invited to something."

She would be disappointed when he refused, but I smiled anyway. She seemed pleased with her plan.

"Thank you for stopping by, Charlie. Next time, however, go down to the service stairs. Millard is a stickler for the proper order of things."

I gave her a tight smile. "I wouldn't want to upset your butler."

The front door suddenly burst open and a man sauntered inside. He was a little older than me and clearly a gentleman, going by his tailored suit. His tie was askew, his brown hair disheveled, and he wore no hat. Heavy lids drooped over red-rimmed eyes and his slack mouth firmed into a sneer upon seeing Lady Harcourt.

"Good morning, *Mother* dear," he drawled.

Mother? This must be one of her stepsons.

"Andrew." Her tone was as crisp as the morning air outside.

"What are you doing down here, dressed like a harlot?" His gaze slid to the deep V of her bosom, visible through the gap of her unfastened over-gown.

Lady Harcourt clutched the edges of the gown closed. "Miss Holloway has called upon me. She was just leaving."

Andrew regarded me with lazy indifference then dismissed me with a sniff. "You're inviting the riff raff in through the front door now, Mother? How amusing."

She didn't bother with a reply, merely stepping around him. She gave me a forced smile. "Thank you for stopping by, Charlie."

I bobbed a curtsy and left. She shut the door, but not before I heard Andrew tell her to "Be a good mother and keep the noise down" while he slept. What a horrid man.

I thought about Lady Harcourt and her stepson on the

...ed
...y just
...cked a

...joining their
...they all owed
...hey answered his

...ne."
...kled. "Aye, but they

...nd that only riled them more.
...o one wins every round of dice

...devil, the cur," muttered the ma...
...e contents of his glass.
...other, and the second man t...
...ellow-toothed grins.
...players attacked him?" I a...
...ded them full tankards. "That
...n they couldn't prove he cheate...
...d a look about him." The man ...
..."Reminded me of a gypsy I on...
...snake he was, always cheatin...
...him."
A gypsy? That was rather ext...

38

omnibus to Kentish Town. Or, more specifically, th
they'd treated me. Servants were supposed to be inv
maid wasn't worth acknowledging, except when
give her an order. Lady Harcourt hadn't introduce
stepson, and he'd not addressed me at all. None
ered me. I wasn't in the least concerned abo
Harcourt or her family thought. But it did
something that I found more upsetting. Tv
was important to the ministry, a curiosi
necromancy and because I'd lived as a bɾ
when I'd revealed myself to be female, '
of a respected vicar. Now I'd sunk to bɾ
were a step below vicars' daughters.

It was no wonder Lincoln treɑ
since I'd accepted the position of h
except during our training. It waʿ
to keep me in my place and ɾ
station. I'd wanted a friendsʰ
but it was becoming clear nɾ
happen. The only thing mɑ
ing, was keeping their m
too much of a gentlemaɾ
would be enough for m

I was trying to
thoughts when the omnɪ
building of The Red Lion. I caɴ
and he pulled the coach to the curɾ
passenger to alight. I hurried back to the ᴜ
surprised to find that it was open. Only two olɑ
hunkered down at each end of the long polished bar ɪɴ
bookends, their gloved fingers grasping tankards as if they
were anchors in a storm. Both looked around as I entered and
straightened. One even shot me a gap-toothed smile.

"Mornin', miss," he said. "Come join me for drink." He
patted the stool beside him.

I hesitated. A mere two months ago, such an offer from a
grubby, grizzly fellow would send me scurrying out of the

"Weren't that fellow asking about a Jimmy last night too?"
said the man on my left. "Tall cove, black eyes, longish hair."

Lincoln. I affected a gasp. "Oh no! Is my brother in some
sort of trouble, do you think?" Mother will be so upset," I
clicked my tongue and shook my head. "Jimmy is forever
getting himself into difficulty. We were worried he was in
over his head this time and was too ashamed to come home.
My poor, fool of a brother. I must find him before this other
man does."

"You be careful, miss," said the innkeeper. "The black-eɾ
fellow is dangerous. He fought off several fellows. I onɭ
finished cleaning up the mess they made." He piɾ
hessian bag off the floor. Broken glass clinked inside

"How did the fight start?" I asked.

"Some folk didn't take too kindly to him
game of dice, then winning every time. Whe
him money, he said he'd wipe their debts if
questions."

"That sounds like a fair exchange to
One of the old drinkers chu
suspected him of cheating."

"Could they prove it?"

"No," said the innkeeper. "ʌ
They were sure he cheated. ɴ
unless they're weighted."

"Had the luck of the
my right. He downed ʰ

I bought him aɾ
thanked me with ʷ

"So the dicɾ
innkeeper haɾ
very fair wh

"He ha
his nosɾ
eyed
trusɪ

e l'ɑ
g builds.

Many Jimmys conɾ
g away. "It's a common nɑ

black hair and eyes of that kind, but his bearing was that of a gentleman, not a carnival trickster.

"And he was asking too many questions," said the other fellow. "If he just took the money and left, he might have got away with it. But he had to go and ask questions."

"The wrong ones, by the look of it," said the innkeeper. "And of the wrong people."

"Was one of the dice players Jimmy, do you think?"

"P'haps." The innkeeper shrugged then edged away. I got the feeling he was hiding something.

The man on my right slapped his palm down on the counter. "Jimmy Duggan!"

The innkeeper glared at him, but the man was too busy grinning at me to notice.

"Jimmy Duggan was one of the dice players. I remember now. He wouldn't answer the gypsy when he asked if he'd been to the cemetery recently."

Lincoln had asked a direct question like that? Good lord, his interrogation technique was worse than I thought.

"What's he want to know about cemeteries for?" asked the other patron with a shiver.

"Jimmy Duggan is my brother," I told them, sitting forward on the stool. "Do you know where he went after the fight?"

"No," said the innkeeper. "He left with his friend."

"What was his friend's name?"

"Don't know."

"Pete Foster," said the man on my right. He was being particularly helpful so I touched his arm to encourage him. "Do you know him too, miss?"

"No. He must be the one encouraging Jimmy to get up to no good." I pinched the bridge of my nose. "Jimmy's a good fellow, and he wouldn't do anything wrong on purpose. Mother and I are so worried. Is there anything else you can tell me about them? Do they have other friends?"

"They came in alone and left alone." The innkeeper shrugged. "That's all I know."

"Sorry, miss," said the man on my right. "If he stops by again tonight, I'll tell him you were looking for him."

I doubted Jimmy and Pete would be back so soon, now that they knew Lincoln was after them. I thanked him and hopped off the stool. It all seemed rather hopeless. I'd learned their names, but not where to find them. Perhaps Lincoln could do something with the information.

"Did the man with the black eyes leave after Jimmy?" I asked.

They glanced at one another and shrugged. "I didn't see him go," the innkeeper said. "Did you?"

The man beside me shook his head. "Must have slipped out when we weren't looking."

I bought them each another round, thanked them again then left. With a sigh, I trudged up the street. On the one hand, it had been a waste of time visiting The Red Lion, but on the other, I'd at least learned both grave robbers' names. I'd also learned something else just as important—I was capable of getting answers if I asked the right questions in the right way. It was a small victory, but only in the war against myself.

I was close to the destination of my third stop for the day, so I decided to leave luncheon until afterward. I'd passed by the handsome red brick Kentish Town orphanage many times when I lived in a nearby lane, but had taken very little notice of it. It was a large building compared to the others in the wide street, and had perhaps belonged to a wealthy merchant in the days when the land was used for farming. It now looked odd, set back from the street amid a row of joined townhouses, but impressive for the same reason.

It was the third orphanage I'd visited since learning of my adoption, but I went in with high hopes. Kentish Town wasn't too far from Tufnell Park, where my adopted parents had lived. I was shown into a small office with a poorly rendered painting of the queen hanging on the wall. The balding bespectacled man at the desk looked annoyed by the interruption. He steepled his fingers and blinked at me over the top of his glasses. According to the carved wooden plaque on his desk, his name was Mr. Hogan.

"Do you have an appointment?" he asked.

"No, but I hope you can help me anyway."

"You need to make an appointment." He returned to the open ledger on his desk. "I'm very busy."

"I understand, but I'm also very busy and can't come back. Please," I added when he gave no reaction. "I was adopted as a baby by a couple named Holloway—"

He glanced up. "Holloway?"

My heart skid to a halt. "Do you remember them?"

"Of course not." He frowned. "But you're the second person in two days to ask about a baby adopted by them."

"The second? Who was the first?"

He steepled his fingers again. "I received the request by letter, and I won't divulge the name on the correspondence. It's unethical."

"Of course." It must be Lincoln, also trying to discover my real mother's name and if she was still alive. She was, after all, a necromancer too, and the ministry needed to know if she still lived.

"I can tell you what I wrote back, however. There are no records of any babies adopted from here by a Mr. and Mrs. Holloway. Now, if you don't mind..."

"Of course. Thank you for your time, Mr. Hogan."

He was once more looking down at his ledger before I even rose from the chair.

I saw myself out into the windy, grim street and was contemplating whether to catch an omnibus or walk home when I spotted a man watching me from the other side of the road. He quickly walked off, but not before I saw that it was the same man who'd stepped off the omnibus outside The Red Lion along with me. I clutched my reticule tighter and hurried away. I checked over my shoulder every few steps, but he seemed to have gone. Perhaps I was silly to worry. He might simply have business in the area too. My recent experiences had made me over-anxious.

It began to rain when I reached the Lichfield gates. I ran up the drive but was thoroughly wet by the time I entered the house through the back door. Cook was alone in the kitchen and I joined him by the warm range.

"You're wet," he said.

"How observant of you."

"Best change into something dry. Soup'll be ready when you return."

"Are the others about?"

"I'm here," said Seth, striding into the kitchen from the same direction I'd just come. He joined Cook and me at the warm range and stretched his hands over the simmering pot of soup.

"Oi," Cook snarled at us. "You be dripping on my floor."

"It's pouring out there."

"Don't mean you can drip all over my floor."

"I'll wipe it up after I dry off," I said. "Where's Gus?"

Seth grinned. "Getting drenched while he watches those grave robbers."

"What?" I pulled back my hands and rounded on him. "Where?"

"They live in a hovel in Whitechapel. Didn't Death tell you?"

"No, he didn't. When did he learn where they lived?"

"Last night. He followed them to Whitechapel from The Red Lion. They got into a fight—"

"Yes, thank you," I said through a clenched jaw. "I knew *that* part. But bloody Fitzroy didn't tell me he'd discovered where Pete and Jimmy lived."

"Who?"

"The grave robbers. Jimmy Duggan and Pete Foster are their names."

"Is that so? And how do you know that?"

"Never mind." I removed the pins from my hair and shook it out so it would dry faster. "Excuse me, I need to speak with my employer."

"Wait." Seth caught my arm. "How did your visit with

Lady Harcourt go? Did you find out any more about Gurry?"

I glanced at the door to make sure Lincoln wasn't lurking there. I didn't want him knowing I'd visited Lady Harcourt to learn more about him. It felt as wrong as eavesdropping had, and part of me regretted doing it. "I discovered...very little. Nothing about Gurry." It wasn't my place to tell them Lincoln's story. No doubt they'd asked him at the time of Gurry's death and he'd refused to answer. I was still surprised that Lady Harcourt had told me that Gurry had been Lincoln's tutor. It seemed traitorous, considering they'd once been lovers and she still seemed to consider him a friend.

"I met her stepson," I said, compelled to tell him something. "Andrew. He was just entering the house as I was leaving. I think he'd been out all night."

Seth pulled a face. "Andrew Buchanan, a dissolute little waste of space and air. Stay away from him, Charlie. He's no good."

"I doubt I'll see him again."

"Why's he no good?" Cook asked.

Seth sat at the kitchen table and began removing his boots. "He's Lord Harcourt's second son. The eldest is a fine fellow, but keeps to himself on the family estate. Andrew lives at the Mayfair house with his stepmother, and squanders his inheritance on gambling and women."

"Half the bucks in this city do that," Cook said, stirring the soup. "Includin' you."

"Yes, well." Seth cleared his throat. "I make an attempt to pay my debts, at least, while he racks up more without a care. Nor did I injure anyone in my downfall. Except a few hearts, perhaps."

Cook snorted.

"Andrew Buchanan is a malicious gossip who likes to cause trouble," Seth went on. "He rubs people the wrong way and has never worked a day in his life. He thinks women are there for his amusement."

"And you don't?" I asked.

"Of course not! I treat women like delicate flowers."

"Ripe for the pluckin'," Cook added with a chuckle.

Seth glared at him.

"Poor Lady H, being saddled with Andrew," I said. "Can she throw him out?"

"He can't afford to live elsewhere. Besides, I'd say Andrew is a small price to pay for what she gained through the marriage."

Lady Harcourt had been a common schoolmaster's daughter before she'd married Lord Harcourt. It was odd to think the beautiful, refined woman had begun life no better off than me. What different paths we'd taken. Mine had led me to the lowest rungs of society, while hers had raised her to the upper echelons. Yet I didn't envy her. Not anymore.

"I'm going to change," I told them. "I'll be back for soup."

I didn't get to my room, however. I knocked on Lincoln's door, and when he opened it, fixed him with a glare. He eyed me up and down, and I suddenly felt like a bedraggled rat that had crawled out of the sewers.

"Why didn't you tell me you learned where Jimmy and Pete lived?" I asked with more vehemence than I would have if I hadn't felt embarrassed by my appearance.

One of his severe black brows lifted. "How do you know the second man is named Pete?"

"Does that matter?"

"Yes."

"Perhaps Seth told me."

"He didn't know it."

I crossed my arms. "Gus?"

"He's not here." His eyes narrowed but that didn't stop me from receiving the full force of his icy glare. "You went to The Red Lion, didn't you?"

I swallowed. This wasn't how the conversation was meant to go. I wondered if it would be wise to try to run to the safety of my room or if I should battle it out. He would probably catch me before I reached the door, so I chose the latter. But I ought to have known better than try and win against Lincoln.

CHAPTER 4

"*I* did go to The Red Lion," I said, with as much defiance as I could muster in the face of his frostiness. "I was in the vicinity and thought I might be able to find out more information than you did. It seems you discovered more than you let on, however. I would have saved myself the bother if I'd known."

He grunted. "You're cold and wet. You should change before you catch a chill."

"I'm in more danger of catching a chill from your glare than I am from being wet."

His eyes narrowed. "I don't understand."

"Never mind. You're changing the subject. May I come in?"

"No."

I sighed. "The tavern keeper at The Red Lion told me you got into a fight with Jimmy and Pete, last night, over a game of dice. Did you follow them home after that?"

"I did. Questioning them proved futile. They refused to tell me what they were doing, why, or who they worked for."

"Are you sure they're working for someone?"

"They don't seem intelligent enough to know what to do with the bodies, so I think they are. Whoever it is must be paying them very well, because they told me nothing of use.

45

That's why I followed them. Keeping watch will eventually give me the information I need to determine if their master is guilty of something supernatural or not."

"So why didn't you tell me this when you returned last night?"

"I didn't think I had to keep my maid informed of ministry business, since it doesn't concern her."

"Of course it does. If it concerns you—and Seth and Gus—then it concerns me. Besides, I want to help in any way I can."

"You have enough to do here, Charlie. There's no need for you to do more."

I wasn't sure whether I ought to be offended or pleased. Was he trying to protect me or shut me out? "Being your maid is all well and good, but I'd like to do more, on occasion. If Seth and Gus can, then why not me?"

He backed away, but I moved into the open doorway so he couldn't close the door. "You're not ready to do more, Charlie."

"I disagree," I said tightly. "I am ready. I can defend myself, if necessary, and an extra set of eyes might be handy from time to time. Not to mention my necromancy would be useful."

"You wish to use it," he said flatly. "In public view."

"In private, and only when other avenues are closed to us."

He seemed to consider this for a moment, then he said, "I thought you didn't like your power."

"It's not something I wish to advertise, but I've had time to accept it now. I'm not as horrified at myself as I used to be. My father—Anselm Holloway—made me feel little better than a creature from the marshes, but you...you and the others here at Lichfield helped me to see that I'm not something to be abhorred."

"You are certainly not that," he said quietly.

"Then you will let me help?"

"Unlikely."

"Lincoln!"

"That's enough, Charlie," he growled. "Go and change out of your wet clothes. I'll see you later for training."

"Very well, but I would like to point out that it's unfair that you are allowed to be involved in my affairs and I can't be involved in yours."

"I don't understand."

"I know you're trying to find my mother through the orphanages. We could cover more in faster time if we worked together. Or am I not allowed to search for my own mother because it's taboo ministry business?"

"It will be if it becomes too dangerous for you."

I blinked rapidly at him. "But she's *my* mother." It sounded pathetic—small—and I wished I could take it back as soon as I'd said it. He was probably right in that others might try to use her necromancy too, if they knew about it, just as Frankenstein had tried to use me. But who else knew about her—or me, for that matter? There was unlikely to be any danger now.

"You admonish me for trying to keep you safe?" he asked quietly.

"Frankenstein is gone, and Holloway is in jail. Nobody else who knows or, I suspect, cares what I can do."

"We cannot know that for certain. For now, I'd like you to be careful." He went to shut the door, and this time I backed out. There was no point arguing with him anymore.

His words had reminded me of the man I'd seen get off the omnibus—the same man who'd watched me as I left the orphanage. It was probably just a coincidence, however. Nothing untoward had happened, and he'd not even approached me.

I changed my clothes and returned to the kitchen for soup. Poor Gus was still out in the rain, watching Jimmy and Pete, and since I'd been given the day off, Seth acted as scullery maid and washed the dishes.

"You had a morning off yesterday," he complained as he collected bowls. "Why did he give you an entire day today?"

"I'm not sure." I handed him my bowl and gave him a

47

sweet smile. It didn't work and he stormed out of the kitchen like a boy who'd been scolded by his mother.

"Death be gettin' soft, now there's a woman in the house," Cook said.

"Fitzroy, soft?" I laughed. "Hardly. Come and play cards with me until it's time for training to begin."

He sat with me and pulled the deck of cards from his apron pocket. "I thought you'd given up cards," he said as he dealt. "You bein' no good and all."

"I'm not too bad when I concentrate." I checked my cards and placed the queen of hearts on the table. "Did you know that Fitzroy has a set of weighted dice?"

"I do *not* cheat at dice. Or cards."

I spun around as my stomach plunged. Lincoln strode into the kitchen, looking like he wanted to challenge me to a duel for besmirching his reputation. "Why are you always sneaking about? It's grossly unfair."

"I am not sneaking." He flicked his hand and Cook dealt him in. "Why do you think I cheat?"

"The Red Lion barkeep said you won every throw against Jimmy and Pete."

"That was luck."

"Every time? How many throws were there?"

"Twenty-eight." He threw down a card and swept up the pile. He'd won the round.

"Twenty-eight!" I looked to Cook. "In your experience, has anyone ever won twenty-eight throws of dice in a row?"

Cook glanced from me to Lincoln then threw in his entire hand. "I have bread to bake."

"Coward," I muttered.

"It was merely luck, Charlie," Lincoln said again. "Jimmy and Pete couldn't accept that, even after they inspected the dice." He tapped the table with his finger. "Are you playing or arguing?"

I threw down my best card and won the hand.

"You should have discarded something lower," he said. "My card was only a six."

"What if I didn't have anything lower?"

He looked at me like he didn't believe me.

We played for another hour and he won every round except for those where he deliberately discarded a low value card. It was extraordinary. It was as if he could see my hand. I checked the deck during the break we took for him to have his soup, but I couldn't see any markings on them. If he was cheating, it wasn't obvious how he was doing it.

"You're wasting your time," he said. "I do not cheat. I'm merely lucky at cards. And dice." He sounded offended.

I resisted telling him, once again, that nobody was that lucky. "You could make a fortune at those disreputable gambling dens that you gentlemen like to frequent."

He said nothing, merely finished his soup. Seth, who'd rejoined us, laughed softly. "Where do you think we met? It was at one of those disreputable gambling dens. Mr. Fitzroy did indeed win everything that night."

I recalled Seth telling me the story of how he'd been about to wager his body as a last resort when Lincoln had stepped in and won enough to clear Seth's debts. His price had been Seth's service, which he still seemed to be paying off a year later.

"He was banned that night," Seth said, smiling. "For suspected cheating."

"I didn't—"

"Cheat," I finished for Lincoln. "So you keep saying."

He set the bowl down hard on the table. "It's time for your training." I got the feeling he was going to make me work extra hard today. "Change into your exercise clothes and meet me in the ballroom. It's still raining outside and there's more space in there."

I did as told, leaving him behind in the kitchen. I changed into my training attire of loose fitting men's trousers and an oversized shirt. Even without a corset, women's clothing was too restrictive. I would one day have to learn to fight in it, so Lincoln had told me, but not yet.

The ballroom was located on the first level. I rarely

entered the vast, empty room, as there was no need to clean a space that was never used. Besides, it made me a little sad to see such a grand room go to waste. In days past, the three crystal chandeliers would have presided over revelry and scandal, but now they gathered dust. Perhaps Lady Harcourt could convince Lincoln to hold a ball there, one day, to breathe life into the room. Perhaps after he attended a few elsewhere, he'd want to hold one of his own.

Or not. I rather thought he'd prefer to use the room for fighting than dancing.

Lincoln arrived a few minutes after me in his regular clothes of shirt and trousers. He rarely wore a waistcoat or tie around the house, unless he was receiving callers, and he rolled his shirtsleeves up to his elbows for training. If he knew the effect his state of casual undress had on me, he would probably don the full suit. Sometimes it was a marvel that I could learn anything at all.

"I'm ready," I said, planting my feet on the floorboards to steady my stance.

"I thought we'd try something different today." He nodded at the sideboard and table, pushed up against the wall and covered by dust sheets. On the table, a long knife, short one, and a club had been set out. "Choose a weapon."

"I thought you said I wasn't ready for weapons training."

"We have to start at some point. Inspect the weapons and tell me which one you want to use, but do not pick any up."

"Why not?"

"Don't ask questions."

I crossed the room and inspected the three weapons then turned back to him. "Does Cook know—"

I heard the dust cover flap in the moment before something slammed into my back and a set of arms gripped me round the waist from behind. The warning didn't give me enough time to turn to fight my attacker—Seth, I assumed—but I was able to position my arms so that he couldn't pin them too. Then I jabbed my elbow into his ribs, stomped on his toe, and threw back a punch that had the fortune to hit his groin.

He let me go and I spun round. He was too busy clutching himself and going deathly pale to counter my attack, so instead of attempting to gouge his eyes out, I simply placed my hand over his face.

"I win," I told him, fighting to keep my grin under control. "Are you all right?"

He squeaked a response that I didn't understand.

"Sorry," I said. "If you'd come out from your hiding place more quietly, I wouldn't have had time to react."

"Good," Lincoln said, joining us. "But you should have grabbed the weapons while he was incapacitated then fled."

"You said not to pick up the weapons. I was following orders."

"My orders are irrelevant in the event of an attack. You must do everything you can to escape, and if that means defying me, then I give you my permission."

"How gracious of you." I clutched Seth's shoulder. A little color had returned to his cheeks, but he still looked in some pain. "I didn't think I hit you that hard. I couldn't muster as much strength as I would have if I were facing you."

"It's the most sensitive area on the male body," Lincoln said. "Remember that, aim for it, then run if you can. Your primary goal is to get away from your attacker, not defeat him."

Seth rubbed his crotch and finally released his nether regions. "Jesus, Charlie, not so hard next time. I might need it later tonight."

"I am sorry." I bit my lip and glanced at his crotch. "I hope it still works."

"So do I!"

"And so does your lady friend, I'm sure." I grinned and he managed a wobbly smile in return.

"Leave us," Lincoln growled at Seth.

The poor man walked gingerly from the ballroom. "I

haven't done any permanent damage, have I?" I asked Lincoln once Seth was out of earshot.

"Unlikely."

"Good. I'd hate to deprive the ladies of their favorite pastime."

He narrowed his gaze at me.

"That was a joke," I said.

"Young ladies shouldn't make such crude jokes."

"I'm hardly a lady, and that's tame compared to what I used to say." Fitting in with gangs of boys required far cruder jokes than that. "Will you allow me to help you investigate now?"

"I will consider it."

"Are you going to teach me to fight with weapons?"

He shook his head. "That was a ruse to get you near Seth's hiding place. Training will resume as normal. That little exercise proved to me that your reflexes are fast, your hearing excellent, and your nerves steady. But you still need to become stronger and build your repertoire of maneuvers before you learn how to fight with weapons."

He'd rendered me quite speechless. I'd never thought I'd hear such praise from his mouth. I was still basking in his words when he suddenly grabbed me round the waist in almost the same manner that Seth had. Except I'd not had a chance to keep my arms free. With them pinned to my sides, I was only able to stomp on his toe, wriggle and kick backward, failing to connect with his legs.

"That wasn't fair," I said, giving up. If I couldn't beat him, I might as well enjoy the feel of his arms around me.

"No attack is fair. During training, you must always be alert. Whenever you are out walking on your own, you must always be alert."

I tilted my head to peer up at him. His jaw was at my eye level, his throat near my lips. I relaxed against him and rested my head on his shoulder. His long, slow exhale fanned my hair. His heart gave a single, booming thud against my back. It stirred my blood, raised my hopes.

"Lincoln," I whispered into the smooth skin at the base of his throat.

His arms loosened so that I was able to turn into him and place my hands on his chest. His heart beat rapidly, erratically, and even as I registered that, I pushed hard against him with one hand and slammed the palm of my other under his chin, snapping his head back.

I went to step out of his embrace entirely, but he'd already recovered and grasped my forearms. I was facing him now, however, and had the use of my legs. I stomped on his toe then lifted my knee to smash it into his groin, but he knocked it away with his hand. With one arm now free, I swung a punch into his stomach and another at his jaw, but missed.

In the blink of an eye, he'd grabbed both my arms again and lowered me to the floor with more gentleness than an attacker would have. He sat on my thighs and stretched my arms over my head. He gripped both my hands in one of his and planted the other on the floor beside my head.

I bucked and growled in frustration, but I couldn't dislodge him. If he were a real attacker, I'd be in a lot of trouble. It was a stark reminder that I needed to improve.

"You win this round," I muttered.

He didn't release me. The shutters came down over his eyes, leaving only a slit through which he watched me. His face drew close to mine as he leaned forward to lock my hands in his own big one. Heat flared beneath my skin and pulsed through my veins, throbbing in time to my rapidly beating heart. His free hand cupped my cheek. His face lowered until his mouth was near mine. His spicy scent filled me, rendering me stupid. I could think of nothing but this powerful man, and the way I ached for his kiss.

"Sir, when—? Oh." Seth stood in the doorway, his mouth flopped open.

Lincoln sprang to his feet in a blur of movement. "What do you want?" he snapped.

Seth backed out the door. "I'm, er, sorry to interrupt, sir."

"We're training." Lincoln held out his hand to me and I

took it. His touch was clinical and he let me go as soon as I was steady on my feet. "Charlie is yet to defeat some of us."

I searched his face for signs that he was as affected as me by what had almost happened, but there were none. His mouth was set in an uncompromising line, his eyes were black voids. With my heart still in my throat, I walked as steadily as my shaking legs would allow to the table and clutched the edge through the dust cover. With my back to the men, I gasped in air in the hopes my nerves would feel a little less frayed. It didn't work.

"I was going to ask when you wanted me to relieve Gus," Seth said.

"I'll go after dinner," Lincoln said.

"For how long?"

"All night."

"Is that wise, sir? Shouldn't you rest?"

"I'll rest tomorrow. Charlie, training is complete." His footsteps receded from the ballroom and I closed my eyes. So he was going to fight against his feelings and ignore what had almost happened. I didn't know why I expected anything else.

"Are you all right, Charlie?" Seth asked from close behind me.

I nodded.

I thought he'd walked off, but then he sat on the edge of the table beside me. "Will you allow me to give you some advice?"

"If you must."

"Forget him. He's too volatile, too wild."

What an odd thing to say. "He's not an animal."

"Isn't he?" He sighed. "If you'll permit me to speak freely?"

"Of course."

"You crave a family, a place, a home."

"Lichfield is now my home, and you are all my family." My throat clogged with tears that I couldn't swallow past. Why did I want to cry? I hated crying, especially over a man. There were sadder things that deserved tears. Things that had happened to me in the past that had failed to unravel me like this.

"I know," he said softly. "That's why you shouldn't do anything to jeopardize what you have here. He'll throw you out if he feels your presence is making him weaker."

I spun round. "How am I making him weaker?"

"If he develops feelings for you, it makes him vulnerable. Fitzroy hates vulnerability in himself, and if you make him weak..." He shrugged. "He would force you to leave."

I blinked back tears and shook my head. "He wouldn't," I whispered. "He's not that cruel."

"Isn't he? Anyway, like I said, that's *if* he develops feelings for you. I'm not entirely certain he's capable of feeling anything."

"You're wrong about him, Seth."

"Am I? I've known him longer than you."

"That doesn't mean you know him better."

"Women," he muttered as he pushed off. "Moths have more sense. They know to stay away from flames like him."

I watched him go, my heart a dead weight in my chest. How many moths were circling Lincoln's flame? I wished I didn't care so much. It would make life far easier if I could do as Seth wanted and shrug off my feelings. Lincoln certainly seemed capable of shrugging off his desire for me.

* * *

"CHARLIE, WAKE UP." Lincoln's deep voice nestled into my dreams. I wanted to hold it close, sink into its silky depths. His vigorous shaking of my foot was far more disruptive, however.

I sat up and he let my foot go. I rubbed my eyes. "What is it? What's wrong?"

"Come with me."

I blinked at him. He was fully dressed and not looking the

least sleepy. He must have come straight from Jimmy and Pete's place. "Where to?"

"Whitechapel."

"Why?"

"You wanted to help," he said turning away. "Now is your opportunity. Dress in boys' clothes and your cloak."

I scrambled out of bed as he shut the door behind himself and waited in the corridor. I pulled on the boys' clothing I'd worn the day I'd arrived at Lichfield, and a black hooded cloak, gloves and boots. My hair would have to stay loose. I doubted he'd allow me the time to pin it back.

Without word, he strode ahead of me through the darkness. Neither of us needed a light to move around the house at night, but I was slower at descending the stairs than him. It would be just my luck to miss a step and tumble down. He waited for me at the base of the staircase then strode off again, through the kitchen and other service rooms and out the back door. I had to take two steps to his one to keep up.

A horse tethered to a bollard blew foggy air from its nostrils. The light of the glowing moon glinted off the metal stirrup as Lincoln held it for me. I hesitated, but not for more than a heartbeat. If he'd made the decision to invite me to help on a whim, I didn't want him thinking too much about it and risk having him change his mind. I might never get the opportunity again.

I hoisted myself into the saddle and tried to correct my balance. Seth had given me some riding lessons but I wasn't very good; I much preferred to have both feet on solid ground. It felt somewhat more natural and comfortable with trousers on, as I sat astride like a man instead of sidesaddle. I was beginning to think I could get used to riding if I always sat astride—until Lincoln mounted and disrupted my composure.

He sat in front of me and directed me to hold on. I circled my arms around his waist and rested my cheek to his back. Even through the layers of clothing I could feel his warmth and the ridged muscles of his stomach. Every part of him felt taught, but I got no chance to ponder that when the horse moved. It didn't walk or trot, but flew down the drive to the gates. At least it felt like flying, the beast was going that fast. I held on, not only with my hands and arms, but with my thighs and feet too.

"Charlie." Lincoln's hand closed over mine at his stomach. "Relax your fingers. I need to breathe."

"I will relax them when you hold the reins in both hands again."

He let me go and I loosened my grip a little.

"Are your eyes open?"

"Of course." I opened them and was glad that it was too dark to see much. The few working streetlights provided enough light for me to realize we were going exceedingly fast. I resisted the urge to close them again and instead began to count to pass the time and take my mind off the fact I was riding at an alarming speed.

It still seemed like an age before we slowed. We'd reached Whitechapel. I knew the area well, having spent more months in the miserable precinct than I would have liked. Where not a soul was out on the cool, damp night in Highgate, there were signs of life in Whitechapel, from the homeless, huddled on front porches, to the whores offering themselves to us as we passed. Their threadbare clothing looked too thin for the bitter autumn night. I wished I'd brought some coins with me to hand out.

Lincoln ignored them all. We rode through the shadows, down narrow lanes that stank of human wretchedness until we finally came to a stop behind a row of buildings. Lincoln dismounted and opened a gate then led the horse through to a small courtyard. It was empty except for a small cart, a pail and some empty crates. He closed the gate again and held the horse steady while I dismounted without assistance.

"Is this where Jimmy and Pete live?" I asked.

"They live around the corner. This is a butcher's shop. They stole another body earlier this evening, deposited it here and then left."

Bile rose to my throat. "They're selling human meat for people to eat?" Oh God, how horrid.

"I don't think so, but I don't know for certain."

"So you wish me to use my necromancy and find out from one of the body's spirits what it is they plan to do?"

"I doubt the spirits will know. They have probably crossed over and wouldn't have witnessed anything. It's unlikely they even know their bodies have been disturbed."

"Then how can a spirit help? What do you need me for?"

"To raise one so he can frighten them into telling us."

"Oh. That's a good idea. It might work. But you don't think your interrogation techniques are enough to scare them into giving you answers?"

"It wasn't when I questioned them at The Red Lion. They're being paid very well, or being offered another incentive to keep the secret. Either I kill one of them to frighten the other into loosening his tongue, or we frighten them in some other way."

"I think you've made the right choice."

"We shall see."

"Do you think I can manage it? Raising a dead man when his soul has already crossed over, I mean. I've never done it before." I knew from reading Lincoln's books that a necromancer must summon a soul that has crossed over to the afterlife by name then instruct him or her to re-enter a dead body, not necessarily their own. I knew from experience that a soul that has not yet crossed doesn't need to be summoned by name. Simple instructions suffice in that case.

"You can manage it," he assured me.

"But I don't know any names."

"Gordon Moreland Thackery was inscribed on the headstone of the latest victim."

"Oh. Well done." I pulled my cloak tighter around my neck to keep out the chill. "Take me to the body."

"I picked the lock earlier," Lincoln said as he pushed open the door to the butcher's shop. It was as dark as his eyes inside and he didn't light a candle.

"I can't see."

His hand slipped into mine and he led me down a short corridor. The door clicked closed behind me. Our footsteps echoed on the floorboards and my breath sounded loud in the dense silence. He stepped on a creaking board and stopped. He let go of my hand and a sudden surge of fear bubbled inside me. I huddled in closer to him and was relieved when he struck a match and lit a candle that had been placed on a small recessed ledge at the top of a flight of stairs.

He returned the box of matches to his inside coat pocket then, of all the odd things, he fussed with my hood, ensuring it was pulled low over my forehead and around my ears. He was clinical, his gaze not meeting mine.

"Keep warm," he said, lowering his hand.

"Is the body down there?" I whispered.

He nodded. "Charlie?"

"Yes?"

"Prepare yourself."

We went down the steep narrow staircase and Lincoln slid back the bolt on the door at the base and pushed it open. A blast of cool air hit my face and I shivered. He stepped into the room first, blocking my view, but I entered close behind, not wanting to be left alone in the dark corridor.

He raised the candle high and I gasped. Behind the carcasses hanging from hooks suspended from the cool room ceiling was not one human body, but four. And they all stood upright, staring back at me with empty, dead eyes.

CHAPTER 5

"Are you sure they're dead?" I whispered.

"They are. I checked earlier." Lincoln angled himself between the pig carcasses and gripped the arm of one of the human bodies. He swiveled it around to show me the large hook gouged into the back of the cadaver's neck above the jacket collar. The toes of its burial shoes scraped the packed earth floor, and the rest of the clothing hung loosely from the emaciated figure.

My stomach rolled and I pressed a hand over my nose and mouth, although there was no smell in the cool room. "That's vile." They were being treated the same way as the pigs, as if they would be carved up for meat and served to a customer in the shop. At least some dignity had been preserved by keeping the bodies clothed.

"How long do you think they've been in here?" I asked.

"Two months, perhaps. I'd say that's the first one they took, most likely from Highgate the day you spied them." He pointed to the body of a short man on the end. In life, he would have been perhaps thirty or so, but now his flesh was gray and sagging, and much of his hair had fallen out. "The blocks of ice can only preserve them for so long."

I noticed the wooden crates containing ice set around the

small room for the first time. They were stored beneath the marble shelves and behind the feet of the bodies themselves. I pulled my cloak tighter.

"Do Jimmy or Pete work here?" I asked.

"I don't know yet, but tonight was the first time since we began watching them that they visited. They must be associated with this place somehow."

"I wonder what the butcher wants with them." I ventured closer, avoiding looking at the pig carcasses and instead focusing on the last human on the right. His skin wasn't as decayed as the others and he still had most of his hair. He looked only a little older than me. He seemed to be the most recent addition to the cool room, so he must be Gordon Thackery.

"Are you ready?" Lincoln asked.

"No, but I doubt I ever will be." I stood a few feet from Thackery and blew out several breaths. Lincoln set the candle down on a shelf nearby and slid a knife from his sleeve. I wasn't sure why, since I could control the soul after I'd raised it.

"Gordon Moreland Thackery, can you hear me?" My voice echoed around the small room, although I'd kept it low and quiet. "The spirit of Gordon Thackery, I need you to join me here in the world of the living again." When nothing happened, I added, "I summon you."

A white mist coalesced out of the air above the body. It drifted back and forth then formed the shape of Gordon Thackery, right down to the bent nose. "Who're you, and what do you want?"

My pulse quickened. Despite knowing I controlled spirits, raising the dead still alarmed me. "My name is Charlie," I said. "I wish you no ill."

"Then let me return."

"I can't. I need your help. Someone has removed your body from its resting place." I nodded at the dead figure in front of me.

The mist swirled around the body, shimmering in the

candlelight. Its ghostly hand reached for the cheek, but didn't touch. "What is this?" He shot toward me, stopping so close to my face that I had to lean back or be covered in spirit mist. "Have *you* done this?" He raged. "Him?"

Lincoln moved up beside me, his arm touching mine. He couldn't see or hear the spirit, and it must be difficult to follow a one-sided conversation, but he didn't ask me to repeat Gordon Thackery's words. His solid presence was reassuring.

I tried to keep my voice steady, my gaze direct. The spirit was confused and angry at being wrenched from his afterlife. I couldn't blame him for that. Of course, it was also possible that he hadn't been a good man in life.

He can't harm you, Charlie.

"Not us," I told him. "These bodies were dug out of their graves by two men, possibly acting on another's instructions. We don't know why, and despite our best efforts, they won't tell us."

"Have you tried beating the answers out of them?" Gordon asked with a sneer.

I couldn't help smiling. "Yes, but they still kept their secrets. We decided to scare the answers out of them instead."

"How? They can't see me, only you can. Are you a medium?"

"Not precisely. I'm a necromancer."

He frowned. "That word is unfamiliar."

"I summon the dead from the other side and direct them into a body to bring it back to life…in a way."

"Blimey." He looked impressed and horrified in equal measure. It was an improvement over his anger. "A little thing like you can do that? Can he?"

"Not him."

He nodded, thoughtful. "That makes you a very powerful woman."

"So will you help us to stop the men doing this?"

"Do I have a choice?"

I thought about lying, but decided there was no point.

"No. We need you to do this for us, and I can make you. I'm sorry, but I assure you that I will release you afterward."

The mist swept away and circled his body again. Ghostly fingers rubbed his chin. "What if you die before you can release me, Charlie? What happens to my spirit then?"

"I...I don't know." I glanced at Lincoln. If his books didn't specify then it was unlikely he would know. It was a question to ask my real mother—if she was still alive.

"Then you'd better not die," Gordon said.

"I don't plan to."

He studied his body, taking particular interest in the hook in the back of the neck. "Will I feel pain?"

"The dead feel nothing. You'll have a little trouble with controlling your movements at first, but it won't hurt."

"Good." Misty fingers passed through what would have been his hair, as if it were a long held habit from life. "I have a troubled history with pain. I don't like it, you see. A bad state of affairs for a soldier." He laughed without humor. "My weakness did this to me."

"Killed you?" I asked, startled. "I don't understand."

"Opium. Black tar. The soothing bliss of oblivion from the pain caused by my injuries. I got shot in the leg in Burma and couldn't cope with the pain upon my return to London. Opium offered the only relief."

"But you became addicted," I finished. "And your addiction killed you."

"I'd say so. I don't recall much. Out of my mind, you see. Opium does that to a fellow."

Lincoln touched my arm gently. "Ready?" he asked.

I nodded. To the spirit, I said, "The sooner we start, the sooner we can finish. Float into your body."

He looked uncertain, but tried it anyway. Once the entire mist had disappeared, the body jerked on its hook like a recently caught fish. He stretched his fingers and lifted his head. The skin on his face was so pale it almost glowed in the wan light, and the blank eyes made the cavities seem more sunken. Even as I acknowledged each sign of death, the rest of the body came slowly to life, one limb at a time. Gordon's spirit seemed to be testing out each finger, every muscle, seeing if his parts still worked. It was both fascinating and gruesome. I couldn't turn away.

He reached back and unhooked himself. The body crumpled to the floor. Lincoln stepped forward and held out his hand. Gordon hesitated then accepted it. Lincoln helped the dead man to stand and steadied him as he balanced himself on legs that must seem both familiar and not.

"Are you all right?" I asked.

Gordon nodded stiffly. "I feel...nothing." His voice was as brittle as a dry twig. He lifted his trouser leg and studied a raw, pulpy scar on his shin. If I wasn't mistaken, the wound had been caused by a bullet. With a nod of satisfaction, he let the trouser leg go.

"You will regain some strength soon," I told him. "Indeed, you will become very strong. Stronger than you ever were in life."

The muscles on his face twitched, but I couldn't determine what expression he was trying to make. He studied his hands and I worried I'd told him too much. If he'd been an unscrupulous character in life, he might try to kill us.

I kept my distance. As long as I could speak, I could control him.

Lincoln too moved, but not toward the resurrected Thackery. He dodged past me and around the pig carcasses and lunged for the door—the door that was closing fast.

He didn't reach it in time. The door slammed shut and the bolt on the other side slid across.

We were locked in!

Lincoln pushed against the door but it didn't budge. I joined him and pounded on it. "Let us out! There are people in here. Living ones," I added weakly.

Lincoln closed his hands over mine and held them firmly. "He intended to lock us in, Charlie. He won't set us free."

I bit down on my lip and searched the room for another way out. But there were none. We were in a windowless basement, and the only exit was locked from the outside. The cold seeped through to my bones.

"Did you see who did it?" I asked him.

He nodded. "It was Jimmy. I heard his footsteps in the moment before he closed the door."

"I heard nothing."

He rubbed his thumbs over my knuckles then let me go. "We'll be out soon. Step aside." I expected him to try to break the door down, but he turned to Gordon instead. "Have you regained your strength?"

The white face of Gordon folded into a frown. He tried picking up one of the pig carcasses, but dropped it. He tried again and again, each time lifting it a little higher, until the fourth try when he hefted it over his head.

"Ready." His voice held no trace of the rasping brittleness, and his smile was controlled, certain. He almost looked alive, especially since it was rather a nice smile.

Fitzroy and I moved away from the door. Gordon gave it a tentative push, but when it didn't budge, he ran at it and slammed his shoulder into it. If he could feel pain, it would have hurt. He laughed.

"Will a piece of me fall off if I overdo it, do you think?"

I pressed my lips together to stop myself smiling. It seemed inappropriate to laugh at such a joke, particularly when we were in danger of freezing to death if we didn't get out.

Gordon ran at the door again, using his shoulder as a battering ram. The crack of wood splintering and hinges snapping announced his victory. Lincoln helped him finish the task and set the door aside.

I fetched the candle and was about to ask Gordon to go up the stairs first, but Lincoln was already out the door. I held my breath, but heard no sounds of fighting. I followed Gordon out to the small courtyard. Our horse was missing, and so was Lincoln.

I ran to the gate and spotted him running to the end of the lane. He stopped and signaled us to follow. Gordon lumbered ahead of me, stretching out his legs in giant leaps and once, spinning around on light feet. He grinned at me.

"Care to dance, Miss Charlie?"

I smiled politely. "Perhaps later. We're in rather a hurry." Thank goodness it was too dark for him to see how appalled I was by his suggestion. Dancing with a dead man wasn't my idea of a pleasant way to spend an evening.

"This way," Lincoln said, moving off again as soon as we joined him.

I trotted to keep up. Gordon had no such difficulty. "Where are we going?" I asked.

"To visit Jimmy and Pete." We rounded a corner then hurried down a lane that suddenly turned left and stopped at a high wooden fence. The lane was so narrow in that part that I could stretch my arms wide and almost touch the buildings on either side. Something scurried and scratched in the pile of bottles and newspapers in the corner, but otherwise silence surrounded us as thoroughly as the darkness. The candle had blown out when I'd quickened my pace.

Lincoln pressed his ear to a door in the end building. Gordon joined him, and I stepped closer, but both men shook their heads no. I rolled my eyes but neither would have seen.

"They're in there," Lincoln said, rejoining me. "I can hear Jimmy telling Pete how he saw people in the butcher's cool room, and how one of the dead bodies they'd exhumed was walking and talking. He didn't seem to have recognized me. I think he was too distracted by Thackery to notice much else."

He looked to Gordon. Gordon gave a flat smile. "He sounds upset. His friend doesn't believe him. He called him a soft-headed, yellow-bellied little turd. Pardon my language, miss."

"That's quite all right," I said. "Shall we show Pete that Jimmy isn't soft in the head?"

He rubbed his hand through his hair, dragging out a clump by the roots. He frowned at the limp strands as they fell onto the cobbles. "What will you have me say?"

"Make it clear they know who you are," Lincoln said. "Ask

why they dug you up, and who is behind the scheme. If you get a name, find out where he lives. We'll remain out here, hidden."

Lincoln and I kept to the shadows on the far side of the lane. "They can't hurt you, Gordon," I added when he hesitated.

Instead of breaking the door down, he knocked. I wasn't sure that was a good idea, until someone opened the door. With a startled cry, the man on the other side tried to close it again, but Gordon thrust his foot into the gap then forced the door wide. The man inside fell back onto his arse. He scampered across the floor until his back hit a bed, then he slid under it and buried his head beneath his arms.

The second fellow had fallen off a chair at the small table. He gawped up at Gordon, then he too scooted backward. "Get away from me! Devil! Monster!"

"Be quiet," Gordon ordered, stepping into the room. It appeared to be a one-room home with a small cooker, table, one chair and two beds that wouldn't have been long enough for either of the men.

The man under the bed whimpered and curled into a ball. I couldn't see his face, but the other fellow was perhaps my age and was of a sturdy build.

"Who're you?" Gordon asked. "Why did you disturb me?" His voice had taken on a deep harshness that suited the role of dead man come back to life. If I hadn't just seen him dancing along the street, I would have been terrified.

"I'm Pete," said the nearer man. He nodded at his friend under the bed. "That's Jimmy. We didn't mean no harm, sir. Honest to God, we're just poor coves tryin' to make a decent wage. Don't hurt us, sir."

The one under the bed continued to whimper. The occasional word drifted out to me. It sounded like he was praying.

"How does digging up my body make you money?" Gordon asked.

Pete's gulp was so loud I could hear it from outside. "How

is it you're walkin' around again, if you don't mind my askin'?"

"I do mind. I asked you a question." Gordon stepped forward but Pete held his ground. He seemed less afraid now that he realized Gordon wasn't a crazed demon.

"I can't say," Pete said with a shrug. "We ain't allowed to speak to no one about it."

"Is that so?" Gordon glanced around then lifted the bed beneath which Jimmy cowered.

Jimmy screamed.

"Shut up," Gordon growled. He set the bed back down, grabbed a fistful of Jimmy's jacket and dragged him out. He clamped a hand over Jimmy's mouth.

Jimmy gagged and I admit that my stomach somersaulted. I wouldn't want a dead man's hand covering my mouth, even if that hand wasn't as decayed as some of the others in the cold room.

Lincoln touched my back, settling my nerves.

"When I remove my hand," Gordon said to Jimmy, "you will answer my questions. Understand?"

Jimmy nodded, not taking his wide unblinking eyes off Gordon.

"He won't like that we told," Pete warned his friend.

"No one need know," Gordon said. "All I want is answers, then I'll return to my grave."

"You won't hurt us?" Pete asked. "After we tell? You won't drag us down to hell?"

"First of all, I wasn't in hell. Second of all, I don't plan on lingering here. I'd rather return to my afterlife. But I need answers or I can't rest completely. Do your small brains understand that?"

Pete and Jimmy both nodded quickly. Gordon removed his hand and Jimmy spat on the ground then wiped his mouth with his sleeve.

"We don't know why he wanted you," he blurted out before Gordon even posed a question. "He told us which bodies to take and we did it."

"We're just following orders," Pete said, getting to his feet. "It ain't our fault."

Gordon let Jimmy go and the man backed up to his friend. "There ain't much work to be had around here and he paid well," Jimmy said. "Who'd say no to that kind of work? Not us."

"Who's paying you? The butcher?" Gordon asked.

Both men shook their heads. "That's my uncle's shop," Pete said. "He agreed to store the bodies there and let the captain in to see them whenever he wants."

"The captain is the man who paid you?"

Jimmy nodded.

"Does he have a name?"

"It's just Captain to us," Pete said. "We don't know his name, or where he lives, so don't go tryin' to beat the answer out of us."

"Jesus, Pete." Jimmy jabbed his friend in the ribs with his elbow. "Don't go puttin' ideas in his head."

"Is he a ship's captain?" Gordon asked.

Beside me, Lincoln nodded his approval of the question.

"Don't know," Pete said. "Maybe army."

"Nah." Jimmy shook his head. "He didn't bark orders like them army folks do. He were quieter. Didn't speak much, but we didn't see him often. Only when he wanted us to get another body."

"He were real precise, like an army man," Pete said. "Told us exactly where the bodies would be, and how far down they would be buried."

"So he asked for specific bodies? By name?"

"Aye, sir."

Gordon seemed as surprised by that as I was. I wondered if he knew or suspected who the captain was now. He'd mentioned being in the army himself. "What does he look like?"

"Like a toff," Pete said. "Mostly bald, wears spectacles."

"About your height," Jimmy added. "Thin fellow."

"Aside from depositing the bodies in the cool room, what has he done to them?"

Both men shrugged. "Nothing, far as we can tell," Pete said. "My uncle says the captain looks in on 'em sometimes, and asks to be left alone in there. Real strange."

"Is that it?" Gordon asked. "Is there anything more you can tell me? Do you know where to find him? How to contact him?"

"No, sir. He always comes here when he needs us," said Jimmy.

"So what you are going to do now, sir?" Pete asked.

"I leave," Gordon told him. "*You* stop digging up bodies for the captain, or anyone else."

"You going to haunt us if we don't?"

"Yes."

Jimmy gulped. "Thank you, sir. We'll stop right away." He jabbed Pete again.

But Pete's boldness had returned. He stepped forward and peered into Gordon's eyes. I'd trembled the first time I'd stared into a dead man's eyes, but Pete didn't flinch. "Is this some kind of magic trick to get us talkin'? You ain't the first one to ask these questions. Maybe the gypsy put you up to it, or the pigs."

"You've sparked some interest," Gordon said. "Nobody likes a grave robber. You're revolting, depraved."

"Aye, but the pay's good." Pete poked him in the shoulder. "I think you're usin' the night to play tricks on us. We shouldn't have fallen for it, Jimmy. It ain't the body in the cool room come back to haunt us. It's just a cove who's covered his face in chalk—"

Gordon grabbed the finger and wrenched it backward. Bone snapped. Pete cried out and cradled his finger close to his chest.

"Bloody hell!" he screamed. "You're mad!"

"Dead, not mad." Gordon picked up a knife from the table and grinned. The two men backed away. "Since that wasn't enough proof, here's something more definitive." He placed the blade between his teeth and rolled up his left sleeve. He turned his arm over for them to see. "Nothing hidden up there. My arm is real." He splayed his fingers on the table and drove the knife through the back of his hand. I heard the sickening crunch of bone from where I stood outside.

Jimmy and Pete jumped, their huge eyes on Gordon's bloodless hand as he pulled the knife from the flesh. Jimmy crossed himself and blubbered through a prayer again.

"It ain't no trick," Pete said, more to himself than his friend who wasn't listening anyway. He suddenly took off, running out the door and down the lane.

Lincoln could have stopped him, but he let him go. "He's told us all he knows," he said.

"What if he runs to tell the captain?" I asked.

"He claims not to know where to find him. I doubt he'd be believed anyway."

"Come back!" Jimmy screamed. "Don't leave me with this demon!"

"I'm not a demon," Gordon told him mildly. "I'm a resurrected dead man."

"Jesus," Jimmy spluttered.

"Not Jesus. Gordon Thackery." He strolled out of the room and wiggled his fingers in a wave at the blubbering Jimmy. "Be sure to remember my name if you tattle any tales."

Jimmy slammed the door shut.

None of us spoke as we left the lane behind and headed back to the butcher's shop. We spotted Lincoln's horse being led away by a stooped man in a cloak. Lincoln intercepted him before the man even realized he'd crept close. A few words were all it took for the thief to scamper off.

"What happens now?" Gordon asked me.

"I'll release you so you can return to your afterlife."

Lincoln rejoined us, leading the horse. The jittery animal balked and tried to push Lincoln to the side, but he calmed it with a hand to its neck and some quietly spoken words. Its ears flicked back and forth and the nostrils flared, but it didn't shy away again.

"He smells death on me," Gordon said. "I know horses well, and I know when they're afraid. He's afraid of me." He sighed. "It's too bad. I would have enjoyed one last ride while I was here."

"Perhaps I should release you now," I said. "It would be for the best."

When he didn't answer, I grew worried that he was going to protest and demand we let him stay. But finally he nodded. "It has been rather fun, but it must end. Pity."

"Not yet." Lincoln indicated the gate to the butcher's yard and Gordon swung it open.

"You have another task for him?" I was about to warn him of the perils of allowing a dead man to walk the streets for any length of time, when he shook his head.

"A final journey. Including yours, Thackery, we have four bodies to transport back to the cemetery. The cart won't take them all."

"Of course," Gordon said. "But you're not going to notify the police? Those two blighters should be put in prison."

"I'll take care of it in the morning."

Gordon seemed satisfied with that answer, but I knew Lincoln better and suspected he wasn't going to notify the police but try to learn more about the captain and the reason behind the thefts.

"It's good of you return them," Gordon said, as he pushed open the door to the butcher's shop.

Lincoln found equipment to hitch up the horse in a store-room, while Gordon brought up the bodies. They piled them onto the cart and I sat alongside Lincoln as he drove. Our pace was slow enough that Gordon was able to walk. We must have looked an odd sight, with limbs hanging out of the cart, but the streets were entirely empty now.

It had begun to rain again. I hunched into my cloak, drawing the hood close to my face. Neither Lincoln nor Gordon seemed to mind the chill and rain. Indeed, Gordon lifted his face to the sky and opened his mouth like a child catching rain drops. I smiled. It was the first time I'd felt comfortable in the presence of a body I'd resurrected. I didn't fear Gordon at all.

"You must have been a good man when you were alive," I told him. "I think I would like to have known you."

He snapped his mouth shut and stared at me. Despite the hollowness of the sockets and the emptiness of his eyes, I didn't feel as if I were conversing with a dead man. "Thank you, Miss Charlie. I appreciate the sentiment, but I doubt you would have liked my company. Perhaps before my injury, but not after."

"The opium changed you," I said quietly.

"The cure for the pain was no cure at all. I wish someone had warned me before I tried it. It's like a beautiful lover. Beguiling and tempting at first, then it gets greedy, always wanting more. By the time you realize it's ultimately bad for you, it's too late. It already has its claws in too deep."

I knew little about opium addiction. There were houses where you could smoke it, but I'd never been inside one. The people who came and went from them were sometimes respectable members of society, many of them injured soldiers searching for relief from painful injuries. I'd never met an addict. From what I'd been told, opium rendered the addicts useless for hours after smoking it. They lost their lives to it, figuratively as well as literally.

"Do you know the man Jimmy and Pete referred to as the captain?" Lincoln asked.

"I think so," Gordon said. "If it's him, then I can't say for certain if he is, or was, an army man. I met him *after* I was invalided out. I use the term 'met' loosely."

"You were suffering the effects of opium at the time," Lincoln suggested.

Gordon nodded. "He would visit me, talk to me, but my memory fails me and I can't recall what was discussed or his name."

"Drat," I muttered.

"I do remember that he gave me something."

"An object?" Lincoln asked.

"A liquid. He would spoon feed it to me."

"How odd," I said. "Was it water, perhaps? Soup?"

"That sounds like the act of a good Samaritan." Gordon's dry, flaky lips flattened. "That doesn't fit with what we know of our grave robber."

"No," I said quietly. "You're right. Do you think he was poisoning you?"

"Possibly. But why? The addiction would have got me anyway."

"Did he visit you at the opium house or at home?" Lincoln asked.

"The opium den. I rarely went home. I lived and died among strangers who profited from my weakness. It's not a noble way to be, Miss Charlie. I hope you never have to see the miserable souls wasting away their lives on the stuff."

"Where is the house?" Lincoln asked, abruptly.

"Lower Pell Lane, off Ratcliffe Highway, at the docks."

"I know it."

I blinked at Lincoln. "How do you know it?"

"I've been there. A Chinaman named Lee is the so-called pharmacist."

Gordon snorted. "He's no pharmacist."

Lincoln didn't elaborate and I doubted I'd get further information out of him. That didn't mean I wouldn't try at a later time.

"What about them?" I pointed to the bodies behind us, squashed ungainly into the back of the small cart. "Do you recognize them from Mr. Lee's den?"

Gordon shook his head. "That doesn't mean they didn't frequent that hell too. I wouldn't have noticed the queen if she'd wandered in wearing a crown."

We pulled up the cemetery gates and deposited the bodies where the groundskeepers couldn't fail to see them in the morning. "I do hope they put the right body back in the right grave," I said, stepping back to inspect our handiwork.

"The extent of the decay on each should help them determine the order in which they were dug up." Lincoln passed his hand over the eyes of one of the corpses to close them. "Thackery?"

Gordon lay down on his back, hands by his sides. He looked quite peaceful. "Ready," he said.

I knelt and touched his hand. It wasn't necessary to do so to release the spirit, but I wanted to give him a connection to the living world right to the end. "Thank you, Gordon. You've been very helpful. Rest easy, now. Return to your afterlife. You are released."

White mist floated up and the now empty body subsided as if it had expelled a deep breath. I closed its eyes then gave the spirit of Gordon Thackery a small smile.

He returned it. "If you ever require my services again, Miss Charlie, please summon me. I'd be happy to help." He waved then his spirit mist dispersed and blew away.

"He's gone," I said rising.

Lincoln held his hand out to me to assist me up into the cart. "Are you all right?"

"Yes." My answer surprised me. I *was* all right. The experience hadn't been awful at all.

Lincoln climbed up beside me and urged the horse forward.

"Let's hope they stay buried this time," I said, looking back at the bodies. "Do you think the captain will try to retrieve them again?"

"Perhaps. I do know that he'll need to find other diggers. I doubt Jimmy and Pete will venture near the cemetery again for some time."

"Gordon did perform rather well." I chuckled, but it ended with a yawn.

"So did you," he said quietly.

I glanced at him, but he was looking directly ahead. It was difficult to tell what he was thinking at the best of times, but the darkness made it impossible. "Does this mean you'll allow me to do more work for the ministry?"

"If and when required."

"I suppose this makes me Her Majesty's Necromancer." I

laughed softly. "It sounds rather grand, if one ignores the macabre nature of it. I wonder what official positions receive? A medal? A sash?"

"A warm fire and soup."

"I prefer hot chocolate."

"I'll make you a cup when we get home."

I rested my head against his shoulder. To my surprise, he neither moved away nor tensed. I closed my eyes and stifled another yawn. "I wonder how many spirits my mother—my real mother, that is—raised."

"We may never know."

"If she's still alive, we can ask her."

He was silent, and I suspected he was trying to decide whether to warn me not to hold out hope of her being alive. I wasn't a fool. I knew she was most likely dead, after all this time, but I still wanted to find out for certain.

"We should make a list of all the London orphanages and cross off the ones we've both visited to save time. We can begin with the one in Kentish Town."

"That was next on my list."

I jerked upright. "But you already wrote to the administrator there and asked about my adoption."

"No I didn't."

"But you told me you had."

"You never mentioned which orphanage you'd just returned from. I assumed it was the one in Clerkenwell where I'd last been. I haven't written letters."

"It wasn't Clerkenwell," I whispered. "The administrator of the Kentish Town orphanage said someone had asked the same question as me, and I assumed it had been you. Lincoln, that means someone else is searching for information about my adoption."

CHAPTER 6

*T*he library's fireplace threw out enough heat to keep the entire room warm. I sat on the crimson and gold Aubusson rug and stretched my toes toward the hearth. By the time Lincoln returned with a large cup of hot chocolate, my clothes were steaming and my hair curled at the edges.

"You're not having one?" I asked as I accepted the cup.

"I don't like chocolate."

"Strange man." Stranger still that it was the first time he'd voiced an opinion on something as mundane as chocolate. I realized I had no idea of his likes and dislikes, although some of them I could guess. I imagined he loathed social events like balls, for example.

"Are you warm?" he asked.

I nodded. "Are you going to sit down?"

"My clothes are damp."

"The furniture will dry out. Or the rug."

He hesitated then sat on the armchair. I thought he'd excuse himself and retreat to his rooms, so his presence felt like a small victory.

"If you remove your jacket and boots, you'll dry faster," I said.

"I'll keep them on."

So much for small victories. I stared in silence at the flickering flames. Their dance mesmerized me, the warmth made me drowsy. It must have been almost dawn and I was dog tired, but I wasn't prepared to excuse myself from Lincoln's presence. It was rare that we spent time alone outside of training.

I pulled my knees up and, feeling his gaze on me, rested my cheek on them and tilted my head to face him. I'd been wrong, however. He wasn't looking at me but at the fire.

"Will you keep watch over the graves?" I asked. "In case the captain returns for the bodies?"

"Seth and Gus can take turns tomorrow. Today." He rubbed his forehead. He must be exhausted. I'd at least slept a few hours, but he'd been up all night. "It's unlikely the captain will be back now."

"If he learns where the bodies went anyway, that is."

"Pete and Jimmy will have to tell him something, but whether they tell the truth or not, I cannot guess."

"I wonder if the captain will be angry."

"Probably. We've likely set him back."

"I wonder what it is he's doing. I can't begin to think of a reason that would require the bodies be stored for months on end in a cool room. If he were a doctor, surely he would have dissected them by now." I shivered and hugged my knees tighter.

"Perhaps."

"Have you ever noticed how you give non-committal answers?"

"Sometimes." The corner of his mouth twitched, and this time I was certain it was a smile.

I smiled in return. It felt like another victory. Two in one night! No, three. He'd not corrected my usage of his first name in the cart. There was no better time to try my luck for a fourth win. "You're going to visit Mr. Lee's opium den to try to find out more about the captain, aren't you?"

The black orbs of his eyes narrowed to pinpoints. "Why?"

"I want to come with you."

"No."

"But—"

"No, Charlie."

I stretched out my legs and stroked the soft rug with my fingers. "There may be death there. Recent death. I could talk to a spirit while you question Mr. Lee."

"I don't want you near that place."

I sighed. "Lincoln—"

"Fitzroy," he barked.

I squared my shoulders. I didn't deserve to be shouted at! "I am not a delicate flower that wilts at the first sign of danger, *sir*, so do not treat me like one."

"I am your employer," he said through an unmoving jaw. "I'll treat you any way I bloody well like."

"I would be concerned if we weren't arguing about you being over-protective toward me."

He pushed off from the chair and rose above me. "While you live under my roof, you live by my rules."

"And if I choose not to?" I held my breath. Would he throw me out? Would he go along with the committee's suggestion and banish me from London?

"If I want your help at Lee's, I'll ask for it," was all he said.

It didn't answer my question, but it was an improvement on an outright refusal. "That's all I want—your due consideration. I can be of assistance, Linc—Mr. Fitzroy. Tonight proved it."

He drew in a deep breath that expanded his chest, then he strode out of the library.

* * *

IT WAS after midday when I arose to the sounds of voices downstairs. One of the voices was Seth's, the other softer and feminine. It must belong to Lady Harcourt, the only woman who visited Lichfield. I dressed quickly and headed down via the main staircase, but stopped on the landing, out of sight, above them. Seth's heated tone was not one I'd heard him employ with her before.

"Why not?" he prompted her. "Don't I have a right to be there?"

"Of course you do." Her voice was barely above a whisper. She glanced around, but did not think to look up the stairs to where I hid. "But it's not my ball or my invitation."

"Would you invite me if it was?"

"Of course," she soothed.

"Even if it caused a scandal?" When she didn't answer, he added, "It would, you know. It would make you the subject of gossip and ridicule."

"It might cause a scandal, but I wouldn't be tarred by it. A little gossip and ridicule doesn't bother me. If it did, I wouldn't be here."

He grunted, but I couldn't decipher what he meant by it.

"Darling Seth." She patted his cheek. "I know your current predicament troubles you."

"You cannot possibly have a clue, Julia."

"Clearly your memory is short."

He grunted again.

"You will find a way out of it, Seth. I'll do anything I can to help."

He snatched something from her hand—an envelope?— and waved it in her face. "You could have helped with this. If you managed to get Death invited, why not me? I scowl far less than him, and my heritage is not a mystery. I'm also easier to get into bed and far less discerning about whom I take there, something for which I would have thought Lady Plumton grateful."

She plucked off one of her gloves, finger by finger. "That's part of the problem. You're not particularly discreet."

"Ah," he said with a theatrical sigh. "If only that were my singular fault."

"But alas you have many?" She grinned and took back the envelope. "I'll wait in the parlor."

"He could be some time."

"Will you join me until he returns?"

He glanced over his shoulder toward the service area. "Why not?" He held out his arm and she took it. Together they strolled through to the parlor.

I crept down the stairs and headed to the kitchen where I found Cook alone. "Is there anything for breakfast?" I asked.

"Cold sausage. I ain't got time to heat it up, now her ladyship's here." He stirred the contents of the bowl wedged in the crook of his arm.

"She has requested tea?"

"She be stayin' for lunch. I weren't goin' to put out much, what with Fitzroy and Gus not here, but now I have to cook somethin' special."

"You can't serve sandwiches?"

He glared at me.

"I suppose not. Can I help?"

"You can get your own breakfast and stay out of my way."

I saluted him, just as Lincoln strode into the kitchen. "Good morning, sir. Did you come in from the courtyard?"

He nodded. He remained by the door, his arms folded, and watched Cook beat the contents of the bowl. I stabbed a sausage in the pan on the stove and ate it whole. It was warm, despite what Cook had said. He might be in a sour mood, but he'd known I would come down hungry.

"Lady Harcourt's here," I told Lincoln.

"I know."

Cook slowed and looked up at his master. I stared at him too, waiting for him to say he was about to go in to see her. He didn't. Was he avoiding her?

"Somethin' I can get you, sir?" Cook eventually asked.

Lincoln inclined his head at me. "Charlie." He turned and walked out.

I blinked at him then looked to Cook for an answer. He shrugged. "You better go," he whispered.

I fetched my apron from the hook and raced after Lincoln. I'd just finished tying it when he stepped out of the little room that was supposed to be the butler's office but we used for storing the tennis and croquet equipment. Some of his hair had come loose from its leather tie and skimmed his jaw line. It was looking particularly wild, and coupled with the intensity of his gaze, I braced myself. What had I done now?

"I need to speak plainly to you," he said.

I swallowed. "Please do."

"We didn't end the night on a good note."

"No-o," I hedged.

"Charlie…" He glanced over my head and drew in a deep breath. "I want to thank you."

Oh. Well. I hadn't expected gratitude. "For bringing Gordon Thackery back?"

"In part, but also for how you handled him once he was here. You charmed him last night. If you'd left him to my company alone, I doubt the events would have gone quite so effortlessly well."

It was positively effusive praise, and for a moment I was rendered speechless. After our quarrel in the library, I hadn't been sure what he'd thought of the role I'd played. I'd even begun to suspect he regretted asking me to raise Gordon's spirit at all. "I appreciate your thanks, Mr. Fitzroy, but I'm happy to help. It was no trouble. I rather enjoyed it, dead bodies notwithstanding. Gordon was quite the gentleman. I'm only glad he was so willing. It wouldn't have been pleasant to have to coerce him."

"You liked him."

"I did. I suppose he charmed me as much as I charmed him." I laughed softly, but it faded as his eyes darkened. I cleared my throat. Since he neither moved away nor said anything further, I decided to push my luck. "Does your newfound gratitude mean you'll take me to Mr. Lee's after all?"

"Not unless I can find a use for you there. At the moment, it's better that I work alone."

"Very good. You're learning."

He lifted both brows.

"Your response today is more considered and diplomatic

than the one you gave last night. I'll make allowances for your tiredness and forgive you completely." I shot him a bright grin to show him I was teasing.

"Thank you," he said drily. "And I'll make allowances for your persistent nature and forgive you for asking me yet again."

I gasped in mock horror. "Mr. Fitzroy, did you just make a joke?"

"No." He walked off, leaving me standing in the corridor trying to determine what sort of mood he was in. I gave up when Seth joined me and we entered the kitchen together.

"What's Lady H here for?" Cook asked him.

"Death's been invited to a ball tomorrow night, and she's delivering the invitation."

Cook snorted. "He won't go."

"That's what I told her. He'd rather rip his own arm off than dance with silly girls."

"Why would he dance with silly girls?" I asked. "Surely there will be some sensible ones there."

"Sensible *women*, yes, but not girls. And it's the girls who are in need of husbands, hence their pursuit of one of the few eligible bachelors in the city. The far more interesting women are mostly taken, except for the occasional dried up widow."

"I doubt Lady Harcourt would appreciate being called dried up."

"Except her, but he's already taken a dip in those waters and didn't like it."

Cook, standing by the stove, snickered.

I followed Seth into the servants' dining room, which also doubled as a small parlor. We didn't use it often, preferring the warmth and coziness of the kitchen. Besides, he'd taken to polishing shoes on the dining table.

"Is Gus watching the cemetery?"

Seth nodded and checked the clock on the mantel. "I'll relieve him soon."

"I suppose there'll be a committee meeting to inform them of the latest developments." I picked up a pair of Lincoln's shoes, which had been sitting on the bench for two days, and joined Seth at the table.

He slid the polish toward me. "Fitzroy says not."

"Why not?"

He smirked. "He wants to wait, as we don't know if anything supernatural has occurred yet. Besides, they only create an unnecessary layer of bureaucracy that wastes time."

"Is that your opinion or his?"

"Definitely mine. I can't imagine what he thinks, and I wouldn't dare guess."

"Very wise." I buffed off the black polish then set down the shoe and picked up the other. "I wish I knew what they were talking about. Do you think he has already refused the invitation?"

"Why don't you go and listen in? You like to eavesdrop."

I dropped the shoe. "Uh…"

"I've learned a great many things from eavesdropping, so I'm not going to tell you not to do it. Just be careful you don't get caught, especially by Death."

I picked up the shoe. "You make it sound as if I do it frequently. It's not my fault people say things when I happen to be nearby. I don't eavesdrop on purpose."

He tapped my nose with his finger and frowned. "Sorry. I left a smudge."

He handed me a clean cloth and I rubbed my nose. "Is it gone?"

He shook his head. "You'll need soap."

Cook beckoned me from the doorway. "Soup course be ready."

"You take it to them," I told Seth. "I can't. Not looking like this."

He scraped the chair back and stood. "Sorry, Charlie, I've got to relieve Gus." He hadn't even finished polishing the shoes.

"That's not fair."

"You look like an adorable chimney sweep when you pout."

I shot him a withering glare. He flashed me a grin.

I hurried to the parlor and bobbed a curtsy to Lady Harcourt. Without raising my chin, I announced that luncheon was ready. "If you'd like to make your way to the dining room, I'll serve soup in a moment."

"What happened to your nose?" Lady Harcourt asked. "It's black."

So much for keeping my head low. "It's shoe polish."

"That stuff is difficult to remove."

"Yes, thank you," I said tightly.

"How did you manage to get it on your nose?" Lincoln asked. His voice sounded light, almost amused.

"Seth did it."

His jaw hardened. If he had been amused, he certainly wasn't now.

Lady Harcourt arched her brows at him, and I half-expected her to say "See?" but she said nothing. No doubt she thought I was flirting with Seth and he with me. She'd not wanted me to live in a house full of men. Apparently she didn't trust them or me. I'd thought it presumptuous of her at first, but now that I'd had time to think about it, I'd decided it said more about her than us. Not that I would dare say so to her face. One did not accuse a lady of having loose morals.

I returned to the kitchen then delivered the soup to the dining room. Gus arrived home during the next course, and I served him up a steaming bowl. He gulped the soup down and asked for more before I'd had time to clear away the dishes in the dining room.

"I'm glad to see you have a healthy appetite," I told him as I finally sat down with Cook for our own lunch. "I was worried about you, out in the rain the other night."

"That's kind of you, Charlie," he said, "but a bit o' rain never hurt no one."

I wasn't so sure about that. I'd seen children die from being out in the cold and wet too long. "Fitzroy explained everything that happened last night?"

"Aye. Seems you had an adventure." He accepted the bowl

85

and dipped his spoon in. "You're braver than me, calling up the dead like that."

"Bravery has nothing to do with it. It was simply necessary. Did you see anyone who matched the captain's description at the cemetery?"

He shook his head. "Not a soul."

Lincoln joined us after Lady Harcourt departed and briefly questioned Gus too. Then he ordered me to join him in the parlor.

"I have to wash up," I told him.

"Later."

Once in the parlor, he shut the door and rounded on me. I had no difficulty deciphering his emotions on this occasion. He was definitely mad. All that was missing was the steam rising from his ears.

I gulped. "Have I done something wrong?" I tossed my head to counteract the pathetic smallness of my voice. I hadn't done anything to deserve his sudden coldness.

"You visited Lady Harcourt and asked her about Gurry."

I'd forgotten about that. "She told you?" The traitor! So much for thinking we had an understanding and she'd keep silent. I shouldn't have assumed.

He stepped closer to me so that we were mere inches apart. I could smell the scent of his soap, feel the vibrations of his anger. "Why did you go to her?"

"I needed to know who Mr. Gurry was and why you killed him."

"*Needed* to know?"

The force of his glare pushed me a step back. I gripped the wing of the nearby armchair and tried to muster a show of righteous defiance, but it wasn't easy when I didn't believe I was in the right. He had every reason to be angry with me but, in my defense, I had every reason to know the truth. "It's only fair that I know what the other people living here have done in the past."

"Is it?" he ground out.

I tilted my chin. "Yes. You murdered Mr. Gurry, Mr.

Fitzroy. By all accounts, he begged you for mercy and you still killed him." With so many other things on my mind, I'd forgotten about Gurry, but now it all rushed back to me. Lincoln had done something so awful that I shouldn't have set it aside so easily, and yet I had. I'd closed my eyes to that side of him and only seen what I wanted to see—a good, if somewhat emotionless, man. But I knew that only a fool closed her eyes to such a heinous crime. I hated that I could be such a fool.

I took a step away from him and rubbed my cold arms.

"And has this knowledge helped you in any way?" he snapped.

"It's made me more aware of the man you are."

He went very still. Not even his chest moved with his breathing. "Do not presume that it tells you anything about me."

"I don't. Chiefly because I believe there must be a reason why you did what you did. Lady Harcourt didn't know what that reason was, however. She only told me that he was your tutor."

He searched my face. What did he hope to see in it? Whatever it was, he must have been disappointed, because he turned his back to me. "You should have come to me," he said in that quiet, calm voice that meant he'd reined in his temper, but only just. It was still simmering below the surface, ready to explode at any moment.

"Would you have told me? Will you tell me now?"

His broad shoulders rose and fell. "I...can't." He strode out of the parlor.

I sagged against the armchair, feeling battered and bruised by the encounter. While I felt sick for being found out, I only regretted trusting Lady Harcourt, not searching for answers. There *had* to be a good reason for Lincoln to have killed that man, Gurry. But if so, why wouldn't he tell me?

Or was I wrong, and the only explanation was that the tutor had brought out the violent monster inside Lincoln; the one he managed to keep well-hidden most of the time.

CHAPTER 7

I didn't see Lincoln again for the remainder of the afternoon. I dusted the entire house until Gus fetched me to train with him. Apparently Lincoln had given him instructions to do so. Seth was still out. The gloomy day promised rain so I suggested we use the ballroom again.

The exercise helped clear my head and distract me from the conversation with Lincoln. By the time we'd completed moves that were designed to strengthen me, I had completely set it aside. I rarely trained with anyone other than Lincoln, so it was good to go up against Gus. He was a scrappier fighter, his footwork not as polished as either Lincoln or Seth's, and that made him somewhat less effective. I was able to extricate myself from his headlock and send him crashing to the floor by the end of the session.

Cook applauded from where he sat on the covered table. "You made a bored man very happy, Charlie." He grinned at me. "I been wantin' to set him on his arse since I met him."

Gus got to his feet and dusted off his hands. "She would do it to you in half the time, you oversized slab of lard."

That only had Cook grinning wider. He hopped off the table. "Want to learn how to throw a knife so it always hit its target?"

I'd seen how accurate his knife throwing was. He'd planted a meat cleaver into Anselm Holloway's shoulder when my adoptive father had attacked me in the courtyard. It would be a useful skill. "Yes, please."

"We should run it by Death first," Gus warned.

"He ain't here," Cook said, signaling for me to follow him out the door.

"Why wouldn't he want me to learn to throw knives?" I asked.

Gus fell into step alongside me as we trotted down the stairs. "He will, when he feels you're ready."

"Why aren't I ready now?"

He sighed. "I don't know. All I know is, he hasn't given permission."

"Stop worrying, Gus. It's not like you."

We headed out to the courtyard at the back of the house. It was an area set aside for receiving deliveries and for the servants to use as a recreational space during their spare time. Although I'd sat on the bench seat and read often during the early weeks of my arrival, the colder weather had driven me indoors lately.

"There be any wooden barrels in the stables?" Cook asked Gus.

"Aye, but you can't use those. They'll be no good to anyone if you put holes in 'em. There's some spare planks in the carriage house."

He disappeared into the building adjoining the stables, while Cook returned to the kitchen. They both emerged a few minutes later, wooden planks and knives in hand.

Gus set three planks up on their ends and leaned them against the wall of the storehouse at one side of the courtyard. Next he drew a smiling face on the middle one with chalk. "A point if you hit the face. Extra if you get an eye."

He joined us and Cook handed me a knife. "The heavy end be thrown first," Cook said. "A knife with a heavier blade than handle should be held by the handle. One with a heavier handle, hold it by the blade. What's yours? Blade or handle heavy?"

I tested its weight by balancing it on my palm. "Neither."

"Good. It be a balanced knife. Best for beginners. Mine be blade heavy." He gripped his by the handle and I did the same, taking careful note of where he placed his fingers and thumb. "Don't hold it too tight or too loose. Now put your left foot forward, but keep your weight on the right. Bend your arm. Not so close or you'll cut your ear." He adjusted my arm for me. "Move your weight onto your front leg, unbend your arm, and release the knife when it be fully stretched out. Watch me."

He did everything he'd just instructed me but in rapid motion. The knife lodged in the eye Gus had drawn.

Gus whooped and clapped.

"Where did you learn to do that?" I asked Cook.

"My pa taught me. He were a knife thrower with a travelin' troupe of carnival folk. They performed at country fairs and the like."

"You didn't follow in his footsteps?"

"For a bit, aye, but the travelin' life weren't for me."

"How did you come to be here at Lichfield?"

"I were assistant cook for Lord Gillingham."

I pulled a face. Gillingham was one of the committee members and he'd made it abundantly clear that he didn't like me. What wasn't clear was whether he didn't like me because I was a necromancer, had lived on the streets, or both. "He stole you from Gillingham?"

"Gillingham dismissed me, the little turd."

"Why?"

"Thought I'd been drinkin' the wine from his cellar on the sly, but it weren't me. Were his cook, but the cook blamed me. The cook were jealous because I cooked a meal for his lordship's guests one night when he were sick, and they all thought it were the best they ever had."

"Did you defend yourself and tell Lord Gillingham you didn't drink the wine?"

"Course, but then the cook found out I been to jail for theivin' a few years back, and there were no hope I could stay after that. Ain't no one who wants a thief in their house."

"Except Mr. Fitzroy," I said wryly. I'd also been a thief and had only escaped jail by raising a dead man's spirit and frightening the guards. "Did Fitzroy feel sorry for you and decide to employ you here?"

Both Cook and Gus snorted. "He don't feel sorry for nobody," Cook said. "He employ me because I the best cook in London."

Gus rolled his eyes.

"Go on, Charlie," Cook said. "Your turn."

I set my feet apart like he'd shown me and held the knife near my head, arm bent. I released it in a smooth motion. It missed all the planks and bounced off the brick wall. "What did I do wrong?" I asked, going to retrieve it.

"Your aim be off."

"I gathered that. Anything else?"

"Maybe stand closer. You be weaker than me."

I came in another foot from my previous position and set myself up again. I was just about to release it when Lincoln rode into the courtyard on his horse.

"What is this?" he growled, dismounting.

Gus rushed over to gather the reins.

"Target practice." I held up the knife and indicated the planks. "Cook is teaching me how to throw them to wound someone."

"I didn't give permission."

"It was only a little practice. Why do we need your permission?"

"Because I am your employer." He stalked into the house, flinging his cloak from his shoulders.

I handed the knife to Cook, rolled my eyes, and went after Lincoln. "That is not a reason."

"You need to learn to obey my orders, Charlie. You all do. If you want to help with ministry business then you need to learn to do as I tell you. I can't have you all going off in different directions on a sudden whim. It's imperative you do as I say, or plans will fall apart."

I quickened my pace to keep up with him. "While that does sound reasonable, we are simply training here at Lichfield. We're not out on ministry business. I think you're overreacting."

He suddenly stopped and rounded on me. "Do you? Then you won't be surprised to learn that I'll dismiss Cook."

"What? You can't!"

He walked off again. "He should know better."

We'd reached the stairs now and I was beginning to breathe heavily from the effort of following him. "You're being unreasonable."

He said nothing, just took the stairs two at a time.

"Mr. Fitzroy, slow down." He didn't. "This is absurd. I won't let you dismiss him. He won't get another position in a large house, not with his history."

"You have no say in the matter. You're a maid."

"I don't care!" I shouted, stopping on the landing. "Dismiss me too, if you will. It was my fault, after all. I asked him to instruct me." I resisted the urge to look back down to see if Gus and Cook were listening and would tell Lincoln that wasn't true.

"*He* should know better," he said again. He didn't sound quite so angry, and I suspected I was getting through to him.

"You'll regret this tomorrow."

"Will I?" He came back down the stairs toward me, but remained on the step above so that I had to crane my neck to look at him. "You presume to know me that well?"

I stepped up beside him and folded my arms. "I think I do, yes."

The muscles high in his jaw bunched. "You're wrong, Charlie. You don't know me at all."

"Bollocks."

His eyes narrowed.

I took his silence as permission to continue. "I do know

you will regret speaking to me like this. I also know you'll regret dismissing Cook."

"Why would I?"

"He's a bloody good cook, for one thing. His sponge cakes are delicious. More to the point, it would be several days before we could replace him, and you do not want to eat my cooking. I imagine Seth and Gus are equally inept in the kitchen. Cook also saved my life. So, please," I said, softer, "keep him on. It was a trifling thing he did, after all."

He placed his hands behind his back and regarded me from beneath heavy-lidded eyes. "Why are you so intent on defying me lately?"

I baulked. "Am I?" I shook my head. "I disagree."

He ached a brow.

"Yes, well, while that does sound insolent, I would hardly call standing up for Cook defiant. You never said not to learn how to throw knives. I actually don't see the problem with it."

"I will oversee your training. Not Seth, or Gus, or Cook."

"You weren't here."

"And I will not have my staff going against my orders," he said, walking up the stairs again.

"You never actually gave a direct order not to teach me knife throwing."

He paused and glanced over his shoulder at me.

I shrugged. "If you're going to be particular about this then so will I."

He marched up the stairs again. "Tell Cook he can stay," he tossed back. "He's fortunate to have you as his champion."

* * *

LINCOLN DIDN'T JOIN us for dinner, but came downstairs afterward and announced he was heading out to Mr. Lee's Lower Pell Lane establishment.

"Again?" I asked, setting aside my mending.

"There is no again. I haven't been yet." He threw on his

riding cloak and picked up the gloves he'd set on the kitchen table.

"I thought that's where you were this morning."

He shook his head without looking at me. Indeed, he'd not met my gaze since entering.

Gus yawned and slumped further into the chair. "So where were you this morning?"

"The orphanage in Kentish Town." Upon my quiet gasp, he finally met my gaze. "I asked Mr. Hogan, the administrator, if he'd kept a copy of the letter he'd received from the person inquiring after your adoption."

"And?"

"And he hadn't. Nor could he recall where he sent the response. If he were my employee, I'd dismiss him for ineptitude."

"He must receive a lot of correspondence." I picked up my sewing again to hide my disappointment. "Thank you for trying. I know you're very busy."

I wasn't aware he'd moved closer until his gloved hand rested on the table in my line of sight. "Someone wants to know more about your origins, Charlie. They're possibly even searching for you."

"We don't know that certain."

"No."

"If they wanted to know where I'm living, they could simply question Anselm Holloway. It's not like he's difficult to find, locked away in a jail cell." I glanced up at him. "I won't live here as a prisoner."

"I know."

His response surprised me, after his earlier over-reaction. Then it had seemed as if he were trying to protect me to the point of being unreasonable, but now I wasn't so sure.

"Will you take one of the men with you?" I asked.

"Seth is still out and Gus can't stay awake."

Gus grunted and sat up straight. "I'm awake!"

Cook snorted.

"Besides, I don't wish to alert Mr. Lee to my interest,"

Lincoln said. "A single gentleman whom he already knows can make discreet inquiries. An entourage will raise questions and shackles."

"Why have you been to Mr. Lee's before?"

"Why does anyone go to Lee's? Don't wait up for me. I'll probably be out all night."

I blinked at his back as he walked away. Once he'd left the kitchen, I turned to Gus. "Did you know he'd been to an opium den before?"

"No, but nothing about him surprises me," Gus said, settling back down into the chair.

"Aye," Cook chimed in from where he sat beside me. "Best not to think about all the places our leader has been. He be a worldly sort."

Worldly was one thing, but frequenting an opium house was quite another. There was only one reason to go to a place like Lee's—to smoke opium.

I returned to the mending, wondering if I would get any sleep at all as I alternately pondered this new piece of information and worried about him. One thing would help me rest easier, however—he seemed to have calmed down and forgiven Cook for the knife-throwing incident.

* * *

COOK INFORMED me over breakfast that Lincoln had not yet returned. I tried not to look worried, since he didn't seem to be. Gus had relieved Seth at the cemetery a few hours earlier and the latter was now asleep upstairs in his attic room.

"Cheer up," Cook said as he handed me a boiled egg in a cup. "There be sponge cake later."

"Delicious! Are we expecting guests?"

"Don't think so. Fitzroy asked me to bake it."

"But he hardly ever eats cake. Why would he ask for it specifically if he's not expecting guests?"

His hairless eyebrows lifted. "You can't guess?"

"No."

"He knows it be your favorite."

I scoffed. "I doubt that's it."

He smirked but said nothing further. Perhaps he was right and the cake was a peace offering for his bad temper. Since it wasn't something he actually had to bake himself, it was hardly a very convincing one.

I cracked the top of my egg open with a spoon and peeled off some of the shell. "He's rather hot and cold lately. Have you noticed that?"

Cook sat with me, two boiled eggs in front of him as well as a slice of toast. "He been that way ever since you moved in."

"That's not a comfort. Indeed, I feel rather guilty now, thank you."

He held up his hands. "I just be tellin' it as I see it."

I couldn't know if he was right or not, but I felt Lincoln's bad humor had increased recently—since he'd learned that I'd asked Lady Harcourt about Gurry. I hated to think that my prying had put a wedge between us that might never be fully removed, but I wasn't completely sorry. How else was I meant to learn more about him?

Seth finally awoke late morning, about the same time that Lincoln returned, along with Gus. The latter had deep blue-black circles under his eyes and a spider web of red lines on his eyelids. He pounced on the soup Cook placed on the kitchen table in front of him and devoured it in a few gulps.

Lincoln set a large rectangular box on the table and took a seat. A blue silk ribbon was wrapped around the box, tied up in a bow. Silk ribbons were expensive. Seth, Gus, Cook and I all exchanged glances, but if Lincoln noticed, he didn't say. He merely sat at the table and accepted the bowl of soup Cook placed in front of him. He ate with less greed than Gus, but asked for more when he'd finished.

"Don't spoil your appetite for cake," I told them.

"There's cake?" Gus asked.

"Sponge. I believe we have you to thank for it, Mr. Fitzroy."

Lincoln's gaze slid to Cook and turned frosty. "We haven't had one in a while. I thought it was time."

"Actually, we had one only last week."

"I forgot."

"Is that so? And here I thought you forget nothing." I thought it best not to tease him too much, since he was trying to broker peace. Poking the bear would be unwise. "Sponge cake will go nicely with a cup of tea later."

He accepted the second bowl of soup from Cook and gave me a somewhat hesitant nod.

"Do you want me to return to the cemetery?" Seth asked from where he was leaning against the doorframe.

"Not yet," Lincoln said. "There's been no sign of the captain so far, and I suspect he'll be hesitant to return there. He's unlikely to risk trying to retrieve them."

I removed my apron and joined him at the table. "That will set him back, if he was specifically after those bodies."

"I'd say he was. He picked them for a reason. I questioned Mr. Tucker this morning and he claims three of them are from his cemetery, the first one taken and the last two."

"Gordon Thackery being the very last."

"The first was the one you witnessed, Charlie. His name was Lieutenant Martin Jolly, and another was Captain John Marshall. Mr. Tucker also spent yesterday traveling to the other London cemeteries. He discovered the second body to be dug up came from Kensal Green."

"Did he learn his name?"

"William Bunter. All except Bunter were in the army."

"Or was he, but it wasn't inscribed on his tombstone?"

He shook his head. "I checked with his family. Bunter was a shopkeeper in the family's Piccadilly ready-to-wear shop."

I eyed the box. "You did some shopping while you were there? What did you purchase?"

"Blimey," Gus muttered with a roll of his eyes. "Just like a woman to think about shopping in the middle of an important discussion."

"A cloak," Lincoln said.

"What's wrong with your old cloak?" I asked.

He regarded me with those deep, black eyes of his and I clamped my mouth shut. I'd overstepped the boundary he'd laid between us again. I needed to learn to behave as a maid should.

"My apologies," I muttered. "So not all the dead men were linked through the army."

He shook his head.

"There must be another connection," Seth said, joining us at the table. "There has to be a reason why the captain chose to dig up those four specifically."

"The Bunters mentioned their son had been acting strangely before he died," Lincoln went on. "He would disappear for days on end without word, and when he returned home, he was inexplicably tired. He also seemed to be losing money but claimed not to be gambling. He'd grown thin too."

"Opium," Cook said quietly.

Lincoln nodded. "I suspect so. The Bunters didn't know where William went during his missing days. He wouldn't tell them, despite their pleas."

"What did you discover at Mr. Lee's house?" I asked.

"He admitted that a man matching the captain's description frequented the house from time to time, but never partook of the opium. Lee claimed not to know what the captain was up to. He paid well for privacy."

"And Lee allowed him to be alone with the men while they were so vulnerable under the opium's effects?"

"The likes of Lee don't care about anyone's safety," Gus said. "Only money."

"I'm unclear on how much Lee did know exactly," Lincoln told us. "He could be withholding information."

"Is his English good? Perhaps you need a translator."

"We understood one another."

Seth leaned in to me. "Mr. Fitzroy speaks perfect Chinese."

"Cantonese, and a little Mandarin."

How impressive. I wondered how many other languages he'd mastered. "What else did Mr. Lee tell you?"

"That the captain hasn't returned since the morning of Thackery's death, and that perhaps all four of our dead men frequented his establishment in the weeks and months before their deaths, but he can't be sure. It stands to reason that most were soldiers."

"Gordon said opium relieves the pain of war injuries."

He nodded. "Soldier's curse, some call it."

"Mr. Lee doesn't note down his customers' names?"

He shook his head. "The addicts like the anonymity he offers." He rose and picked up the box. To Seth and Gus he said, "Tucker and his staff are going to keep a close eye on Thackery, Marshall and Jolly's graves and report any visitors to me. We'll focus on watching Lee's instead."

"I'll go," Seth said, also rising. "Gets me out of scullery duty."

"What if the captain goes to a different opium den next time?" I asked. "If he thinks he's been found out, he'll be wise to change his pattern if he wishes to continue doing whatever it is he's doing."

Lincoln nodded, thoughtful. "We'll ask at other places I know."

"After a rest," I told him. "You must be exhausted."

He didn't answer, but strode out of the kitchen, the box under his arm. "Charlie, come with me."

"You've been summoned," Gus intoned in an imperial voice.

"Let us know what's in the box," Seth said, pushing me in the shoulder to hurry me up.

I wasn't sure if I was going to find out, or simply be given specific duties for the afternoon. I expected to be admonished for not blacking the fireplace in the parlor, but he went to the library instead. It was the one room that was perfectly clean. The more I cleaned in there, the longer I could spend browsing through the books.

He stood at the table and held out the box to me. I paused by the door, half expecting Seth or Gus to creep up behind me to watch, but there were no sounds. The house had fallen silent. Only my heartbeat made a noise as it pounded against my ribs.

"What is it?" I asked.

"The Bunters' shop didn't sell gentlemen's clothing."

"Oh."

"Take it." His curt reply dismissed all excitement. It was probably just a new apron.

I came further into the room and accepted the box. "Thank you."

"Don't thank me until you've seen it. If you don't like it, Mrs. Bunter said I may return it and you can choose another."

I placed the box on the table and carefully undid the bow, not wanting to damage the beautiful length of silk. My heart's hammering picked up speed as I lifted the lid with trembling fingers. I suspected that whatever was inside would be lovely —one didn't wrap up aprons with silk ribbons.

I set the lid aside and removed the plush black garment from the box. It was a short cloak, trimmed in gray fur, with a curlicue pattern was embellished all around. The royal blue silk lining was the same shade as the ribbon.

"My goodness," I said on a breath. I studied it from all angles, and brushed the soft plush against my cheek. "I...I don't know what to say. Are you giving this to me?"

He folded his arms over his chest. "You don't like it?"

"I do, it's beautiful. Thank you. But...where shall I wear it? It's much too fine for going to the market with Cook. I don't want to ruin it."

"Wear it whenever you want. That's why I bought it—to be worn." He sounded put out but I didn't see how my question could cause offence. The cloak must have cost him a considerable sum, and I didn't want to wear it just anywhere. It was the sort of cloak one should wear strolling around the park with wealthy and titled friends. My friends consisted of the other Lichfield Towers servants, and my old cloak was more than adequate in their company.

"Why did you buy it for me? You already gave me a cloak when the weather turned cool."

"This one will be warmer. I noticed you shivering the other night."

"Oh. Thank you, Lincoln. It's the loveliest thing I've ever owned."

He inclined his head and, with his hands behind his back, marched out of the library. He hadn't even said anything about me calling him Lincoln. I held the cloak against my chest, half expecting him to return and take it from me, to give to someone more deserving, like Lady Harcourt. But he didn't, and I stayed there in the library for some time, stroking my new cloak.

* * *

I WASN'T EXPECTING Lincoln to conduct my training that afternoon. Between rest and work, he had very little spare time. But after sleeping for a mere four hours, he found me helping Cook in the kitchen and ordered me to change and meet him outside, on the lawn at the front of the house.

The day had cleared up nicely but the miserly sun failed to take the chill out of the air. It was perfect weather for the vigorous exercise regime Lincoln put me through for the next two hours. The lack of warmth didn't stop me from sweating by the end of it, but not quite as much as I had two months ago.

There was no sign of his ill humor anymore, or the strangeness that had shrouded our encounter in the library. He was all stiff formality as he ordered me to repeat the various maneuvers, over and over. It was just as it always had been between us. I almost preferred the simmering anger. It was at least an emotion.

We still had quite a bit of our session to go when we had

to stop for a visitor. The carriage rumbled up the long drive and it was some time before I realized who it belonged to. Lincoln must have recognized the horses and driver because before the carriage turned so we could see the escutcheon painted on the side, he ordered me into the house.

"Change into your uniform," he said quickly. "And stay in the kitchen."

I intended to do exactly as he asked, and only paused on the steps to see who had arrived unannounced in such grand style. As the carriage swept into a wide arc and pulled to a stop in front of Lincoln, I groaned. The escutcheon was that of a snake wrapped around a sword. Lord Gillingham's crest. I headed up the steps.

"You there! Girl!" Gillingham's barked order set my teeth on edge. I stopped, turned and inclined my head in question. I refused to curtsy to that man.

"What do you want?" Lincoln asked as Gillingham stepped down from the cabin.

The sun picked out the flecks of gray amid the red of his beard. He planted the end of his walking stick on the gravel and regarded first me then Lincoln with those insipid eyes of his. "Lady Harcourt has called a special meeting. It seems I am the first to arrive."

"A meeting? Why wasn't I informed?"

"I am informing you now." He went to walk off, but Lincoln stepped in front of him.

"What is the meeting about?"

"Ministry business." He stepped around Lincoln and pointed at me with the end of his cane. "Why is she dressed like that?"

"That's none of your affair."

"I'm training," I told him. Lincoln glanced over his shoulder at me. His face was positively rigid with fury. "Mr. Fitzroy is teaching me to fight and protect myself in the event of an attack."

Gillingham's red-gold eyebrows rose. Then he burst out laughing. "Is that a joke?"

Neither of us answered.

"You are trying to teach this girl to fight? Good lord, Fitzroy, you're softer in the head than I thought. Do you suppose that dressing her in boys' clothes will give her the strength, speed and aptitude of one? That's absurd."

"Nobody is concerned with what you think, Gillingham," Lincoln said. "Keep your opinions to yourself or leave."

I didn't trust Gillingham's smile. It was all lips and no teeth. "You'll find out soon enough what I and the others think at the meeting. You've been allowed free reign for too long, Fitzroy, and it's gone to your head. That time has come to an end. You cannot be allowed to make foolish decisions when the lives of so many depend upon you."

I had no idea what he was talking about, and if Lincoln did, he gave nothing away. He didn't even answer Gillingham; he simply turned and strode up to me. "Come inside," he said in a low voice.

"Wait a moment," Gillingham called. "Girl, come and collect my hat and scarf." He pointed into the cabin where the hat and scarf sat on the seat.

I went to fetch them, but Lincoln caught my arm. "Let him get them himself."

"It's all right. I am the Lichfield maid, and he's our guest. I ought to do it."

"He's no guest of mine," he growled.

"We have to tolerate him, for now, if a meeting has been called. It's all right," I said again. "I'll do this. You go inside and tell Cook to prepare tea."

He hesitated before removing his hand. I trotted down the stairs to Gillingham and the carriage. I reached into the cabin, but just as my fingers touched the silk of his hat, the crunch of gravel had me whipping around.

Teeth bared, Gillingham lunged at my head with his walking stick.

And Lincoln was too far away to stop it hitting me.

CHAPTER 8

I dove to the side so that the stick hit the carriage, not me, and landed on my hands and knees on the gravel. My palms stung, but I jumped up and went to grab Gillingham's arm and twist it as Lincoln had taught me.

Except he got there first. He stood between us and grabbed Gillingham's wrist. He snatched the walking stick and snapped it in two over his knee. It was the second stick of Gillingham's that he'd broken in as many months.

"Pathetic," Gillingham said as another carriage rolled up behind his. He laughed; a brittle, dry laugh that was as humorless as the man himself. "She's a maid, Fitzroy, and a creature of death. You shouldn't—"

Lincoln clamped a hand to the other man's jaw, shutting his mouth with an audible clack of teeth. His fingers dug into the soft flesh of Gillingham's cheeks and the sound he made could have been that of choking, a protest or cry of pain.

"Lincoln! Let him go!" General Eastbrooke shouted from his carriage. The two drivers exchanged alarmed and uncertain glances.

Lincoln's face only hardened, something I'd not thought possible. His mouth twisted and the black orbs of his eyes were so dense that I was afraid he might never see his way out of his rage.

Oh God, he could break Gillingham's jaw.

General Eastbrooke tried to pull Lincoln off Gillingham, but Lincoln made no sign that he'd registered his presence. I laid a hand on his arm too, but that did nothing, so I pressed my palm against his cheek.

He blinked.

I stroked my thumb over his face and he blinked again. He removed his hand, shoving Gillingham away as he did so. "Don't come near her," he said in a voice so raw that I hardly recognized it. He took my hand and pulled me with him. I had to run to keep up with his long strides.

"I was only testing her," Gillingham grumbled. "You claimed to be training her to defend herself. I wanted to see if you were getting results."

"Is that so?" General Eastbrooke sounded amused. "And how did she go in your little test, Gilly?"

Gillingham grunted and if he gave a response, I didn't hear it.

Once inside the house, Lincoln let me go. Only then did he seem to see me. He took my hands and inspected the palms, then ordered me upstairs. "See to the grazes."

"Will you be all right?" I asked, searching his face for signs that he might try to kill Gillingham in my absence.

He nodded stiffly. "Of course. Go."

I headed upstairs to my room and washed the bits of gravel off before changing into my maid's uniform. I used the service stairs to get to the kitchen, rather than the main staircase, to avoid any encounters with other committee members.

Gus looked up from where he was arranging cups and saucers on a tray at the kitchen table. "Charlie, what happened?"

I glanced from him to Cook, putting the final dusting of icing sugar on the cake. "What do you mean?"

"Death came in here looking like he wanted to murder someone, ordering us to get cake and tea into the parlor for the committee members. Did Lord Gillingham do something to annoy him again?"

"Annoy? That's one way of putting it. Set the cake on that tray and I'll carry it in." I went to fetch the cake plates and forks from the cupboard.

"He asked me to serve," Gus said. "I don't want to annoy him any more than he already is by disobeying."

"You can still serve. I'll take in the cake and you take the tea things. Two trays, two servants."

He relented without argument so Lincoln mustn't have said "Don't let Charlie do it." Even if he had, I would have fought to perform my role. I wasn't going to let Lord Gillingham think he'd frightened me when he hadn't. On the contrary. I was pleased with myself for foiling his so-called test. He'd bolstered my confidence without intending to. I must be sure to tell Lincoln that later. It might make him a little less angry.

I heard his voice before I reached the parlor. He was recounting the evening we'd found the bodies at the butcher's and learned about the captain from Pete and Jimmy. There were a few holes in his story, however, and the committee members pounced on them.

"How did you return the bodies to the cemetery?" Lord Marchbank asked.

"I appropriated the butcher's cart."

"And moved them on your own?"

"Am I not enough?"

I entered, with Gus behind me, and set the tray on the table near Lincoln. I avoided his glare and set about slicing the cake. Ordinarily I would place the tea things near Lady Harcourt, as she liked to perform hostess duties, but this way I would have to remain in the parlor longer. I glanced at Lord Gillingham as I handed him a slice of cake. Both of his cheeks sported bruises above his beard, and there was a rigidity about his shoulders that hadn't been there before. He didn't acknowledge me, for which I was grateful.

"Lincoln," Lady Harcourt said, accepting a cup of tea from Gus, "how did—"

She stopped when Lord Gillingham put up his hand. "Wait for the maid to leave," he said.

"All of my staff are aware of what happened," Lincoln told him. "They're ministry employees and as such need to know ministry business."

"Did you hear that?" Gillingham directed his spluttered appeal to General Eastbrooke and Lord Marchbank. "He's lost all reason! Involving a maid in our affairs is dangerous, as well as ludicrous. Particularly *this* maid."

"Calm down, Gilly," Eastbrooke said with a shake of his head. "She already knows what we're about, and Lincoln won't tell her anything he thinks ought to be kept from her. You know that."

"Bloody mistake," Gillingham muttered.

"If anyone can be trusted, it's Lincoln," said Lady Harcourt. "May we move on? I have a question. How did you get the grave robbers to tell you about the captain?"

Lincoln tore his steely glare away from Gillingham and fixed it on her. "I used my charms."

She stared directly back, unsmiling. Gillingham snorted.

"You beat the stuffing out of them, didn't you?" Eastbrooke said around a bite of cake. "Be sure to keep your name out of it. We don't want any more trouble with the police."

Lincoln shook his head when I offered him cake. His gaze met mine and for a brief moment, it seemed to warm. But the moment was fleeting and the pits became dark, cold wells again.

"You should have learned more from them," Gillingham said. "You've got no name of the man paying them, no place of residence, and only a general description. If it were me, I'd have scared something more useful out of them."

If it were him, he'd probably have soiled his trousers.

"Not good enough, Fitzroy," he muttered into his teacup. "Your *charm* didn't work on this occasion."

"That isn't fair," I snapped, rounding on him.

Lord Gillingham gulped too much of the hot tea and coughed until his eyes watered. I took the moment to continue, ignoring Lincoln's warning of "Charlie, don't." It wasn't fair that he be blamed, and it was about time they became aware of how useful I could be.

"It wasn't Lincoln who scared them off but the body of a dead man."

"What do you mean?" both Eastbrooke and Marchbank asked.

"I raised one of the bodies in the butcher's and used him to scare answers out of Pete and Jimmy. It worked effectively. The men were tight-lipped until that point and weren't going to give us anything. While *we* think they gave us enough to continue the investigation, if you do not, then it's my fault, not Mr. Fitzroy's."

"You did *what*?" Gillingham exploded. "Are you mad, girl? Fitzroy, you allowed her to do this?"

"I ordered her to do it," Lincoln said. "Not that it is your affair, what I do and how I manage ministry business."

"It bloody well is!" Gillingham had the sort of coloring that reddened easily, but his face had turned positively crimson.

"That's enough!" Eastbrooke shouted. "You're out of line, Gilly. Lincoln's methods may not be conventional, but they are effective. It's precisely because of his unconventional methods that he's good at what he does. You know that as well as anyone in this room. Now pipe down and listen to what he has to say."

"Unconventional and ungentlemanly."

Lady Harcourt dropped her teacup into the saucer with a clatter to draw everyone's attention. "He is more of a gentleman than you, Gillingham, in every sense of the word."

Gillingham sneered at her, but she simply picked up her teacup again and took a sip. I tried to catch her eye and smile my approval, but she didn't look my way.

"If the necromancer is living here, she might as well be useful," Lord Marchbank said quietly, with a nod in my direction. "As long as she's discreet."

"How discreet is it to have a dead man walking the streets?" Gillingham muttered in a last gasp effort to speak his mind. He remained silent on the topic after that, thankfully. Another protest and Lincoln may have decided to break the man's jaw after all.

"I've investigated further," Lincoln went on, picking up the story. "The four men whose bodies were taken were probably all opium addicts. The captain visited them at either one or more opium dens while they were still alive, and he targeted them specifically after death. It's unclear why. The grave robbers think the captain may be an army man, but his description says otherwise. He wore spectacles and doesn't have a strong build. That, coupled with his interest in cadavers, makes me think he might be a medical officer in the armed forces rather than a regular officer."

I hadn't thought of that but it was a good guess, based on what we knew.

Everyone looked to the general. "You don't expect me to know him, do you?" He shook his head. "There are countless captains in the medical corps. Besides, I retired some years ago."

"There isn't enough information to go on," Marchbank agreed. "We need a name."

"There may be countless medical officers," Lincoln added, "but how many have been dismissed for dubious behavior?"

"It's possible he did something of a similar nature during his tenure, I suppose." The general stroked his mutton chop whiskers and stared into the middle distance. "No one comes to mind, but I'll look into it."

"Good thinking, Fitzroy." Marchbank nodded his approval. I liked the middle-aged nobleman on the whole, even though his visage was perhaps the most frightening of all the committee members with his scarred face, crooked nose and gruff manner. He certainly looked nothing like the soft Gillingham, yet of the two, I'd rather spend time in Marchbank's company.

Gus had already left the parlor and I'd lingered as long as

I possibly could without raising suspicions. I went to walk out but Lincoln, standing near the door, caught my elbow.

"Stay," he said quietly. "This concerns you." He let me go and addressed the rest of the room. "Someone is trying to find Charlie's mother."

"Damn," Eastbrooke muttered. "I was afraid of this."

"How do you know?" Lady Harcourt asked.

"We became aware of it when we visited an orphanage. Someone had already been there and asked the same questions."

"*We?*" She arched her brows at him. "Have you been looking for her too? Together?"

"Yes," he lied.

I arched my brows at him too, but he ignored me.

"Damn," Eastbrooke said again. "I thought nobody except Holloway knew she was adopted."

Gillingham shook his head. "The threat should have been removed as soon as we learned of the adoption."

I gasped. "Removed? You would kill my—kill Holloway?" I looked to Lincoln but he was stony faced.

"What did you expect, girl?" Gillingham snapped.

"But what if he hasn't told anyone?"

"Who else could it have been? He is the only one living who knows you are a necromancer and adopted."

"Aside from all of you."

He half rose from his chair, his face turning a mottled red once more. "How *dare* you accuse us of betraying the ministry!"

"I'm not accusing you of betrayal, but of searching for my real mother without informing anyone."

"Be seated, Gilly," Eastbrooke snapped. "The girl is right. She hasn't accused anyone of anything. But I must inform you, miss, that everything of a supernatural nature must go through the ministry first. You and your mother are supernatural creatures, and as such, any investigation surrounding you both must be tabled at a meeting *before* Lincoln takes care of it."

"I am *not* a creature, sir." I had the feeling his little speech had been more for the party's benefit than mine specifically. Reminding them of their duty to not act without official sanction, perhaps?

"Of course you're not, Charlie," Lady Harcourt said. Her soft brown eyes settled on me. "The general was talking in broad strokes."

"We must learn who it is and how he knows about her," Marchbank said.

"Charlie and I will continue to search for her mother," Lincoln told him. "Hopefully we'll learn more about the other party as we do so."

"You'll be quite busy then. Can you manage, Fitzroy?"

"Of course. My staff will help."

Marchbank rocked out of the deep armchair and lurched to his feet. "Their household duties will suffer if you spread them too thin."

"We'll be sure not to let standards slip," I told him.

Marchbank grunted. "A house this size ought to have more staff. Have you considered employing some extras?"

"That would only cause complications," Lincoln said. "I don't need a large staff. Not all the rooms are in use."

"Pity," Lady Harcourt said, setting down her teacup and also rising. "I do wish to see the ballroom filled with music and dancing. It's quite a magnificent room."

"Are we done?" Marchbank asked. "I have to get ready for dinner. Lady Marchbank will expect me home to receive the guests."

General Eastbrooke chuckled. "Makes me glad I never married. The army was my wife and my children for so long, I don't think I could have adjusted to a domestic life in retirement. I like living alone."

No wife or children? But if that were the case, then which family had Lady Harcourt been referring to? I'd heard her tell Lincoln that he was protective of his family, yet it seemed he'd been brought up in General Eastbrooke's house, alone except for tutors. Surely there'd been someone there whom she called his family, even though they may not have been his natural ones. Could she mean the general's household staff? Lincoln certainly didn't treat us the way a gentleman ought to treat his servants, so perhaps that habit had begun in his childhood when he was close to the only people he saw regularly, the maids and footmen.

I wondered if he would tell me. So far he'd been close-lipped about Gurry, and only given me the bare facts about his upbringing when I asked. Perhaps I was asking the wrong questions. Lincoln had been brought up to be the ministry's leader, so his childhood was inextricably linked to the ministry itself. Perhaps if I asked about its history, I would learn something about his. If nothing else, I would gain an insight into the organization I now worked for—*if* he gave me answers.

"Fetch Gus to retrieve cloaks," Lincoln said to me. "Take the rest of the cake with you."

"I want another slice," Gillingham protested, holding out his empty plate to me.

Lincoln picked up the tray with the rest of the cake on it and handed it to me.

"I think it would be wise to leave now," Lady Harcourt warned Gillingham.

I left with the tray and walked quickly to the kitchen. The sponge—*my* sponge—was half eaten, but at least I would get some. I smiled as I recalled the look on Gillingham's face when Lincoln refused him another slice.

"What're you smiling about?" Gus asked when I reached the kitchen.

"Nothing." I set the tray down. "This is for us, but first we have to get coats for the guests. They're all leaving."

"'Bout bloody time."

"I'll make tea," Cook said as Gus and I left. "It be ready in five minutes."

We were about to enter the entrance hall when Lady Harcourt's lyrical voice carried to us. I put my arm out to stop Gus and shook my head. I didn't want to disturb them.

"He didn't mean that, Lincoln," she cooed.

"Who didn't mean what, Julia?"

"The general. You are his child, as much as any natural one could have been."

There was a slight pause after which he said, "You couldn't be more wrong."

I heard a carriage roll away outside, its wheels crunching on the gravel. Lord Marchbank, I assumed, hurrying home to his wife and dinner guests. He must have fetched his own coat. Lady Harcourt and Lincoln seemed to be alone. Gus moved past me to join them and I followed.

He retrieved the cloaks from the hooks and handed Lady Harcourt's to me. Lincoln held out his hand for it and I passed it along.

"Why did you call the meeting, Julia?" he asked her in an idle voice as he helped her into the coat.

Her gaze flicked to me and Gus and she gave a slight shake of her head.

"Answer me," Lincoln said. The idleness had vanished, replaced with iciness.

"They needed to know what you've been up to. We all do. The sketchy details you gave me this morning weren't enough, and I doubted you would elaborate if I asked."

He strode past her and held open the door. "Don't go behind my back again. Is that understood?"

The black choker at her throat moved with her heavy swallow. "I didn't go behind your back, Lincoln. I called a meeting. As a member, I am allowed to do so." Her hands shook as she pulled on her gloves, but her chin remained at a defiant angle.

The general and Gillingham entered from the parlor. "Is all well?" the general asked, eyeing each of them.

Gillingham didn't seem to notice the tension in the hall and strode up to Gus. He snatched his cloak and marched to the door.

"Perfectly," Lady Harcourt said with a smile for Eastbrooke. "Walk me out, please, Gilly."

Gillingham stopped in the doorway, sighed, and put out his elbow for her to take. They left together. Lincoln followed them out with General Eastbrooke, and Gus and I returned to the kitchen.

I sank onto a chair and accepted a cup of tea from Cook. The steaming liquid helped settle my nerves, but I suspected a slice of cake would do more.

"Glad that's over with." Gus sat opposite me and stretched his legs out under the table. "So what happened after I left the parlor?" His thick brow bunched into a frown as I recounted the meeting to him and Cook.

When I finished, I proceeded to cut the rest of the cake into four slices. I was about to take my first bite when Lincoln entered.

"That was supposed to be all for you," he said with a nod at the cake.

"There's enough left for the four of us." I pushed a plate toward a spare chair while he poured himself a cup of tea at the stove. "Seth will have to miss out."

He joined us but didn't eat the cake. Cook, Gus and I gobbled ours up then Lincoln pushed the plate in front of me. I ate his slice too.

"You be dining here, sir?" Cook asked.

"Just something quick before I go out. I'm returning to Lee's, and I'll investigate some other establishments during the night."

I dabbed my mouth to catch all the crumbs. "It was clever of you to suggest the captain is a medical officer in the army."

"It's a possibility."

"A likely one, I think. I wonder if the general will learn more. It can't be difficult to find details of doctors dismissed from the medical corps for misconduct."

"That's if he was dismissed," he said. "He could still be practicing. His army record could be an exemplary one."

"True, but wouldn't he be stationed overseas? He wouldn't have been able to visit the men here regularly over the last few months if that were the case."

"He might have been stationed here, or on long leave for an illness." He shrugged. "But hopefully you're right. A dismissed officer will be more conspicuous in the records than an active one." He continued to watch me, but I couldn't begin to fathom why.

After a moment, unable to stand it any longer, I got up and collected the dishes.

"Charlie," he called after me before I disappeared into the scullery. "Will you go to another orphanage tomorrow?"

"I...are you giving me time off to do so?"

He nodded.

"Then yes, I will. Thank you." I disappeared into the scullery and stacked the dishes in the tub. I couldn't stop my smile as I went to fetch water. He'd not only given me time off, but he'd actually trusted me to leave the house when he knew someone was searching for my mother, and potentially me. It meant he trusted me enough to protect myself.

One day, he would hopefully trust me enough to take care of myself alone at night in the streets, but for now it was enough that he accepted that I could do so in broad daylight with lots of people milling about.

He probably wouldn't have let me go if he had known someone had followed me the other day, however.

CHAPTER 9

*L*incoln was out all night and hadn't returned by the time I left the house in the morning. I paused as I passed through the Lichfield gate, looked left and right, then continued on when I saw no one about. I caught an omnibus into the city, then another over the bridge. I felt terribly conspicuous in my new cloak, among the women wearing practical woolen ones, but by the time I alighted in The Borough, I no longer cared. Indeed, I felt rather grand and important. A gentleman even gave up his seat for me and another doffed his hat.

Although I kept alert, I was quite sure I hadn't been followed when I arrived in Bermondsey. The orphanage was small compared to those I'd visited in the north of the city, and unhappy faces peered down at me from second floor windows. They must think me a well-to-do lady in my cloak, and I regretted wearing it again. I wasn't a lady; I was just like them. Or I had been once, as a baby, and then again at thirteen when Anselm Holloway had thrown me out of his home. While I'd chosen to live on the street instead of taking myself to an orphanage or workhouse, I'd been friendless in the city too.

I pulled the edges of the cloak together and knocked.

Thinking of past choices was never a good idea. From now on, I wanted to only look to the future.

After shouting at the elderly administrator with poor hearing, I was able to cross the Bermondsey orphanage off my list. Thanks to his excellent memory, he hadn't needed to check his records. No one by the name of Holloway had adopted a little girl eighteen years ago, nor had anyone been asking the same question in recent days.

I visited another two orphanages on the south side of London and received the same answers. Only the Brixton one had received a letter asking about my adoption. As with Mr. Hogan from the Kentish Town orphanage, the administrator couldn't recall the address he'd sent a reply to and he hadn't kept a copy of the letter. He'd claimed it had been written on plain paper bearing no monogram, and the signature had been illegible. Another dead end.

I caught a train back to the city and was about to search for an omnibus heading toward Highgate when I had another idea. I knew my father's name was Frankenstein, so perhaps my mother had listed it on my birth record. I enquired at the post office in St. Martin's Le Grand and learned that the General Register Office was only a short distance away on the Strand. It was located in the North Wing of Somerset House, an imposing building that was more like a palace with an air of stuffy authority about it. I waited for my turn to be called to a desk where a snowy-haired man with a pointed beard peered over his spectacles at me.

He asked me to write down my name and Frankenstein's on a form then passed the form on to a younger man. The poor fellow was already laden with forms and documents, and I was afraid that even one more might see the lot toppling.

"Wait a moment," I called out to him as he went to walk on.

He blinked at me then at the snowy haired man. "What is it?" asked the older man at the desk in a bored monotone. "We're very busy."

"I'd like to make an enquiry about one more birth." I smiled my sweetest smile at them both. The younger man moved closer and returned my smile. The older one grunted, but he handed me a blank form to complete. I entered Lincoln's name in the space left for the baby's name section before I lost my nerve. I handed it directly to the assistant and laid a hand on his wrist. "Thank you so much, sir. I appreciate you waiting for me."

"It could take a little while," said the older fellow.

"Oh."

"Yours are at the top, miss," said the younger man. He winked at me and headed off.

I sat with several other people who were also waiting and instantly regretted my hasty decision to inquire after Lincoln's birth. It had been made on a whim, and not one I felt proud of now that I'd had time to think about it. He would hate me going behind his back again. I hated myself. I resolved not to look at the response.

I had to wait only half an hour before the young assistant came looking for me. He smiled and fiddled with his tie, but I had no inclination for flirting.

"What did you learn?" I asked.

He spread out his hands in front of him. They were empty. "Nothing, I'm afraid. There are no births registered under the name of Frankenstein."

I smiled through my disappointment, but it felt forced, and he seemed to know it too. His own smile slipped. "I'm not interested in the other matter anymore," I told him as I rose. "Whatever you learned you may keep to yourself."

His face brightened. "That's a relief because I learned nothing anyway. There were no babies named Lincoln Fitzroy born in the last fifty years."

I left the registry office and walked along the Strand in a daze. It wasn't the lack of information on my own birth that confused me, since I suspected my mother was trying to keep Frankenstein from me and, as such, wouldn't have recorded his name on the birth entry. But not finding a record of

Lincoln was a little more surprising. I'd assumed his parents were poor and couldn't keep him. If that were the case, there should still be a record of him.

I dismissed any further questions I had on the matter. I was glad to have learned nothing useful from my thoughtlessness. The sickening sensation I'd felt in my gut ever since sending the fellow off with the inquiry began to ease.

I caught an omnibus from the city to Highgate. Instead of heading straight home, I detoured via the cemetery. The costermonger and his cart weren't there today, thank goodness, and no other passengers alighted behind me. I was satisfied that I had not been followed and was no longer being watched. It was a considerable relief.

I couldn't find Mr. Tucker, so I sought out the chap with the port wine birthmark. I found him sitting under a tree munching on his lunch. He scrambled to his feet, doffed his cap and tucked his chin into his chest.

"I'm sorry to interrupt you." It was like talking to a stray cat. I had to keep both my movements and voice gentle, soothing. "I hope you can answer a question for me about the grave that was dug up."

He nodded.

"Have you been near there since the body was reburied?"

He nodded.

"Is it still buried?"

Another nod.

"Are you aware of anyone taking an interest in the grave since then?"

"No, miss," he mumbled.

"Thank you. That's all. Please continue to enjoy your lunch."

So it would seem we were right; the captain hadn't wanted to risk digging up Gordon again. Our only way to find the man was at Mr. Lee's—*if* he paid the den another visit.

* * *

DESPITE HAVING THE DAY OFF, I completed some chores after lunch. Lincoln had returned while I was out and was resting in his rooms, while Gus kept watch at Lee's. It was quite late in the day when Lincoln joined me in the parlor as I rubbed beeswax into one of the tabletops.

"We can get an hour of training in before I head out again," he said.

I glanced out the window. The sun's final rays cast a sepia glow over the front garden. It would be dark soon. "Not today, if that's all right with you. I want to talk instead."

He rested a hand on the mantel. "About?"

"About the ministry."

He drew in a breath and let it out slowly. "Very well. First, tell me how your investigations went this morning."

I told him which orphanages I'd visited and what I'd learned from them, as well as at the cemetery. I didn't mention my detour to the GRO. "The captain hasn't been back to Thackery's grave."

"We'll find him at Lee's or one of the other opium dens," he said. "Not the cemetery."

"You're very confident, but I don't see how you can be. You can't possibly watch all the opium dens in London. There are only three of you."

"I've paid each proprietor a substantial sum to report to me if a man fitting the captain's description shows up and doesn't partake in smoking. I'm confident my money will bring results."

I smiled. "You've thought of everything."

"I know how these operations work."

"How? You said you knew Lee's..." I couldn't meet his gaze anymore and returned to polishing the table.

"You want to know if I smoke opium."

I shrugged one shoulder. "It crossed my mind."

"I have."

His answer startled me into looking at him again. "Oh. I see. Well."

"Don't you want to know more?"

"I don't want to pry."

"Yes, you do." Despite his accusation, he didn't sound angry or offended. "You have a curious nature."

"Some would say nosy."

The corner of his mouth lifted. "I would rather you asked me questions directly instead of others. That way you'll be sure to get the right answer."

If he wanted to answer at all. "Very well. How did you end up becoming an opium addict?"

"I wasn't an addict. I experimented with it as part of my studies when I was younger."

"You experimented with it?" I echoed. "How does one experiment with opium? And to what end?"

"I smoked it five times over five weeks to study the effects."

"Why?"

He shrugged. "Why not? It's just another piece of knowledge, and knowledge is necessary in my position."

"When you put it like that, it sounds quite innocent. I think of opium smoking as a sordid habit that lures desperate men."

"It can be, if one partakes too often. As Gordon Thackery did, by his own admission. An addict is not a pretty sight."

"I've seen men coming and going from a garret in Bluegate Fields, near where I once lived. We all knew it was an opium house. I'd often see the same men on street corners, begging for money that they would spend at the garret later that night. There was such an air of hopeless about them, as if they were caught in a web they couldn't escape. It was awful."

"That's generally how addiction works. It's difficult to break free once it digs its claws in."

"You never felt the pull of the opium when you experimented? You never wanted to partake more than once a week?"

He shook his head. "Like you, I'd seen what it could do to a man. One of my tutors showed me the addicts like you describe."

"That's an odd thing for a tutor to do. What was the subject he taught?"

"It didn't have an official name. I called it Slums and Scums Studies, but not to my tutor's face."

I laughed. "How many tutors did you have?"

"Twenty-two, but not all at one time. Over the course of several years, I might have three or four different tutors for the same subject."

"Your lessons were private?"

He nodded.

"No other children joined you?"

"No. Why?"

"I'm merely curious." It confirmed my theory that he must have had a lonely childhood. "Were they stuffy old men?"

He paused before answering. "Not all."

I frowned, wondering why he'd paused. And then it dawned on me. "Do you mean to say you had women tutors too?"

Another pause. "Only one."

"What subject did she teach?"

"Women."

I almost choked on my tongue as I tried not to laugh. "Women?"

"I had little to do with females at that point, so the general decided I needed to learn more about them. Since there was only a crusty old housekeeper living at the house, he employed a woman to tutor me in all things feminine. How they behaved and thought, their weaknesses and strengths. I learned a lot from her."

"So it's thanks to her that you're the charming man you are today?"

His eyes narrowed. "She did her best. It's not her fault I was already sixteen and set in my ways by the time she took on the task."

"She must have done something right," I said, finishing off the cleaning.

"Is that so?"

"Lady Harcourt certainly finds you appealing."

"Does she?" he said idly.

I wondered what else his female tutor had taught him. How to please a woman intimately? Or had that task fallen to Lady Harcourt, or perhaps an earlier mistress? How many had this handsome, intriguing man taken to bed?

I wiped my greasy hands on a clean cloth and screwed on the wax tub lid. I tried not to think about his lovers. Being aware of Lady Harcourt was quite enough.

"Are those the only questions you had for me?" he asked.

"No. They weren't even the questions I intended to ask. Thank you for answering them. I appreciate your candor." I bit my lip, acutely aware that he was watching me and that as his maid I had no right to ask him anything about his private life.

"I want you to feel comfortable here," he said, placing his hands behind his back.

"I already do."

He indicated I should sit on the sofa so I sat, being careful not to touch the brocade fabric with my hands. He sat on an armchair opposite. "Go on."

"Tell me about the ministry," I said.

"I thought I already had."

"You've told me what its purpose is now, and why there is a committee, but not its history. You all seem to have quite different opinions about ministry business, and what to do with people like me, and I thought understanding the ministry's past will help me understand its present."

He leaned forward, resting his elbows on his knees. "Don't let Gillingham upset you. His is one opinion among several."

"I know. And he doesn't upset me." Not anymore.

He leaned back and sat very still. He was often still, whether sitting or standing, as if conserving every ounce of energy and storing it for later use. "The ministry grew out of an order that has existed for a long time. It was renamed the Ministry for Peculiar Things when I became its head."

"Things?" I chuckled. "Who thought of that name?"

His lips drew together. "It was more recently given its current name The Ministry of Curiosities. Prior to my taking over, it had been dormant for many years, with no leader and only a committee to remember its function and pass on information about it from generation to generation. And to store the archives, of course."

"How old is it, precisely?"

"Perhaps a thousand years. No one is certain."

"Good lord. It's been in existence all this time? That means people with supernatural abilities have been around for just as long, or there would have been no need to harbor them."

His gaze drifted away. His hands shifted ever so slightly on the chair arm.

"What is it?" I asked. "What aren't you telling me?"

He seemed surprised that I'd picked up on his cues. "The order wasn't originally formed to find and harbor those who knew magic, but destroy them."

I drew in a breath. "People like me?" I whispered.

He nodded. "The order thought anyone who performed magic, as they called it, was unholy, unnatural."

"Like Anselm Holloway does."

"A thousand years ago, the church declared all supernatural people abominations against God, and that put a price on their heads, so to speak. It gave ordinary folk free reign to burn witches, lynch necromancers and anyone else who displayed magical abilities. The order grew from those times of persecution here in England and, for hundreds of years, it thrived as it hunted down anyone accused of witchcraft."

"How awful," I whispered.

"Yes and no. Not everyone has a good heart and conscience like you, Charlie. Magicians and witches have been known to cause great harm. They're people, after all, and as with any group of people there are good and bad. Some did terrible things. The order, however, didn't discriminate.

Good and bad supernaturals all fell victim to their form of justice. Innocents were persecuted alongside the guilty."

"So...magicians and witches are real," I said carefully.

"They are. You're one."

I scoffed. "I'm a necromancer. It's hardly magic or witch-craft. I can't change into a bat, or turn you into a frog. I can only do one thing, and it's only moderately useful."

"From what I've read in the ministry archives, that still qualifies you for being a witch. Most witches and magicians seemed to have a specialty, only one trick they could perform. I found no records of turning anyone into a bat or any other animal, but I did find accounts of mind control, changing one's own appearance, speaking to ghosts, that sort of thing."

I shook my head slowly, not because I didn't believe him, but because it was so fantastical. It was difficult to under-stand the scale of what he was telling me. "Why do we know nothing about witches and magicians now? Well, except for me, that is."

"I've observed others who possess strange powers. They're not hard to find, if one listens to rumors and talks to the right people. I expect they keep to themselves for precisely the reason you did—fear of reprisal. Society would ostracize them at the least, and hurt them at the most."

"I suppose so." Holloway had tried both ostracizing me and hurting me. He'd succeeded at the former and only failed at the latter thanks to Cook and his meat cleaver.

"The order accounted for many, many deaths of supernat-urals in those early centuries," he said. "Times have changed drastically, fortunately. You have nothing to fear from the ministry. No one wants to eradicate supernaturals now."

Except, perhaps, Lord Gillingham. "The others wanted to exile me."

"Exile is not death."

"No," I said drily.

"And I won't let that happen to you, unless you wish to relocate to a tropical island paradise."

I smiled, despite myself. "Lichfield will do nicely for now."

"I'm glad to hear it." His rich, deep voice washed over me, and my smile broadened. He blinked once, then looked down at his lap where his hands bunched into fists. The tender moment was over so quickly, I wondered if I'd misread him this time.

"Why did the order become dormant?" I prompted. "Did it destroy so many supernaturals that few were left and it was no longer needed?"

"That's one theory, but it's more likely it suffered the same fate as the Roman Catholic church here. It was closely tied to the faith, so when England navigated the Reformation in the sixteenth century and ousted Catholics, the order fell into disarray. It was forgotten by everyone but a few who kept the records and stories alive. A handful of caretakers were appointed in each generation, passing on the information to their sons, who would pass it on to their sons, et cetera."

"The current committee members are descendants of the original caretakers?"

He nodded. "I had no choice in their selection. No one did."

"You said sons. What about Lady Harcourt? Does she not have brothers?"

"Lady Harcourt's late husband was the committee member. He didn't pass on the information to his sons, but to his wife. She doesn't know why, but it's possible he didn't trust his sons to be discreet."

Having met Andrew Buchanan, I could see why he thought that. "Why didn't one of the generations resurrect the old order and put it to use again? Why wait until now?"

"They were waiting for me."

I raised my brows.

"Apparently there was a prophecy, spoken by a seer in the mid fifteen hundreds. She foresaw the long years of the order's dormancy, which would come to an end in this century, when a new leader was appointed. She gave particular details about him." He held out his hands, palm up. "It turned out to be me."

How extraordinary, and rather intriguing, too. It made me think of old fairytales with curses, prophecies and evil witches. It even had a knight in shining armor—Lincoln. The story only lacked a princess.

"And so you were brought up in the general's home, trained from birth to be the leader."

He nodded. "He was the eldest member. He had no family of his own and so was considered the ideal candidate."

"But he was never home."

"Precisely. It was deemed best if I didn't become attached to anyone."

I blinked at him. Not become attached? But little children *needed* to feel a sense of belonging and nurturing. I'd seen it in the gangs, with the youngest members. They often attached themselves to a champion who took care of them and provided for them, even loved them. It was human instinct. "Were the servants like a family to you?"

"They were often moved along before I could make friends."

"Oh, Lincoln."

His hands balled into fists on his knees. His lips flattened and I decided not to tell him that I thought his childhood sounded desolate. He would hate my pity. So I asked a more impersonal question instead. "Wouldn't a seer be considered a supernatural and therefore a target of the caretaker committee?"

"That's the irony. Her prophecy not only kept the order dormant for so long, but it perhaps had a hand in changing the position of the caretakers. I couldn't find any reference in the archives to her being punished for her prophecy. It stated the new leader would even use magic to defeat dark forces that want to bring the realm to its knees."

"Good lord. Do you think she meant Frankenstein?"

"Perhaps. He certainly could have caused great harm if he'd managed to build an army of strong corpses."

"And if my necromancy is considered magic, then that fits too." I waited for him to add more, but he didn't. It seemed I would have to broach the subject instead. "Did your mother let you go freely?"

"I don't know. The general has told me so little about her."

"What *do* you know?"

"That she fell pregnant at a young age and wasn't married. That removing me from her was a blessing, for both her and me. She couldn't have afforded to raise me, apparently, and I would have lived a life of squalor."

I wondered if the general could be believed. Lincoln seemed to, although he spoke stiffly, formally, as if he didn't want to think too much about it. If he'd led a lonely, unhappy childhood, it was no wonder he had difficulty expressing himself and showing kindness.

"You were raised to be a killing machine, weren't you?" I hedged.

He looked at me with wide eyes that quickly narrowed again. "Among other things," he snapped.

"I...I'm sorry. I didn't mean to offend. I just meant that you're supposed to save the world from dark forces, so you must have been prepared accordingly."

"I speak a dozen languages fluently and another dozen moderately well. I've memorized entire books, know advanced mathematics, and can put together an engine as efficiently as any engineer. I can create poisons and antidotes, have a thorough understanding of medicine and the workings of the human body. I've traveled across Europe and through parts of Asia and America. I can dance as well as any gentleman, recite poetry, and play the violin. Do you want me to go on?" It wasn't boastful, but matter of fact; as if he wanted me to know that he was more than a killing machine, more than his nickname of Death. As if *needed* me to know. That only made me ache for him more.

"Your catalog of skills is very impressive," I whispered. "I feel rather provincial now."

He clicked his tongue and unclenched his fists. "That wasn't my intention. Forgive me."

"It's all right." I wanted to smile to let him know it didn't matter, but he wouldn't look at me. It was best to return to the topic of the ministry again. Safer. "The committee are still wary of magic and the supernatural, on the whole," I said. "But you don't seem to be. Why is that?"

He cleared his throat. "I mentioned before that I've observed some people who possess powers. They were all harmless, good folk, and I had no reason to fear them or worry that they wanted to take over the country."

"They were not the dark forces the seer spoke of?"

"Not in the least."

I rose and bobbed my head. "Thank you, Mr. Fitzroy. I appreciate your candor. I won't tell a soul what you've told me."

"I know you won't." He rose too. "Gus and Seth will be busy tonight," he added. "So there's something I need you to do for me."

"Would you like me to clean your rooms?"

"Nothing like that. Can you check my tailcoat to see that it's in good order? It's been some time since I wore it. My formal shirt will need starching too."

It took a few moments for my dull brain to realize he was talking about the clothes he would wear to the ball. "You're accepting Lady Harcourt's friend's invitation?"

"You seem surprised."

"I didn't think it your sort of thing."

"It's not."

"Then why are you going?"

"The answer matters to you," he said flatly.

"Yes. No!" I sighed. "I'm curious as to why you would go if you think you'll hate it. Is it because Lady Harcourt wishes it?"

One dark brow lifted slowly then lowered again. "No," he said as he walked away. "Because people I want to see will be there."

"Your family," I murmured, surprising myself. My mind was leaping in all directions, and I wasn't entirely sure if I believed what I'd said or was merely throwing it into the mix to gauge is reaction.

And he did react. He stopped suddenly and turned to face me. I gulped.

"I...I'm sorry." I waved the polishing cloth in dismissal. "You're a gentleman, so I assume your family must be gently bred too and would perhaps attend balls. That's all I meant."

"I told you my mother was a pauper."

"And your father?"

"I was never informed who he was." With his hands clasped behind him, he strolled out of the parlor.

I watched him go, a curious feeling in my chest. It was partly sorrow for the little, lonely boy he'd once been, but it was mostly a sense of triumph. I'd realized something during our exchange—I'd begun to decipher the small cues he sometimes gave away without realizing it. It might be a twist of his mouth, a quirk of his eyebrow, or hardening of the muscles in his jaw. Or it could be an abrupt stop and a defiant, challenging glare—as he'd just given me. A glare that dared me to tell him what I suspected. What I did know now from those minute cues was that I'd been right—his family would be at the ball tomorrow night. His father's side of the family, that was. Just because Lincoln claimed never to have been told who'd fathered him didn't mean he hadn't found out by some other means. He was resourceful. If he wanted to discover something, I had no doubt that he could.

I wondered which noble family he belonged to, and who else knew. The committee must. Lord Gillingham had once alluded to knowing secrets about Lincoln, and Lady Harcourt had said he was protective of his family. She could have meant his mother, but I somehow suspected she meant his father. She'd also known precisely which ball to invite him to, one where his family would be in attendance, therefore increasing the chances of him going.

He must like to keep his eye on them from time to time, perhaps even talk to them. I could understand the allure.

I wondered if his father knew that Lincoln was his son.

* * *

THE ONLY MENDING Lincoln's formal tailcoat required was for a loose button to be removed and sewn back on. I ironed his best shirt and made a note to send the collar out to a nearby laundry for starching into a circular shape on their special steam iron. In the evening, I read in the library for a little but grew lonely and went in search of Cook. Everyone else had gone out to make inquiries at opium dens.

I found Cook stropping a knife blade on a cleaning board at the kitchen table. I must have startled him because he glanced up quickly. The moment's inattention caused him to cut his thumb.

He swore like a sailor and swiped up a cloth, wrapping it around his thumb. Blood soon seeped through.

"Are you all right?" I dropped the sewing I'd brought with me on the table and tried to get a look at his thumb, but he wouldn't unwrap it. "Let me see."

"It bloody hurts."

"I'm sure it does. Is it still attached?"

He gingerly unwrapped the cloth. The cut oozed blood, but after a close inspection, I was satisfied the thumb wasn't going to come off. The cut was deep, however, and required stitching. Fortunately I knew where the medical kit was kept, and how to suture a wound. Lincoln had shown me soon after we'd met. I'd not done it since, and not without supervision, but I was sure I could manage.

Cook wasn't quite so certain. It took some convincing, and half a bottle of Lincoln's best brandy, before he would unwrap it for me again. He couldn't bear to watch as I threaded the sterile needle and sewed up the cut. He whimpered like a child the entire time.

"And here I thought you were a big, strong beast of a man," I told him as I tied the thread ends. "You're nothing but a baby."

"It bloody hurts!"

I kissed the top of his bald head. "I know. You cradle your hand while I make you some hot chocolate."

He sat there while I packed away the kit and he didn't get up as I broke the chocolate pieces into the saucepan. I made a cup for him and one for me, and I tried to get him to return to his usual gruff self by getting him to talk about the carnivals his father used to take him to as a child, but it was no use. I sent him to bed when he finished his chocolate.

I cleaned his knives and washed the saucepan and cups then sat down to my sewing. I pulled the lamp in close so I could see the dark blue ribbon against the pale blue fabric of the dress. It was the only dress I owned that wasn't a uniform. I'd only worn it once, preferring to keep it for special occasions. Unfortunately, there'd been no special occasions. I'd worn it one time when I went out, merely to get some use out of it. I resolved to wear it more now that I'd sewn Lincoln's ribbon into the waistline.

I was packing my pins away when I heard a brisk knock at the back door. It must have been almost eleven o'clock; far too late for callers or deliveries. I thought about fetching Cook, but whoever it was might have given up by then. The knock came again, more urgent this time.

"Who is it?" I called out.

"I come from Mr. Lee," came a small voice. It belonged to either a child or a woman, but I still didn't open the door.

"What do you want?"

"Mr. Lee sends a message for Mr. Fitzroy."

"What about?"

The person hesitated, perhaps considering if he or she should deliver the message to someone who wasn't the intended recipient. "Mr. Fitzroy wanted to be told if the captain returned."

I unlocked the door and opened it. A boy no older than fourteen stood there, shivering in clothes too small for his growing limbs. I ushered him inside and through to the kitchen, and he immediately went to stand by the warm range, like a moth attracted to a flame.

"Has the captain returned to Mr. Lee's?" I asked him.

He peered at me through his long, dirty hair. He had Oriental eyes, but he wasn't a full-blooded Chinese. "Mr. Lee sent me here to tell Mr. Fitzroy."

"Thank you. Mr. Fitzroy will be very satisfied. I'll inform him shortly. Did you get a look at the captain?"

The boy shook his head.

"What is the captain doing now?" I asked.

"Watching someone."

"Watching one of Mr. Lee's...customers?"

He nodded again and rubbed his hands more vigorously. They were dirty and red raw, and the boy's clothes were so thin. He at least wore shoes, but his toes poked through.

"Stay here. Don't steal anything." I hurried out of the kitchen and up the stairs. I found a spare coat and pair of gloves in Seth's room and ran back down to the kitchen again. The boy was exactly where I'd left him. I handed over the garments then asked him to wait. I found some bread and cheese in the pantry and handed the lot to him.

"Thank you for reporting in," I said to the lad, who now stared back at me as if he'd seen a remarkable vision. "You may go now. Be careful. It's dark out and the streets are dangerous."

"Thank you, miss." He scooped up the food and his new possessions and dashed for the door as if he were afraid I'd change my mind.

I locked the door behind him and considered what to do. I didn't know where Seth, Gus and Lincoln were, precisely. They could be anywhere in the city. And Cook was in no state to head out. It was up to me.

Lincoln would be furious if I went alone. So I wouldn't go alone. I'd find myself a bodyguard. And I knew just the place where hundreds, if not thousands, could be found, if one were a necromancer.

CHAPTER 10

*T*he glow of my lantern wasn't bright enough to penetrate the fog that blanketed the cemetery grounds. Its ghostly form swirled about my trouser legs as I padded over the dense layer of fallen leaves and picked my way between graves. It wasn't easy to avoid tree roots and headstones, which seemed to emerge from nowhere, but I managed not to fall over or get lost. I knew my way to my mother's grave, and Gordon Thackery's wasn't too far from there.

It wasn't so much the lack of visibility that stretched my nerves to breaking point but the silence. There was no wind, and the fog dampened all sounds. If anyone followed me, I wouldn't be able to hear them. Even my own footsteps were deadened by the fog and damp leaves.

Before I'd become fully aware of my powers as a necromancer, I would never have ventured into a cemetery at night for fear of ghouls and demons, but now that I knew I could control spirits, that fear had vanished. I was perhaps safer in a place where I could call up the dead than I was anywhere else. All I needed was a name and a body, and I was surrounded by names on headstones and bodies in graves.

But I only wanted one. Gordon had proved himself to be a

good soul, and he'd offered to help again if we needed him. I hoped he hadn't changed his mind.

I recognized the large tree that the grounds keeper had sat under. Gordon's gravestone was nearby, the earth still bare from his reburial.

"Gordon Moreland Thackery's spirit, can you hear me?" My voice was swallowed by the fog. I cleared my throat and tried again, louder. "I summon Gordon Thackery here to speak to me."

A smoky wisp shot out of the fog, straight at me. I dropped the lantern and fell backward with a yelp.

"Are you all right?" the ghostly figure asked. "I am sorry, Miss Charlie, I have no control over my speed when I arrive."

"Gordon! It's so nice to see you again."

He smiled. "I would help you up..."

I stood and picked up my lantern. "Are you, er, well?"

He chuckled. "My afterlife goes well, yes. And you?" He looked me up and down. "How long has it been since I was last here?"

"A few days. I need your help again, but only if you're up to it. I don't like disturbing you like this."

"I would be glad to help if I can." The misty spirit spun round. "Where is your man?"

"Don't let Mr. Fitzroy hear you call him my man. He's my employer. He's not here tonight, which is why I need you. I want you to act as a sort of guard for me. I have to visit Mr. Lee's opium den. The captain is there, and this might be our only chance to find him. Unfortunately, Mr. Fitzroy and his men are out looking for him elsewhere, and I only got the message from Mr. Lee now. I'm afraid if I miss this opportunity, it could be some time before we find him again."

"It's rather brave of you to undertake the task alone."

"I won't be alone, I'll have you."

He frowned. "Lee's is not a place for ladies."

"Thank you, Gordon, but I'm not a lady and I've been in far more disreputable places, I'm sure. I lived on the streets for five years."

His lips formed an O. He nodded. "Very well. If you're up for an adventure then so am I."

"Excellent! Shall we get started?"

We both glanced at his grave. Last time, his body had already been above ground. This time it had to break free of a coffin and dig through several feet of earth. "I wish I'd thought it through a little more," I said. "Do you think you can manage?"

"Let's see." The mist swirled and dove down into the grave, disturbing nothing, not even the nearby leaves at my feet.

I waited. Nothing happened. I set the lantern down near the head of the grave and flipped the hood of my old cloak back. Still nothing happened. It must be too much of a task. He had to somehow push off the coffin lid with all that soil pressing down on it. He might have superior strength, but—

The earth pulsed. I rested a hand on the headstone and leaned closer to get a better look. The soil was definitely moving, as if something underneath pushed it up. *Come on, Gordon, you can do it.*

Dirt trickled down from the center of the grave as it rose upward to form a mound. Then a hand punched through. For the second time that night, I yelped and fell backward. I scrambled to my feet again and watched, fascinated, as Gordon pulled himself free of his grave. Any innocent bystanders would have run screaming from the cemetery, but I was transfixed.

When he finally stepped free, he smiled at me. "I'm a little filthier," he said, inspecting himself. "How do I look otherwise?"

Like he'd decayed more in the short space of time since I'd last seen him. His eyes and cheeks had sunken further and his skin now sported a tinge of green, although to be fair, it was difficult to see in the poor light. "Er...like a dead man."

"That bad?" He screwed up his face. "I suppose it's inevitable. I wonder how long it will be before I'm nothing but bones."

"A little while longer, yet." I don't know why I wanted to reassure him. He was very matter-of-fact about his decay; I, on the other hand, was somewhat saddened by it. "Are you ready?"

He dusted off some of the dirt from his suit, but he was still covered in it. His hands in particular were filthy. "I'd offer you my arm, but I don't want to sicken you."

"I'm not sickened," I said, holding out my hand.

He hesitated then with a smile, offered his elbow. I slipped my hand into it, picked up the lantern, and headed out of the cemetery with him like an ordinary couple going for a stroll. I giggled at the macabre image we cut, earning a smile from Gordon in return. Unfortunately, one of his teeth fell out, and he shut his mouth again.

We passed through the Highgate Cemetery gate and I nodded at the two horses tied up nearby. "It's too far to walk so I brought transportation." I'd managed to saddle them on my own; Seth had taught me how. I'd brought the two most docile horses in the stables and prayed they wouldn't be spooked by the ethereal quiet of the foggy night, or by Gordon.

I'd left a note on the kitchen table for Cook. I didn't want to wake him and he wouldn't have been as useful as Gordon anyway. Hopefully I'd be back before he or one of the others read it. No doubt it would cause alarm, despite my assurance that Gordon could protect me.

"Do you know the way to Lee's?" he asked me.

"Not precisely. Lower Pell Lane is near the docks, but that's all I know."

"I'm well familiar with it," he said drily. "I could find my way there with my eyes closed."

He held my horse while I mounted, then spent a moment to familiarize himself with the other. It shied away from him at first, but a few gentle words and pats coaxed it to stand still and allow him to mount. Even so, its ears twitched back and forth and its nostrils flared.

We rode south as quickly as I dared. With no traffic to get

in the way, it was an easy ride, thank goodness. Gordon was more comfortable on horseback than me, as most gentlemen would be, and he frequently had to stop and wait. We dismounted in a tavern yard around the corner from Lower Pell Lane and paid a tired looking stable lad to mind the horses. Gordon clung to the shadows as I completed the transaction.

Despite the late hour, a few drunkards came and went from the tavern but took no notice of us. Dressed in my boys' trousers, I blended in. We were a few streets north of the actual docks, and aside from taverns and alehouses, there were shops selling wares that travelers or sailors might need. All were shut up for the night, some with lamps valiantly trying to ward off thieves, all with heavy locks on doors.

I held my lantern high and walked swiftly to keep up with Gordon. We headed away from Ratcliff Highway, through an arch, along a narrow passage and into a courtyard crammed with tenements. Faded signs hung above doors announcing that lodgings could be had within. There were other signs too, in a script I couldn't understand.

Gordon fixed on a door with the symbol of a dragon etched into the wood. "This is it," he said. "Lee has rooms inside and a man on the door. He'll scream blue murder if we're police, but shouldn't put up a fuss when he sees it's just two lads, especially if I use Mr. Lee's name. He's had this establishment a few years now, ever since the authorities began cracking down on the dens, and he had to leave his shop for something more discreet. Be prepared, Miss Charlie. It's a hovel."

I drew in a deep breath and nodded at the door. "I'm ready."

He pulled up the collar of his suit to cover his chin and mouth and drew some of his hair over his face. A few strands fell out as he did so. He knocked and the door was opened by a Chinaman with a long black ponytail and sleepy eyes. His age was difficult to discern, but his face was quite youthful. The smell of smoke drifted to us, tickling my nose.

Gordon bowed before the man could fully see his face. "Is Mr. Lee in? I've brought a friend with me this time."

The Chinaman bowed and so did I. When he straightened, he indicated we should go through. "Mr. Lee at home," he said and sat again on a stool by the door.

We headed up a flight of wooden stairs. The burning smell grew stronger, but it wasn't quite the same smell as a fireplace. It was more acrid, and the closer we drew to the room at the top of the stairs, the more my eyes watered.

Gordon opened the door and the fumes almost overpowered me. I coughed into the haze of smoke and wiped tears from my stinging eyes. Gordon took my arm. His eyes were fine. He would be unaffected by such mortal things as opium fumes.

As my eyes adjusted, I saw that the room was quite small. Clothing and bedsheets hung from the ceiling on string, but for what purpose, I couldn't say. If Mr. Lee did his laundry in there, it would never be free of the smoke. A large bed occupied most of the room, but there were two other narrow beds as well, two chairs, a table and stove. When I realized how many people lay on the three beds, my jaw dropped. There were two on each of the smaller cots, lying curled on their sides, and at least four or five on the bigger bed. It was difficult to determine the number as the limbs were splayed here and there, and the bodies packed together. One or two raised their heads upon our entry, but most simply lay there in a stupor, writhing every now and again, like snakes. Even more men sat or lay on the floor, pipes drooping from their mouths. Most stared vacantly, but a few were intent on their conversations or lighting their pipes.

An ancient Chinaman shuffled over to meet us. As with the fellow downstairs, he wore his hair in a long ponytail. His face, however, was quite a shock. It held little more life than Gordon's. The pallor was almost the same, the eyes and cheeks were just as sunken, and the bones at his shoulders protruded through his clothing. The corpse-like figure bowed at us and we bowed back.

"Mr. Lee," Gordon said. "It has been some time since I've been."

Mr. Lee searched Gordon's face for signs of recognition. Either he found some or he thought he must be a friend since he'd greeted him by name, because he ushered us inside. He didn't seem to realize he'd welcomed a dead man in. Now that I was closer, I could see the smokers more clearly. They were from all walks of life; some with English faces, but others different shades of brown, Oriental and one even appeared to be a woman with red hair that fanned out on the pillow like a disheveled aura. She opened her heavy lidded eyes, muttered something, then closed them again and rolled on her side, away from us.

Mr. Lee led us to the table, where a small lamp burned and some pipes had been laid out beside a box. He indicated we should sit, and I realized he was going to prepare us an opium pipe.

I shook my head. "No, no. We're looking for someone. A man." I left Gordon to explain while I moved around the room, checking each face. Of the Englishmen there, none wore spectacles and all were under the effects of opium. If the captain had been there earlier, he wasn't there now.

I rubbed my temple and my fingers came away slippery with sweat. I removed my jacket and slung it over the back of one of the chairs then plopped down on the chair itself. My legs felt heavy, as if they didn't belong to me, and I worried I wouldn't be able to walk out again.

A hand settled on my shoulder, startling me. I jumped, but it was Gordon. Except his hand bore no skin. It was only bone and sinew now. How had he deteriorated so quickly? I blinked and his hand returned to normal. How peculiar.

"Are you all right?" he asked me, frowning.

"I think I'm seeing things."

"Hallucinations. It's the opium doing that to you. You're small and unused to it. It'll affect you easily. We'll go soon."

I nodded again, but wasn't sure how well I managed the motion with such a heavy head.

"There's another room through there." He pointed to a doorway I hadn't seen before. There was no door, only a curtain hanging from a string. "That's where the wealthier customers go. That's where we'll find him."

"Him," I repeated dully. "The captain?"

His hand patted my shoulder then he headed toward the curtain. Mr. Lee settled down onto a floor cushion in the corner of the room and picked up a pipe. He didn't seem to care what we did.

I hauled myself to my feet and followed Gordon. The room beyond the curtain was just as smoky but a lamp burned through the haze, providing more light than the candles in the main room. There was only one bed with one man lying on it, his body so thin that he was almost flat. Another man sat on the bed at his side, his back to us. He held a syringe against the unconscious man's arm. He was going to inject him!

"Stop!" I cried, lunging forward. I lost my balance and Gordon caught me, but I lost sight of the men in the process.

Then someone appeared at my side. Not Gordon. He wore spectacles and seemed quite alert, compared to the opium addicts. The captain! He held up a syringe filled with dark red liquid. Blood?

Bile rose to my throat. I covered my mouth and somehow managed not to vomit.

"Who're you?" the man said in cultured, crisp tones.

"Good evening, Captain," Gordon said.

I'd sunk to my knees at some point, and now looked up to see the man known as the captain stare at Gordon, his jaw slack. He lifted a hand to Gordon's face, but pulled back without touching. Gordon smiled and the captain recoiled altogether.

"My God." The captain shuffled backward and fell on the bed. The figure in it groaned but didn't move. He was still alive, but an air of death hung around him. I could sense it, despite my addled brain.

I got to my feet and lurched to the bed. I rested a hand on

the man's chest and felt for a heartbeat. It was terribly weak and slow. He wouldn't last much longer.

"What were you doing to him?" I shouted.

But the captain wasn't listening to me. He was intent on Gordon. He looked as appalled as he was fascinated. "Thackery?" he squeaked. "What trick is this?"

"No trick."

"My god!" The captain set aside the syringe and got up again. "Come here so I can see you. Are you Gordon Thackery's twin?"

Gordon chuckled, and the brittle sound sent a chill down my spine. I was glad I wasn't the focus of his attention at that moment. I was the focus of no one's attention. My legs once again felt too heavy to hold me up, so I sat down on the bed. My foot hit something solid. A bag, like the sort doctors carry. I bent down to inspect its contents but it was whipped away by the captain.

He clutched it to his chest. "Who're you and what do you want?" he snapped at me.

"I want to know what you're doing to these men." I indicated the near-dead fellow on the bed, and Gordon. "Tell us why you're killing them? What are you doing with them? What do you want with them after their death?" A thousand other questions and thoughts flittered through my head like bees, all buzzing about. My mind would see one, run for it and try to grasp it, but the bee would dash off before it could be caught. It was maddening, confusing. I pressed a hand to my forehead.

"Answer her," Gordon growled. "I'd like to know what you want with me too, now that I'm dead."

The captain hugged his bag tighter and tried to edge past Gordon toward the door. Gordon blocked his path. The captain swallowed heavily. Now that he was closer to Gordon, he must be able to see the signs of decomposition. He'd gone quite a bit paler.

"Y—you're...Gordon Thackery."

Gordon nodded. "I have no twin."

"Y—you're dead."

"Quite. Tell me, Captain, did you kill me? I don't seem to recall much from that night, except that you visited me here."

The captain began to shake all over and a drop of sweat trickled down the side of his face. "Let me out! Let me out of here!"

Nobody came to his aid.

He tried to dodge Gordon but couldn't. Cursing, he opened his bag and pulled out a gun. He didn't point it at Gordon, however. He pointed it at me.

"No!" I cried. "Don't shoot!"

Gordon put up his hands in surrender and stepped aside. The captain ran past, flipped the curtain aside, and disappeared.

"You promised me discretion!" he shouted at someone, presumably Mr. Lee. Then the main door slammed shut.

As I once more struggled to stand, the Chinaman who'd been guarding the downstairs door suddenly appeared. He held a pistol, although at first I thought it was a black lizard. The part of my brain still functioning normally realized that it was a hallucination.

"You, out," he ordered Gordon and me. "Mr. Lee want no trouble."

"We'd better do as he says, Miss Charlie," Gordon said. "Mr. Lee may have sent for you, but I'm assuming this is more than he bargained for."

"Agreed." I was about to get up when the body on the bed gave a final gasp then went still. A moment later the spirit rose from it, glanced around, and was about to take off when it saw me watching him and not his body.

"Good evening," I said. "My name is Charlie Holloway. I'm a necromancer."

"A bloody what?"

I waved my hand. It was too difficult to explain. "Can you tell me what that man wanted with you? The man known as the captain?"

"Jasper? What's it to you?"

Jasper! I must remember that. "It's a long story, but he's linked to some grave robberies."

He shrugged. "Why should I care?"

"Because your body may be the next one he steals from its final resting place."

That got his attention. The spirit swooped closer. "Did he kill me?"

"I don't know. He might have, or you might have died anyway. I do know that he's feeding a substance to opium addicts while they are barely conscious, then, after their death, digging up their bodies. Can you tell us any more than that?"

The spirit's features bunched into a frown. "That bloody cur. If he hadn't run off like a coward, I'd bloody kill him."

"Sir? Answer my question, please."

"I don't need to answer nothing, now. But I can tell you this. If that man had anything to do with my death, I'll come back and haunt him until he's out of his mind. If you find him, you tell him that from me."

"I'll be sure to." I sighed. "So you can't tell me anything more?"

"No." The mist looked at the ceiling and I thought he was about to disappear when he added, "He fed me something on a spoon sometimes, and said my sacrifice would be worth it."

"Worth it? Worth what?"

"That's all I know." Without even a goodbye, the mist drifted off.

"Well, that was rude," I said, finally pushing myself to my feet. Except my feet wouldn't obey and I fell back onto the bed once more. I tried, and failed, again. I yawned and closed my heavy eyelids. "I might rest here a few moments."

"Not yet," Gordon said. "I got you, Miss Charlie." He scooped me into his arms and turned toward the door. I opened my eyes when he didn't move.

The Chinamen still barred the doorway, but he now shook from head to toe, his eyes huge as he stared at Gordon. Mr. Lee stood beside him, a gun in hand. He seemed more composed, or perhaps he thought the cadaver advancing on him was merely an opium-fueled illusion. Either way, he was unperturbed. He lowered his gun, bowed, and backed out through the doorway.

Gordon went to follow, but the young Chinaman wasn't quite so calm. Sweat dripped from his temples and beaded on his bare top lip. The hand that held the pistol shook as he raised it.

"Put it down." If I'd had any doubts that Gordon had been in the army, his command would have banished them. "Let us pass."

The Chinaman said something in his native tongue, shook his head, and fired.

CHAPTER 11

The sound of shattering glass set off a sequence of seemingly disconnected events. The room went dark—or perhaps I'd closed my eyes. I spun around and around, like I was on an out of control carousel. But wasn't Gordon holding me? My head swam. My stomach lurched. I fell.

I landed on something soft, much to my aching head's appreciation. I passed a hand over my stinging eyes—they were definitely open—and felt around me.

I touched something. An arm, a shoulder, a face and hair. The corpse on the bed. I screamed, but it was lost in the din of noise that had exploded in the room. Voices blended together like an out of tune orchestra, some shouting, others groaning. I heard my name, but I couldn't be certain who'd called it.

I stopped screaming. I pushed myself up into a sitting position. The gunshot! I checked myself over, but I was unharmed.

A fight had broken out near the door where some light filtered through from the main room. Gordon wrestled with a man who seemed to be a match for him. But how could that be? The dead possessed superior strength when raised. No mere human could dodge his rapid-fire punches then get in pounding blows of their own that had Gordon stumbling backward. Gordon reacted by kicking out, but his opponent anticipated that too and jumped out of the way. A kick to the back of Gordon's knees unbalanced him, and in the blink of an eye, my bodyguard was pinned to the floor beneath—

"Lincoln? Is that you?" I squinted into the dimness then got off the bed, only to find my legs wouldn't obey me. I collapsed back onto the mattress.

"Are you all right?" he asked, his breathing a little faster than usual.

"Yes. But why did you attack Gordon?"

Gordon grunted into the floorboards. "A good question."

Lincoln leaned closer to Gordon's face then got off him. "I didn't know it was him." He came to the bed and knelt in front of me. At least, I thought he was directly in front of me. It was difficult to tell. My eyes seemed to be playing tricks on me, and at times he appeared to be several feet away. "We need to leave. Can you stand?"

"Not very well."

He glanced over his shoulder and said a few unintelligible words to the young Oriental man standing near the curtained doorway. He held the gun loosely at his side, but his wide eyes stared at Gordon as my bodyguard stood up. Gordon took a step forward and the Oriental inched back, muttering something under his breath. Mr. Lee was nowhere to be seen.

Lincoln picked me up and I snuggled into him, resting my head on his shoulder. "Thank you," I murmured.

Gordon held the curtain back and we passed through. Mr. Lee was once more sitting on his cushion, a pipe plugged into his mouth. Some of the other smokers were sitting up, their droopy-lidded eyes following our progress as Lincoln picked his way through the collection of bodies sprawled on the floor.

"Thank you, Mr. Lee," I said to the ancient Chinaman. "Please notify us again if the captain returns."

He made no acknowledgement, simply dragged on his pipe and blew out a long chain of smoke. Gordon, my jacket in his hand, went first down the stairs, and Lincoln and I followed behind. Outside, the blissfully cool air soothed my eyes and hot skin. I never thought London's air could smell so sweet, but after the thick fumes of the opium, it was the freshest air in the world.

The young Chinaman had followed us down. He said something to Lincoln in his own tongue, pointed at Gordon, and slammed the door shut.

"I don't think he likes me," Gordon said cheerfully.

"The Chinese don't like spirits of the dead walking through their homes," Lincoln told him. "They believe it brings bad luck."

"That's not very nice." I closed my eyes and breathed deeply again. "They ought to get to know the spirits individually rather than make a blanket ruling against them."

Gordon chuckled. "Your fairness knows no bounds, Miss Charlie." We walked a few paces and then he spoke again, the good humor absent from his voice. "Are you hurt?"

Lincoln's arms tightened around me. When he didn't answer, I realized Gordon was asking me.

"No." I yawned. "What happened? I heard a gunshot then everything went black."

"The Chinaman was about to shoot you, or me. I'm not entirely sure. I managed to turn you and put my body between yours and his, but as it turned out, the bullet missed us both and hit the lamp."

That explained the shattering glass and the sudden darkness. "How could he miss? He was so close."

"I knocked him as I entered the room." Lincoln's deliciously rich voice rumbled from his chest through my skin to my bones. I placed my palm against his chest to feel the vibrations, but he'd stopped talking. I felt his heart instead as it pounded a steady rhythm.

"Well done, both of you," I murmured. "But, Lincoln—Mr. Fitzroy, sir—why were you fighting Gordon?"

"I didn't know it was him. I saw him holding you then drop you on the bed. I thought it was the captain, perhaps."

I smiled as the vibrations of his voice met the thump of his heart. "You were saving me? That's very noble. I can ordinarily take care of myself now, but the opium smoke affected me. I wasn't expecting that."

"Clearly," he muttered.

"How did you know where to find me?"

"I read your note. It was considerate of you to leave one, and not rouse Cook."

"I'm not so affected that I can't detect your sarcasm," I told him around another yawn. "I'll have you know that Cook was in no state to come with me. He almost cut off a limb tonight."

"We'll discuss this in the morning, after you've had a good sleep."

"By discuss, do you mean you're going to rail at me?"

"I'll let that be a surprise for the morning." He didn't sound in the least angry. His arms tightened around me and his warm breath fanned my hair. "Thackery," he said.

My jacket came around my shoulders and I felt like I was being tucked into bed. I must have drifted off to sleep because the next thing I knew, I was on the back of a horse, still in Lincoln's arms. Gordon rode beside us, holding my horse's reins. I still felt like my eyes had sunk deep into my head, and my mouth was bone dry, but my brain appeared to be functioning normally again.

I put my arms around Lincoln and sighed into him. He tensed and I tensed too, but after a few moments, as my body relaxed, I felt the tension leach out of him. Was that because he thought I'd fallen asleep again? I didn't dare look up at him or move a muscle. I didn't want him to feel anxious for holding me. I liked it when he was more relaxed.

Some time later, we stopped, and I finally glanced around. We were at the cemetery, near Gordon's grave. He walked ahead of the horses, a spade in hand.

"Where did you get that?" I asked him.

"One of the groundsmen must have left it out." He clicked his tongue. "They ought to be more careful. There are so many thieves in these parts of late."

He handed the horses' reins to Lincoln then began shoveling soil out of his grave so that he could access the coffin. The effort would have left a living man breathing heavily and sweating profusely, but he simply leaned on the spade handle and smiled at me when he finished.

"I have to go now, dear Miss Charlie. Thank you for the adventure. I enjoyed most of it." He gave Lincoln a flat-lipped smile. "You've got a lot of tricks up your sleeve, sir. I've never met anyone who fought like you."

Lincoln inclined his head in a nod. "Next time, declare yourself."

Gordon's lips tightened even more. "If I get an opportunity, I will."

Gordon bowed to me. "Good bye, Miss Charlie. Take care. Don't go inhaling anything you shouldn't."

I grinned. "Thank you, Gordon. I appreciate everything you did tonight." I held out my hand and he took it without hesitation. Some skin flaked off at my touch, but I pretended not to notice. He let me go and bobbed down into his grave, out of my line of sight. "Ready?" I asked.

I heard the coffin lid close then a muffled, "Ready!"

"You are released, Gordon," I said. "Return to your afterlife."

I watched as his misty spirit rose from the grave and hovered above the headstone. He saluted me then swept up into the dark sky.

Lincoln turned the horses around and we rode out of the cemetery. Now that we were alone, and I was fully awake, it felt somewhat awkward. I should ask him to let me ride on my own, but I didn't. Nor did he suggest it. He continued to hold me in his lap, although both his hands were now occupied with all three sets of reins.

"Lincoln?" I said, peering at him in profile. There was just enough light from the streetlamps to see him clearly at such a close angle.

"Yes?"

"I saw no other option." When he didn't answer, I added, "This opportunity might not have come again."

"I know."

"Don't be angry with me. I hate it when you're angry with me for no reason."

"It's always for a reason."

"It doesn't always seem that way from my position."

I felt rather than heard his sigh. "You don't understand."

"Then make me."

Several heartbeats passed before he said, "I can't."

"Why not?"

"Because I'm not sure I understand myself."

The ache in his voice plucked at my heart. I shifted a little to see him better, but he was staring straight ahead. I touched his jaw and gently forced him to look at me. His Adam's apple jerked fiercely and his warm gaze settled on my eyes.

I stroked the strong line of his jaw with my thumb, wishing I dared touch more of him. "I think you do understand," I murmured. "And I think you're afraid of what you feel."

He jerked his head away, breaking the connection. I didn't need to be touching him to know that his jaw hardened. "You're still affected by the opium."

I didn't bother to protest. I simply sighed and settled my head against his shoulder again.

We arrived home to a house that was more awake than asleep. Cook was nowhere to be seen, but Seth and Gus ran into the courtyard when they heard the horses. Lincoln handed me down to Seth, much to my disappointment. I tried telling them that I could walk, but when Seth set me down on my feet, my legs buckled.

He caught me and looped his arm around my waist. With his help, I was able to stumble to the house. Gus and Lincoln took the horses to the stables and Seth sat me down at the kitchen table. He poured me a cup of water and I drank it greedily.

"You don't look injured," he said, his narrow gaze eyeing me up and down.

"I'm not. The residual effects of other people's opium smoke did this. Apparently it affects novices. The dead are immune, fortunately."

His eyebrows shot up his forehead. "Who died? And did you kill them? Or did Fitzroy?"

"I took Gordon Thackery with me as a bodyguard."

"Ah, yes. I read your note." His eyebrows remained halfway up his forehead as he regarded me with more admiration than concern. "That was clever of you to summon him. Your note also mentioned the captain was at Mr. Lee's. Did you see him?"

"No more questions," Lincoln barked as he strode into the kitchen. "Charlie's exhausted."

I would have argued with him, but I was much too tired. "I think I'll go straight to bed." Both of them came to assist me, but I held up my hand as I rose. "I can walk, thank you."

"Have the effects worn off?" Seth asked, hovering nearby.

"It would seem so." I concentrated on putting one foot in front of the other and maintaining my balance. I yawned as I reached the doorway and had to grasp the doorframe as a bout of dizziness swamped me.

"Perhaps not yet," Seth said with a chuckle.

I thought it was his arm that circled my waist to steady me, but I quickly realized it was Lincoln's. "I'd know those muscles anywhere," I murmured, tucking myself into his side.

Behind us, Seth chuckled again.

I reached the main staircase before another jaw-aching yawn engulfed me. Lincoln must have become frustrated with our slow pace, because he picked me up and carried me up the stairs. I looped my arms around his neck and buried my face in his throat.

"I'm so fortunate to have you," I murmured.

"You're fortunate I'm not furious with you."

I pulled away and frowned at his profile. "Why aren't you angry with me? It's most unlike you."

He didn't answer and I forgot all about my question by the time we reached my room. He set me gently on the bed and, of all things, removed my boots. Having this important gentleman take off his maid's boots so he could tuck her into bed suddenly seemed like the most ridiculous thing in the world, and I began to giggle.

Lincoln drew the bedcovers over me. Even though my eyes had closed of their own volition again, I knew his fingers were near my throat. I could sense him close. "You've disarmed me, Charlie," he whispered. "That's why."

By the time I registered what he was talking about, and pried my eyelids open, he'd gone.

* * *

"Charlie, have you seen my coat and gloves?" Seth asked before I'd stepped both feet in the kitchen.

Gus glared at his friend. "Why would she know where they are? You left 'em somewhere, dolt."

"I can't have. I haven't worn that blue coat since last winter. And who leaves their coat behind, anyway?"

"Men who have to escape from ladies' bedrooms in a hurry."

Seth gave Gus a withering glare. Gus ignored him and turned to me. "Feeling better?"

"Much." I inspected the contents of the pots on the stove. One was filled with simmering beef broth and another contained warm water. "I thought I'd wake up with a headache, but I'm none the worse for my adventure. Is this broth ready?"

"Aye, help yerself."

I fetched a bowl from the cupboard and ladled thick creamy broth into it. "Where's Cook? How is his thumb?"

"More painful than anything that anyone has ever felt before," Seth said. He stretched his legs under the table and crossed his arms. "So he'd let you believe, with all that moaning and groaning."

"We sent him to the hospital," Gus told me. "We couldn't stand listening to his whining no more."

"And Fitzroy?"

"Working upstairs. He wanted to know when you woke up. Seth, go tell him."

"Why me?"

"Because I'm busy watching the broth." Gus was nowhere near the range. Like Seth, he'd stretched his legs out under the table and sat reclined in his chair, as if he might nod off at any moment. "Cook gave me instructions."

"Slack arse," Seth muttered as he got up.

"Thank you, Seth," I said sweetly. "You're very kind. Oh, and now that I think about it, I recall you gave your coat and gloves away to a young boy who desperately needed them. He was freezing, poor lad."

He frowned. "Did I? I don't remember doing that."

"It was a wonderful turn you did."

"When was this?"

"Just last night." I winked, earning me an eye-roll.

"You owe me, Charlie."

"Whatever she owes, I'll cover it," Lincoln said, striding into the kitchen. "But you shouldn't be taking advantage of a novice gambler, Seth."

"I wasn't!" Seth threw up his hands. "She gave away my coat and gloves."

"You have others?"

"Yes."

"Then what does it matter?"

Seth sat down again with a sigh. "How do you do that, anyway?"

"Do what?"

"I was about to come up and fetch you, but you saved me the trouble. Somehow you always seem to appear when you're needed."

"Not always," Lincoln said darkly.

Seth's observation triggered a thought that was lodged in the back of my mind. I couldn't extract it from the fog shrouding most of last night, however, no matter how hard I tried.

Lincoln fetched himself a bowl from the cupboard and filled it with broth then sat next to me. "How did you sleep?"

"Deeply." I struggled to recall how we'd parted the night before. Had he been angry? I didn't think any harsh words had been spoken between us, but there were just too many holes in my memory for me to be certain of anything. He could have told me he loved me and I wouldn't remember.

No, that wasn't true. I would certainly remember that.

"The coat and gloves went to the boy Mr. Lee sent to fetch me. Er, I mean you. He was very cold, the poor lad, and he'd walked a long way in the night. I couldn't send him out again in nothing but his thin shirt."

"There you go, Seth," Gus said, grinning. "You did a good turn, for once. Never thought you'd be the charitable sort."

Seth grunted and returned to his position of repose in the chair. "May we change the subject? What happened at Lee's?"

Gus raised a hand. "First of all, how did Cook cut his thumb?"

"I startled him as he was cleaning knives."

Gus and Seth both chuckled. "Afraid of girls now, is he?" Gus said.

Seth snorted. "It'll be fun to tease him when he returns."

Lincoln lowered his spoon and regarded me. "I understand you saw the captain at Lee's."

I watched him carefully for any signs that he was about to admonish me for not waiting for him, but he seemed perfectly calm. Perhaps he got all his anger out last night, but in my dazed state, I'd not realized. "I did. He wasn't a particularly distinctive fellow, but I would recognize him if I saw him again."

"He won't go back to Lee's now," Gus said.

I bit my lip and concentrated on my broth. "I know. I'm sorry I didn't stop him or find out more about him."

"Shut up, Gus," Seth hissed. "You didn't do anything different to what I would've done, Charlie."

It wasn't quite the comfort he'd intended to be. If Lincoln had said it, on the other hand...

He simply finished his broth in calm silence. It was maddening.

"I do know the captain was holding a syringe full of blood," I said. "He was either about to inject it into the man on the bed, or was extracting it out of him."

"Before or after his death?" Lincoln asked.

"Before. The captain is also a doctor, I'm quite sure. He had a medical bag." *That* I remembered. I'd thought the captain was going to hurt me for trying to look inside it.

"Definitely another Frankenstein." Gus shifted his crossed arms higher on his chest and pulled a face. "That's all we need."

"He didn't cut up the bodies," Seth said, holding up a thumb. "He's not searching for a necromancer." His forefinger joined the thumb then a third finger popped up. "And he wasn't injecting electrical currents into the bodies. He's nothing like Frankenstein. Now who's the dolt, eh?"

"So what does he want with them?" I asked before they could exchange further snide remarks.

"If I had to guess, I'd say he's experimenting," Lincoln said. "The experiments have something to do with the liquid he's spooning into their mouths as they lie dying from malnutrition, exhaustion and too much opium. His experiments must continue after their deaths, hence the need for the bodies."

"You mean he's studying them?" I asked.

He nodded. "Specifically, the effects of the liquid on them."

"How awful."

Seth shrugged. "They're dead. What does it matter?"

"It matters because he might be trying to bring them back to life," Gus said before I could.

"How many times do I have to tell you? He's not Frankenstein!"

"Enough," Lincoln said with quiet malice that cut through the tension. "Bringing them back to life is a possibility. One among many."

I folded my arms too and rubbed them. "I wish I'd learned more about him."

"Did you speak to the spirit after he died?" Lincoln asked.

I gasped and sat up straight. "Yes! I believe I did. He was terribly rude. I didn't like him much. I have a feeling he said something important to me..." I dragged my hands through my hair and down my face. There was definitely something there, on the edges of my memory, but I couldn't catch it. It was so frustrating! "Why can't I remember?" I said, thumping the table.

"Opium," Gus said knowingly.

"Thackery might remember more," Lincoln said.

I nodded slowly. "He might, but I have a better idea. Let's ask the spirit himself. That way we're not relying on Gordon's memory either."

Lincoln stood abruptly, startling me. It would seem my nerves were somewhat jumpy this morning. "Are you recovered enough to go now?"

"I'll fetch my coat."

"Be sure to get your own!" Seth called after me.

* * *

LINCOLN APOLOGIZED for keeping us waiting when he joined Seth, Gus and me at the carriage house. "Deliver this message to the general," he said to Gus, passing him a piece of paper.

Gus pocketed the note and headed out of the carriage house. Lincoln finished helping Seth prepare the horse and carriage, then assisted me into the cabin. He climbed in after me, and Seth took the driver's seat. I wanted to ask Lincoln what the message for the general was about, but held my tongue. Well, only until we passed through the gate.

"Are you inquiring into his own investigation?"

He nodded. "I told him we're getting close to learning a name, but if we fail, the names he's managed to uncover so far will give us something to work on. Hopefully Gus will return with a list."

"Good idea. I like to have a plan of action." And I liked to be involved in that plan. I was rather surprised that Lincoln was allowing me to go back to Lee's with him. Perhaps he thought I'd stay out of trouble with him there, even if the opium affected me again.

The drive was a long one and the silence excruciating. It wasn't unpleasant, but it was awkward, and I didn't really know why. Something must have happened last night but my rotten memory was playing tricks on me. Eventually I could stand it no longer.

"Mr. Fitzroy...last night...did something happen?"

"Many things happened last night. Are you referring to something in particular?"

"You know I am."

His gaze flicked to mine then away. He opened his mouth, shut it, then opened it again. "Nothing happened, Charlie. I carried you to your room and put you to bed. I would hope you know that I would never take advantage of a woman in such a state."

My face flamed, even though I'd asked the question. In truth, I'd expected him to avoid answering. My embarrassment was amplified by the fact that he seemed so nonchalant about it. *His* face didn't redden.

"I, er, of course I do. I'm sorry for implying otherwise."

"Then let's speak no more of it." He turned to the window but his gaze seemed unfocused. Something about last night bothered him.

"I do remember something else," I said.

His head snapped around so fast that it was a blur. "Yes?"

His intense interest unnerved me and it took a moment to regain my composure. "It's regarding the fight you had with Gordon."

He let out a measured breath. Had he been expecting me

to mention something else? Something from later in the night, when he put me to bed?

"It might be nothing," I went on. "It's just that I've noticed how keen your instincts are in a fight. You seem to anticipate blows a moment before they happen. It gives you a definite advantage against a stronger opponent like Gordon."

"Visual cues," he said. "You'll learn to look for them too with practice."

"I doubt it's something one can learn. I've seen Seth and Gus fight one another and their instincts aren't as good as yours."

"What are you implying?"

I swallowed heavily. His steely tone dared me to say it aloud. Dared me to accuse him of something quite extraordinary. I wasn't sure I was up to taking the dare if it meant getting on his bad side, but I'd come this far. It was too late to back away now.

"It's not just in a fight," I forged on. "You often anticipate when someone is about to ask you something, or come to your rooms. You also win at cards and dice much too often to put it down to luck. It's an uncanny gift." I cleared my throat, determined not to wither beneath that frosty stare of his. "Uncanny to the point of supernatural."

He searched my face until finally his gaze settled on mine. I tumbled headlong into the endless depths of his eyes, and I didn't care. Didn't want to escape. Time seemed to stop. We might as well have been in another world inside the carriage. The outside ceased to exist. It was just the two of us, connected by a charge more powerful than an electrical current.

He leaned forward and my heart ground to a halt. Would he kiss me? Berate me?

But he simply rested his elbows on his knees and lowered his head. Unruly strands of hair fell across his face.

"What is it?" I dared ask. "What have I said?"

He half shook his head, or perhaps he was merely turning

away. He drew in a deep breath and let it out slowly. "No one has ever noticed that about me before."

"And?" I whispered.

"And I am coming to terms with the fact that *you* have noticed."

Was that a good thing or bad? I couldn't tell from his reaction. My observation had shaken him, however, and that was something. The unflappable Lincoln Fitzroy was rattled —by me.

"But...what does it mean?" I asked.

He leaned back again and once more held my gaze with his own. "It means you have discovered a secret I've kept from everyone my entire life. Even from the general."

CHAPTER 12

"*W*hat secret?" I asked, hardly daring to breathe.

"I've inherited something other than my coloring from my mother." Lincoln grunted softly. "At least, I think it's from her. I doubt it's from my father."

He was talking as if I knew more than I did about his parents, but I didn't want to interrupt him to ask for details. It was so rare for him to talk at all, I didn't want to startle him into stopping.

"Go on," was all I said.

"She may have been a seer."

Good lord! "But you're not sure?"

He shook his head. "I found a reference to her in the ministry archives. At least, I think the woman mentioned was my mother. The general wouldn't answer my questions when I asked."

That seemed grossly unfair. Surely Lincoln had a right to know about his parents. "So why do you think she was your mother?"

"The text was very old and written in a style that was diffi-cult to read. The general probably thought I'd have no interest in old records, so didn't hide them particularly well. Not then, anyway. It was only a sentence or two, but it stated that the woman who bore the next leader of the order would herself be a seer."

"Did this information come from the same woman who foresaw your birth and role as that leader?"

He nodded.

"No name was mentioned?"

"No."

"But since you are the leader, then the detail must be correct."

"Yes."

I stared at him a long moment, trying to gauge how he felt about having a seer for a mother, and possessing some of her supernatural power, but he'd once more assumed a stony face. "How much can you foresee?" I asked.

He shook his head. "I can't tell the future. I can't *see* very far ahead at all. What I possess is a superior ability to anticipate things before they happen, but not everything. I don't know how people will act or what they'll say, for example. Gambling and fighting seem to be different. I can almost always anticipate the way the die will fall, as well as what my opponent's next move will be."

"That's useful."

The corner of his mouth twisted. "Very."

"I wonder…"

He frowned. "Go on."

"I wonder if your *supernatural* instinct has melded perfectly with your skill and *natural* instinct."

He arched a brow.

"You're highly skilled when it comes to combat of all kinds," I explained. "Anyone who has practiced for years would possess excellent instincts in a fight. But couple that natural instinct with your hereditary one, and you've managed to take it to new heights. Perhaps if you were as skilled in non-combative interaction, you could anticipate what people would say and do. It seems your inherited ability enables you to occasionally guess when someone is seeking you out, or is speaking about you, but that's all. If you were more sociable, your instincts with people could improve too."

"Is that your way of saying I don't have much empathy?"

I smiled. "Some would say you lack charm and witty conversation. Not me, of course."

"Witty banter is a waste of time. I'd rather get to the point of a conversation."

"Sometimes the witty banter is the point of the conversation."

"Then those conversations and the people who have them are dull."

I rolled my eyes and tried to contain my smile. "Then you're not going to enjoy yourself at the ball tonight."

"Probably not."

My smile faded altogether as he turned to look out the window again. The last time we'd spoken of the ball and the reason he was going, he'd wanted me to think he didn't know who his father was. I didn't dare ask again and risk his ire.

"Thank you, Mr. Fitzroy," I said. "I appreciate you confiding in me. I won't tell a soul."

"I know."

The certainty with which he said it shocked me a little. Then it warmed me. I would do everything in my power to keep his secrets if it meant that much to him.

The carriage slowed as we turned onto Ratcliffe Highway. We came to a stop, and Lincoln opened the door and alighted first. He helped me down and we headed into Lower Pell Lane, leaving Seth with the horse and carriage. It looked less forbidding during the day, but more derelict. Paint peeled off ever door and window frame, while the windows themselves were gray from soot. The buildings looked as if they'd sprung up haphazardly, with a wall of brick here, a crumbling plastered one there, and a wooden arch connecting them. Children played on the street, their own imaginations as their toys, while their mothers hung out washing from the upper levels.

Lincoln knocked on the dragon's nose carved into Mr. Lee's door, but there was no answer.

"Is Mr. Lee in?" I asked some of the children hovering nearby.

Several of them nodded, others merely shrugged. One of the older ones stepped forward, and I recognized him as the boy who'd brought me the message the night before. I smiled at him, but he didn't smile back.

"Mr. Lee is out marketing, miss," he said.

"We've come to see the body of the man who died there last night," Lincoln said.

"They took it away in a cart."

Damn. We were too late. The captain had returned and claimed the body already.

"They?" Lincoln asked the lad.

The boy lifted one shoulder. "Men. There was writing on the cart. English writing. But I can't read." He drew some lines in the air.

"An M," I said.

"That's all I remember," the boy said with another shrug.

"You've done very well. Thank you." I opened my reticule, but Lincoln already had coins in hand. He gave the boy two and one each to the other children. They beamed and rushed off with their loot.

"M?" I said to Lincoln as we left the lane. "Is that linked to the captain, do you think?"

"The captain wouldn't have returned. He was too scared of both Gordon and of capture, or he would have put up a stronger fight, perhaps even shot someone. M is most likely for Mortuary. The authorities have collected the body. I know where to find the nearest one."

Seth drove us the short distance to St George in the East church, Wapping. The mortuary had been built behind the church, almost on top of a cluster of gravestones. It was unattended and the door locked. Lincoln dismissed my idea to seek out a clergyman and instead used some long pins he withdrew from his pocket. He had the lock open in a moment.

"Impressive. Did one of your tutors teach you to do that?"

He nodded. "Mr. Jack Plackett was a master thief in his time, but was an ancient cripple when he came to tutor me. He was as sharp as a knife, though. I learned more useful things from him than from any of my other tutors."

"Including your female tutor?"

"Not for lack of effort on her part."

I covered my smile with my hand. It seemed inappropriate to laugh in a mortuary.

He pushed open the door. "Do you mind if I go in first?"

"I was hoping you'd offer."

He hesitated. "You should stay out here."

"But we both know I'm not going to."

His lips flattened. "Then prepare yourself."

I stood back while he entered, then followed. I wish I'd taken his advice to prepare myself more seriously. The mortuary wasn't what I expected. Bodies didn't lie on tables and shelves but on the floor, wherever there was a space large enough. Nor were they covered for modesty; they lay naked and exposed. I wondered if the wealthier parishes treated their dead in such a shabby manner.

I counted six bodies, some quite decayed and four of them grossly bloated, their skin pulled tight over swollen bellies and faces. Those four must have drowned, a common cause of death this close to the docks. The only woman had her head smashed in, and the sixth body belonged to our man from Mr. Lee's. He was in the best condition of the lot, but was extraordinarily thin. His skin was like worn paper, and it was a miracle the bones didn't protrude through it.

I drew in a sigh when I saw him and instantly regretted it. The smell of rotting flesh was much fouler than the butcher's cellar. I covered my nose and mouth but it was too late. The putrid odor clogged my throat. I gagged.

"Charlie, are you—?"

I raced out of the mortuary and threw up in the bushes. To

my horror, Lincoln's warm hand touched the back of my neck. I pulled away, not wanting him to see me like this, and certainly not wanting his sympathy. I should be used to death by now. I was a necromancer and had seen death up close numerous times; I'd even touched decomposing bodies. My weakness appalled me.

"My apologies," he said.

I held up my hand. "You have nothing to apologize for."

"I should have made you wait outside."

I accepted the handkerchief he passed to me over my shoulder and dabbed my mouth on it. I couldn't return it to him in that state, so I tucked it into my reticule. "I would have looked in anyway," I told him.

"There's no need for you to go back inside. I have the name."

"You do? How?"

"It was written on a card, along with the names of the next of kin, where the body was found, who reported it, and the likely cause of death. Either Lee lied, and he did keep records of his clients, or there was some identification. My guess is the latter. I'm not sure Lee cares for record keeping."

I drew in a breath, grateful for some fresh air. "I'll summon him, but I won't ask him to enter his body, if you don't mind. Considering the lack of clothing, it seems rather insensitive. But that means you won't be able to hear his answers."

"I don't need to hear them. You're capable of reporting what he says to me."

"What is his name?"

"Bertram Purley."

I looked around to make sure no one could overhear me, then said, "Bertram Purley, I summon you to me. The spirit of Bertram Purley, show yourself."

I thought the mist was a low lying cloud at first, until it coalesced into the form of the dead man from Lee's garret. He scowled at me and then at Lincoln, who was watching me.

"He's here," I told him.

"You again," the spirit growled. "What do you want?"

"To know the name of the man known as the captain. The one who spoon fed a liquid to you."

"Who cares? I'm dead now. It doesn't matter."

"Of course it matters. It matters if we can save other lives. It matters if you'd like your body to stay buried."

The latter argument rather than the former elicited a response. Up until then, he'd looked both bored and irritated. "I told you his name last night, stupid girl."

And to think I'd felt some sympathy for him in the mortuary. "I can't recall what you told me last night. The opium affected me. Kindly repeat it."

"He told me his name was Jasper."

"First or last name?"

"I don't know. Captain Jasper, I called him." The mist swirled around me and up into the sky, only to swoop down again like a bird on its prey. He bared his teeth and snarled. "Why can't I go?"

"I must release you."

"Then do it!"

I looked to Lincoln and repeated the name Bertram Purley had given me. "Do you have any questions for him?"

"No," Lincoln said.

"Go, Bertram Purley. Return to whereever it is your spirit resides."

"I'm stuck in the waiting area," he said as he swept away again. This time he didn't return.

"He's gone," I said. "He had nothing else to tell me."

Lincoln held out his arm and I took it, but before we could leave, the vicar emerged from the rear of the church. He swooped down on us like a black robed version of Purley's spirit.

"You there!" he shouted. "Halt! What are you doing?"

Lincoln drew himself up to his full height and squared his shoulders. He was considerably taller than the vicar, but the clergyman didn't back away.

"That is none of your affair," Lincoln said.

I tightened my hold on his arm. "Don't snap, Brother

dear," I said sweetly. "He was simply asking a question." I felt Lincoln bristle beneath my hand. I hoped he had enough imagination to go along with me. "We're visiting your charming churchyard," I told the vicar. "We'd heard of a distant relative who might be buried here, some years past, but alas, we weren't able to find his headstone."

The vicar blushed and stumbled through an apology. "I see now that you're just an innocent couple. Forgive me, sir, ma'am, but we've had trouble here only this morning and I thought you were he, returning to break the lock again." He nodded at the mortuary behind us.

"Trouble?" Lincoln asked. "Someone has burgled your mortuary?"

"How peculiar," I said. "Who would do such a thing?"

"The lock was broken mere hours ago. I've just replaced it."

"Did you see the burglar?" Lincoln asked.

At the vicar's odd look, I added, "My brother has an interest in law enforcement."

"You're a policeman?"

"Of sorts," Lincoln said. "Tell me what the man looked like and I'll see that the police are informed."

"That's good of you. I reported it to the police, but they said they were too busy to come immediately. I only caught a glimpse, but the man was middle aged, average height. He wore spectacles. I'm sorry, that's all I noticed."

Lincoln touched the brim of his hat and the vicar did the same. "God will see that the police catch him," the vicar said. "He must be reprimanded for his behavior. This is a house of God, not a place for childish games."

Lincoln and I walked swiftly out of the church grounds before the vicar noticed that his new lock had been miraculously unlocked without a key. At least Lincoln hadn't broken it, as Jasper had.

We found Seth waiting with the carriage nearby and climbed in. It was growing late and there was little we could do with the new information. Lincoln said he could find out where Jasper lived, but it would take some time. The easiest way was to see if the captain was indeed an army man. If so, military records would list his last known address.

Unfortunately, the general had gone out, and Gus returned to Lichfield without a response. He, Seth and Cook met us in the kitchen where Cook sat at the table, cradling his bandaged thumb, while Gus sliced up vegetables.

"The general's butler told me he would deliver your message as soon as he returns, sir," Gus said without looking up from the carrots.

"I'll send another message, this time with the name of Captain Jasper," Lincoln said. "It will narrow his search."

"I'll deliver it," Seth said. "I'm going out that way later."

Gus snorted. "To see your bit o' skirt again? Ain't she bored with you yet?"

"*They* don't get bored with *me*. And she's not a bit of skirt. As it happens, she enjoys dressing in men's clothing."

Gus whooped and even Cook's hound face lifted. "Seth," Lincoln warned, most likely for my benefit.

"Does she prefer gentleman's clothes or a workman's outfit?" I asked with a wink for Seth.

He chuckled. "Depends on her mood."

"How is your thumb?" I asked Cook as Lincoln headed out.

"Still bloody hurts," he muttered, holding it to his chest.

"Stop your whinin'," Gus growled. "It's still attached, ain't it? Most cooks I know are missing a finger or two. Goes with the territory."

Cook scowled at him. I patted his shoulder. "I'm sure it throbs terribly," I said gently. "You just rest for a while and we'll take care of everything in here."

Gus shot me a withering glare. "What do you think I been doing while you were out having adventures?"

"I threw up in the bushes outside the St. George of the East mortuary. I don't call that an adventure."

He pulled a face and returned to his chopping, only to be

told by Cook that he wasn't doing it right. I thought it best to leave them to their bickering.

I retrieved my apron from its hook and set to work in the scullery, then cleaned bedrooms and the bathroom. I paused only for a light lunch and to inspect Lincoln's collar when the laundress delivered it mid-afternoon. I took it upstairs along with the pressed shirt and mended jacket and knocked on his door.

He was writing at his desk but set his pen aside when I entered and flipped the lid of the silver inkwell closed. "Thank you, Charlie, I can take them from here," he said, rising.

"I'll lay them on the bed. You'll be the most dashing man there tonight." It wasn't easy to keep the sigh out of my voice, but I managed it.

"Every gentleman will be dressed as finely. I'll blend in."

I rejoined him in the sitting room. "That's not what I meant."

He sat on the edge of his desk, his hands gripping the desktop on either side of him. He didn't say anything further, so I took that as my dismissal.

"Is there anything I can get you?" I asked.

"No."

"Will we continue with our training this afternoon, or do you require time to prepare for the ball?"

"I think I can manage after training concludes." The dryness of his tone made me smile.

"Your hair might take longer than you think," I teased.

"Should I cut it?"

"No!"

Both his brows rose.

"I...think it suits you at that length." It more than suited him. It set him apart from the other gentleman, marked him as a little wild and uncontrollable, which he certainly was. While I ordinarily preferred a man with short hair, I couldn't imagine Lincoln's any other way. "Do you have a black ribbon to tie it? That leather strip won't do."

"There's one in a drawer somewhere. I'll look for it later."

"Very well. Come fetch me when you're ready for training." I smiled somewhat awkwardly and turned to go.

"Charlie. Wait." He knuckles whitened and his gaze didn't quite meet mine.

"Yes?" I murmured. "Is there something you need?"

"Your help."

"To tie the ribbon?"

He shook his head. "With...conversing."

"Oh? You mean you want to know how to engage someone in a conversation that has nothing to do with the paranormal, fighting, or grave robbing?"

"Don't tease me."

"Being teased and knowing how to tease is part of the art of conversing and flirting. Not that I think you ought to flirt just yet," I added quickly. "Leave that for when you're more comfortable with small talk."

"So how does one begin?"

"That depends. You need to adjust what you say according to the people you're with. Perhaps observe and listen for a few minutes before joining in. See what topics interest the group and gauge their general mood, then offer an opinion on something they're talking about. The gentlemen will no doubt discuss politics, and I've seen you read the newspapers. You must be able to say something appropriate."

"And if politics isn't the topic?"

I shrugged. "You're a clever man and very knowledgeable about a wide range of subjects. I'm sure you'll be able to offer something interesting to a conversation."

"Whenever I try, the conversations usually stop dead."

"Perhaps you try too hard. It's best to keep your strongest opinions to yourself until you're fully comfortable with someone. Say something witty—" I cleared my throat. "Say something clever, but be sure it's nothing too gruesome, inappropriate or dull."

"Therein lies the problem. How do I know if what I want to say is any of those before I get a reaction?"

I sighed. This was proving tougher than I thought. "I'm not sure I'm the best person to give advice. The art of conversing in ballrooms is beyond my experience. I'm far more familiar with juvenile jokes that amuse boys than mature banter. And as for flirting, I've never practiced it, I'm afraid. I've never had the opportunity."

He pushed off from the table and came to stand in front of me. "You're wrong. Your skills are equal to any woman I've met. Perhaps it simply comes naturally to you."

My stomach tied itself in knots as I blinked up at him. He wouldn't think it came naturally to me if he knew how his attentions affected me, and how his praise made me want to earn more. "Perhaps," was all I said.

"Your childhood was spent in polite society, and the habits of good manners and conversation were drilled into you by your adopted parents. I grew up isolated from society for much of my life. It's a limitation of my training that the general didn't identify until it was too late."

"Training," not upbringing. Did he see his childhood as one long training session to be endured? How awful and sad; cruel, even. "Oh, Lincoln."

His eyes flared then, and he backed away. He turned to his desk and shuffled a stack of papers. "Thank you, Charlie. You may go."

I opened my mouth to apologize but shut it again. I wasn't sorry for pitying him, only for letting him see and hear my pity. I needed to be more careful in the future.

"Sometimes all that's required is silence and a smile," I said, in a lame attempt to return to our topic. "Indeed, a smile can achieve much, particularly with women." I regretted saying it immediately. I didn't want him to bestow a smile on another woman. I wanted him to bestow one on *me*. Yet he'd never done more than twitch the corners of his mouth, and I doubted he ever would; for me or anyone else.

"I'll keep that in mind. You may go."

One day I would get him to shed a little bit of his pride, just for me. But I suspected that day was a long way off.

* * *

LINCOLN DISAPPEARED into his rooms after our training session. I hovered in the library, a duster in one hand and a book in the other, and waited for him to come down. I didn't want to miss him before he went out. Training hadn't eased the awkwardness between us—it had only amplified it—and I hated to part like that. I hoped he did too and would come looking for me.

It was growing quite late, however, and I was about to go in search of him to see if he'd changed his mind and wasn't going after all, when the crunch of gravel beneath hooves and wheels announced the arrival of a coach. I peered through the window just as Lady Harcourt's footman opened the door for her and she stepped out of the large carriage.

What was she doing here?

I set down the book and duster and went to open the door for her. She seemed surprised to see me and not Gus or Seth. I bobbed a curtsy.

"Good evening, my lady," I said. "Are you expected?"

"I'm not." She smiled as she swanned inside, the hem of her deep blue gown skimming over the floor tiles. It was the first time I'd seen her out of mourning, although it was a dark enough color to keep most sticklers for propriety happy, even with the silver thread embroidered into it. She stood beneath the chandelier and every diamond on her person sparkled. She wore them at her earlobes, over the gloves on her fingers and wrists, and those were merely the ones I could see. The high collar of the gray fur coat probably hid even more at her throat and décolletage. She even had them in her hair and I had to admit her dark tresses set them off beautifully. She was breathtaking.

"I thought I'd collect Lincoln in case he changed his mind," she said.

How odd. She must know that if Lincoln didn't want to go

to the ball, she wouldn't be able to sway him. No one would. "He's getting ready."

She smiled. "And men say we females take too long. Never mind. I'll wait here with you." She glanced at the stairs and lowered her voice. "There's something I'd like to speak to you about anyway."

I glanced at the stairs too, willing Lincoln to come down before she could say anything further. A terrible foreboding had settled into my stomach. "Oh?"

She smiled again, but this time it was like the diamonds she wore—beautiful yet hard and cold. I swallowed heavily.

"You need to raise the spirit of Mr. Gurry for me," she said.

"Lincoln's tutor? No!"

She placed a gloved finger to her lips. "I suspected that would be your first reaction, but listen to what I have to say before you refuse. After we spoke on this matter recently, I haven't been able to stop thinking about it. I need to know why Lincoln killed him. You could speak to him for me. His spirit, that is."

"I won't go behind Mr. Fitzroy's back."

"You mustn't tell him!" She glanced at the stairs again. Then she took my arm and patted my hand. "I know you're curious too, Charlie. Lincoln never has to find out. It's just to ease our consciences on the matter."

"My conscience is eased. I don't care why he did it. He must have had a reason."

"I'm sure he did too, and that's precisely why it's important to get to the bottom of the mystery. Lincoln deserves nothing less than our full support."

"He has my full support already."

"Does he? Come now, Charlie, we both know this matter will bother us until it's resolved. It will always color our perceptions of him. That's why we need to remove it from our minds. You're a better woman than me, if you can do that without knowing the truth."

While she had a point, and I was wildly curious, I couldn't bring myself to go behind Lincoln's back again. He'd forgiven me once, but I wasn't sure he'd do so a second time. Yet I hated to offend Lady Harcourt. I needed her on my side.

"I couldn't even if I wanted to," I told her. "I need a full name to summon spirits that have crossed. Unfortunately we only know the tutor as Mr. Gurry."

"It's Nelson Hampton Gurry." At my startled gasp, she added, "Lincoln isn't the only one capable of looking through ministry archives."

"Oh."

"Come into the library. We don't want him walking in on us." She took my hand and tugged me toward the library, but I wouldn't budge.

I slipped my hand out of hers. "I'm sorry, my lady, but I won't raise Mr. Gurry's spirit. Not for you, or for me."

Her lips pinched together, deepening the tiny lines at the corners of her mouth. "Those are quite strong morals you have now. What a pity you didn't employ them when you went to the General Registry Office."

I fell back a step and my stomach plunged to my toes. "How do you know about that?"

"That's not your concern." She lifted her chin. "Your concern is whether I will inform Lincoln of your betrayal or not. I don't think he'll be too happy if he discovers you've gone behind his back to investigate him."

"But that's what you want me to do now!"

She smiled, and it wasn't at all beautiful. For the first time, I saw the cunning, ruthless woman who'd pulled herself up from being a mere teacher's daughter to a grand lady. I didn't like her. "It's a sticky situation, isn't it? So what will it be, Charlie? Raise Gurry's spirit, and Lincoln is none the wiser, or don't raise it and Lincoln learns of your treachery?"

CHAPTER 13

"*H*—how do you know?" I whispered. Had she followed me? Was it her man who'd caught the same omnibus as me and followed me through the city? No... that was a different day. But...my God, I'd *trusted* her.

Lady Harcourt's nostrils flared. "That's irrelevant."

"I don't think it is."

"It's ministry business."

"And I'm not a ministry employee," I finished for her. "Only a Lichfield one."

Movement on the stairs had us both turning toward Lincoln. "Julia, what are you doing here?" He looked like a prince, dressed in his tailcoat, white gloves and waistcoat, his hat in hand. His hair, tied at the nape of his neck, gleamed like polished jet with the Macassar oil he'd used in it. He cut a fine, handsome figure that made my heart ache even more. No woman could resist such a handsome man if he gave her his full attention. I envied the ladies at the ball, and one in particular. He couldn't take his eyes off Lady Harcourt as he joined her at the base of the stairs.

"I wanted to make sure you arrived at the ball." She beamed at him and held out her hands. He took them and kissed both her cheeks.

I sank into the shadows near the library door, wishing I was anywhere but there, witnessing their friendly greeting. My heart hammered like an anvil; my blood thudded through my veins. I felt like I was caught in a spider's web, unable to run off like I wanted to and forced to watch the exchange.

Caught too by my own actions at the General Registry Office. I was a fool to have gone there. A damned fool.

"Your gown is lovely," he said with stiff formality.

"You haven't even seen it yet." She shrugged a shoulder and her fur coat slipped off. She caught it and twirled for him. Her smile increased when she spotted me watching.

She did indeed look lovely. The slender fit of the dress accentuated her tiny waist and the low cut revealed the swell of her bosom. Her neck seemed even longer, with her hair piled on her head and the off-the-shoulder sleeves. Many men would want to plant a kiss on the smooth skin of her shoulders tonight. It made me feel ill to think that Lincoln might be one of them.

It made me feel worse when I thought of his reaction when he learned I'd betrayed him. Oh God. What had I done?

Lincoln helped Lady Harcourt with her coat then escorted her out of the house. "Goodnight, Charlie," he called back to me.

That's all the attention I received—a hastily tossed out goodnight. It was pitiful, but not as pathetic as my own heartache.

* * *

MY GUILTY CONSCIENCE kept me awake. When the longcase clock in the entrance hall chimed three times, I gave up trying to sleep and padded downstairs in my nightdress with a coat over the top. I curled up in a library armchair but couldn't concentrate on my book, so I took my candlestick and headed to the kitchen instead. Hot chocolate would soothe my nerves and perhaps help me sleep. By the time I reached it, I'd come to a conclusion—I would tell Lincoln what I'd done at the General Registry Office. It would be better coming from me than Lady Harcourt.

The alternative, to raise Gurry's spirit and keep both betrayals from Lincoln, was tempting, but I suspected I would be found out, sooner or later. He was much too clever to remain in the dark for long.

I had just located a small saucepan when the back door unlocked. My heart lurched into my throat. It would be either Lincoln or Seth; neither had yet returned. I found myself hoping it was Seth.

Lincoln strode into the kitchen. His hair was still neatly tied back, but he'd removed his tie and undone the collar so that it flapped open. Thick brows crashed above eyes as black as midnight. Eyes that bored into me with a ferocity that chilled me.

She'd told him already.

"I'm sorry," I whispered. It came out pathetic, small, and I was afraid it didn't carry to him.

"What are you talking about?" he snapped. "What have you done?"

I frowned then shrugged. I had a feeling it was better to act stupid.

He shook his head. "Whatever it is, tell me in the morning. I'm in no mood tonight." Instead of leaving, however, he strode into the pantry. He opened the cupboard where the cooking sherry was kept and poured himself a glass. He downed it in one gulp then poured another.

"How was your evening?" I ventured.

He raised his full glass. "You can't tell?" He drained the glass then slammed it down on the kitchen table. Thankfully it didn't shatter. "What're you doing up?"

"Waiting for you."

He set the sherry bottle down too and came over to me, slowly, like a sleek cat stalking its prey. Heavy lids shielded his eyes, but I didn't need to see them to know he was in a black mood. It was written in the bitter twist of his mouth, the severe set of his jaw, the rigidity of his shoulders.

I gulped and backed up into the range. If he didn't know about my visit to the General Registry Office; why was he mad? "Lincoln, are you all right?"

"It's Mr. Fitzroy. Do you hear me? I am your employer, and you should treat me as such." His hands bunched into fists at his sides, and it took all my courage to remain there and not slink away. He needed to know I wasn't afraid of him when he was like this. He wouldn't hurt me. Telling myself that was one thing, but getting my nerves to believe it was another.

"Tell me what happened at the ball," I said in a calm voice. "Something must have—"

"Stop acting as if you can fix things, fix *me*." With a growl that emerged from the depths of his chest, he wrenched around, presenting me with his back. It rose and fell with his heavy, ragged breathing. "I don't need...you. I don't need anyone!"

I stepped closer and lifted my hand to press it against his back, but I curled it into a fist before touching him. "I don't care whether you need me or not. I will be here regardless."

He wheeled around and loomed over me. Hot anger had given away to cool control and he no longer looked as if he would throw things around the kitchen. But in some ways, the change was worse, because now he looked like he wanted to wound intentionally. "Your affection for me is misguided, naive and childish." The chilly tone sent shivers down my spine. "Me telling you this now is a kindness. When you're older, you'll understand why."

Tears burned my eyes, but I refused to give in to them. I couldn't stop shaking, however. It felt like ice slid through my veins to every part of my body.

"Me, childish?" I snapped. "You're the one throwing a tantrum." I stepped past him and marched out of the kitchen. When I reached my bedroom, I threw myself on the bed and cried into the pillow.

* * *

Gus teased me about sleeping in the next morning, when I came down late for breakfast. Cook, however, slapped him in the chest and told him to "Shut it" when he saw my face. All three of them spent the rest of the morning treating me as if I would break. If they knew I was feeling fragile because of Lincoln, they didn't let on.

They told me he'd gone out but didn't know where. I wasn't looking forward to our first encounter. Lincoln needed to know that he couldn't speak to me that way for no particular reason.

Except he did have a reason, only he didn't know it yet.

When Lady Harcourt arrived, I told the men I needed to lie down. Unfortunately, it didn't stop her from seeking me out. Seth showed her up to my rooms then bowed out and shut the door. He didn't notice my glare because he didn't take his eyes off her.

"You look exhausted," she said, lowering herself onto one of the chairs in my small sitting room. "One would think *you* were at a ball all night."

I didn't answer. My night and my conversation with Lincoln were not her affair.

She pointed to the seat opposite her. "Sit. Don't you want to hear how the evening went?"

"Not particularly."

"Don't be difficult, Charlie. Of course you want to know. You want to know everything about him. It's quite obvious, my dear, and rather sweet. I'm sure most men would be flattered. Not Lincoln, I'm afraid. He doesn't appreciate that sort of thing, and certainly not from his own maid. Take my advice and put aside your infatuation. It won't go well for you, otherwise."

Coming on top of last night's tirade, it was all I could do to hold myself together. Or stop myself from throwing her out.

"He seemed to enjoy himself at the ball," she said. "He chatted with many ladies, some gentlemen, and I think I almost caught him smiling at sweet little Miss Overton. He seemed quite taken with her. She's quite a pretty thing, all big eyes and golden hair. She reminds me of you, Charlie."

Her description of him flirting and conversing was so different to the man who'd come home at three AM that I wasn't sure whether to believe her or not. She might just be teasing me.

"Don't look so disappointed," she said with a tilt of her head. "He will marry, you know. He must." She sighed. "It's something we both need to grow used to. Miss Overton would make a nice match for him, as long as she's careful not to bore him."

"Why do you want him to marry Miss Overton?" I asked, my curiosity getting the better of me. "Don't you want to marry him yourself?"

She plucked the fingertips of her gloves to remove them. "You've become quite bold, for a maid."

"Let's not play games, my lady. We both know what you're here for. Let's get on with it."

"First things first. You asked about me marrying him, and I'd like to answer you." She placed the gloves in her lap and folded her hands on top of them. "I've been married before, Charlie, and it's not a state I want to enter into again. Not lightly, anyway, and not with Lincoln. I know he'd treat me well enough, but there's no advantage for me in marrying him. Do you understand?"

"I do. If you marry someone, it will be a man higher than your last husband."

"Or richer. You must think me terribly avaricious. Or perhaps you understand me." Her crooked smile was almost friendly, knowing, as if she were sharing a secret with a confidant. "We have, after all, come from similar stock."

I didn't bother to tell her that I was nothing like her. I didn't care for wealth or privilege. A home with a solid roof over my head was all I wanted, and people who cared for me.

It was the latter that I thought I'd found in all of Lichfield's residents. This morning, I was no longer certain of that, or even of the solid roof. If Lincoln was still in the same mood as the night before, he might be tempted to throw me out, particularly if he learned about my visit to the General Registry Office.

"Did you see him when he returned last night?" Lady Harcourt asked.

"Why?"

It was a long moment before she answered. "He left abruptly; one would say angrily. I didn't see whom he was talking to before he left, so I have no way of knowing why he was upset. He had no transport home so I suspect he walked all the way."

"I don't know anything," I said. "You'll have to ask him."

"We both know how well that conversation will go," she said with a wry twist of her mouth. "Now, are you ready to summon Mr. Gurry's spirit?"

I gripped the chair arms harder and blinked down at my lap. As I'd watched dawn creep over the horizon that morning, I'd decided not to tell Lincoln about the inquiries I'd made; partly because I was angry with him over his treatment of me and felt he didn't deserve to know, and partly because I felt like a fool for caring about him. If he knew I'd cared enough to investigate him, it would only heighten my humiliation.

"Come now, Charlie, don't think badly of me for asking this of you. I only want what you want—information about Lincoln. It's your own fault if I tell him about your inquiry at the General Registry Office. You refuse me this request and I *will* speak to him about it. You can be assured I haven't told him anything yet, however."

"That's such a comfort," I sneered.

"It'll remain our secret, if you want it to. I promise."

I wasn't entirely sure if her promise meant all that much to me anymore. But I had to trust her. If I couldn't...well, part of me no longer cared. Let him discover every bad thing I'd ever done behind his back. Let him throw me out. It might help me bury this infatuation, as he called it.

I drew in a deep breath. "Mr. Nelson Hampton Gurry. I summon the spirit of Nelson Gurry to this world to answer some questions."

I didn't see the mist until it was surrounding my shoes and coalescing into a human form. It must have filtered up through the cracks in the floorboards. "Who're you and what do you want?" grumbled the ghost of Mr. Gurry. He appeared to be a man of about sixty, with a receding hairline, long nose and strong frown lines scoring his forehead. He must have spent much of his life scowling for them to be so deep.

"My name is Charlotte Holloway," I told him, "and I'm a necromancer."

"A what?"

"Is he here?" Lady Harcourt whispered.

I pointed to the ghost hanging between us like a faint cloud. "There."

"Mr. Gurry," she said in her imperial voice. "Can you hear me?"

"Is she a necromancer too?" he asked. "Or just stupid?"

"She can't see or hear you."

"That answers neither of my questions, girl. You must be stupid too. Typical females," he added in a mutter.

"Mr. Gurry, I would appreciate your civility."

"I'm sure you would, but I don't care." The mist blew away to the ceiling, but returned immediately to me as if I'd beckoned it. "What's going on? What can't I leave?"

"I haven't dismissed you."

"*You* dismiss *me*?" He snorted. "I beg your pardon! If I were alive I would smack you for impertinence."

"And then I would beat you. Yes, Mr. Gurry," I added sweetly, "I am quite capable of doing so, even though I am a female."

His top lip curled in a snarl.

"I'm beginning to see why Mr. Fitzroy killed him," I said to Lady Harcourt. "He's insufferable."

Lady Harcourt stared wide-eyed at me. Gurry's spirit swelled to twice its size then flew at me so fast that I flinched out of instinct.

"You know him?" he spat. "You know my murderer?"

"We do," I said. "He was your pupil, wasn't he?"

"Where is he?" He swept around the room then came to settle in front of me again. "Is that dog here?"

"No. Tell us why he killed you, Mr. Gurry."

"*That's* what you want to know?" His low chuckle plucked at my taut nerves. "Why not ask him?"

"I'm asking you."

"I can't tell you. I don't know. He came across me in a lane one night, years after I'd finished teaching him. He held a long knife. Without so much as a word, he attacked me and cut my throat." He rubbed his neck above his collar. "I pleaded with him for mercy, but he showed none. He's a vicious animal, with no conscience and no soul. Take my advice and stay far away from him."

I glanced at Lady Harcourt, only to find her staring back at me. She urged me with a nod. "Well?" she whispered. "Has he told you?"

I shook my head. "Was it a chance meeting?" I asked Gurry.

"I don't know," he said. "Perhaps not. He was always devious like that, always plotting and scheming. I wouldn't put it past him to have planned the meeting for years. Who knows how long he harbored a grudge against me?"

"Why did he harbor a grudge?"

He turned his back to me. "I already told you, I don't know."

"You have no inkling? Surely you must."

"No."

"Mr. Gurry, please answer me so I can send you on your way."

He circled me slowly, his feet not touching the floor. The lines on his forehead folded together into a deep frown. "He was a willful dog. I tried to train him, but he wouldn't follow orders from the start. I had to employ more and more drastic measures to get him to listen."

"Did you beat him?"

"Of course."

I pressed a hand to my mouth but quickly drew it away. It was too late, however. Lady Harcourt would have guessed Gurry's answer from my question and reaction. She too covered her mouth and left her hand there.

"The general knew," Gurry protested. "He approved. He gave me full reign to do as I saw fit to teach my charge."

The general *knew*? It grew worse and worse.

"I wasn't the only one," Gurry said. "I saw other marks on his back, not inflicted by me. He didn't kill me because of a few beatings, girl. Do you understand? No, he killed me because he's mad, a crazed dog. He shouldn't be allowed out of his cage."

I slapped my palm down on the chair arm. It silenced him, but also made Lady Harcourt jump. I didn't care. I was too intent on what he was telling me, too horrified to think of young Lincoln at this man's mercy, and at the mercy of his other tutors. How many had beaten him?

Gurry was probably right. Lincoln hadn't killed him for the beatings, or Gurry wouldn't be his only victim. Then why? Was Gurry holding something back from me?

"There has to be a reason," I said. "Tell me. I command you."

His lips flattened and he swirled again before standing still. "My methods had begun to work. I'd almost beaten that willfulness out of him when a distraction emerged. I removed the distraction. Perhaps he's angry with me for that." He shrugged.

"What distraction?" I pressed. "Another person?"

"What's he saying?" Lady Harcourt asked. I raised my hand, but she batted it away. "Charlie, you must tell me what he's saying."

"He's a bad seed," Gurry said. "A very bad seed. You can't trust a man with gypsy blood in his veins."

Gypsy! It was the second time I'd heard Lincoln referred to as such. The first time I'd thought it simply derogatory, but now...perhaps Lincoln's mother had been a traveler. She'd been a seer, and he'd told me she had dark coloring, so it was possible.

But it wasn't a word I would repeat to Lady Harcourt. For some reason, I didn't want her to know.

"Nothing important," I told her when she asked again what Gurry was saying. "Cruel accusations, nothing more."

"They are not accusations!" The spirit dashed left and right, around furniture, across the mirror and pictures hanging on the walls, as if trying to disturb them to show his anger.

"Why did Lincoln become distracted?" I pressed.

The spirit chuckled again and came to settle between Lady Harcourt and myself. "It was an annoying little distraction that he was much too fond of. I got rid of it. That's all you need to know."

"Tell me!" I shot up from the chair and faced up to him, but he merely chuckled again.

"Or what?" he sneered. "You can't do anything to me, girl."

"Mr. Gurry, I'm ordering you to—"

The door behind me crashed open. I knew without turning that it was Lincoln. No one else would dare interrupt without knocking. If I needed any further confirmation, I got it from my companions. Lady Harcourt's face drained of color. The spirit of Mr. Gurry flinched and whooshed backward.

My legs felt suddenly too weak to hold me, and I sat down. I wished the armchair would swallow me, but there could be no escaping Lincoln. Fury vibrated off him in waves, leaving me in no doubt that he knew who I was talking to, and why.

Lady Harcourt recovered first. She rose and put out her hand. "Good afternoon, Lincoln. I'm so pleased to have caught you before I go."

"Get out." The quiet order was more brutal than any shout

could have been. I held my breath, waiting for him to explode, but he didn't. He merely stood by the door and watched Lady Harcourt with a ferocity that had *me* trembling.

I knew it would soon be my turn.

She blinked. "Pardon?" Whether she had more nerve than me, or simply didn't see his anger, I couldn't tell. She sailed up to him, smiling sweetly. "Linc—"

"You heard me."

"My dear, what is it? What's the matter?" Her act was a wasted effort, but she didn't seem to realize it.

I did. Perhaps because I knew Lincoln's secret, or perhaps because I knew him better than she did, but I knew he was aware of Gurry's spirit hovering nearby. There was no point in keeping up the charade.

"I said, *get out*." The sharp edge to his voice cut through me, and Lady Harcourt too, it would seem. She paled even further and stepped around him, keeping her distance.

"I see that I'm in the way here," she said from the door. "Charlie, remember my promise to you."

She didn't want me to tell him? Even now that we'd been caught in the act? But that wasn't fair! I watched her rush out with a sinking heart. She *did* want me to lie to him. If I didn't, she would tell him about my betrayal at the General Registry Office.

I wasn't so sure it mattered anymore. If he knew about this, then he might as well know about the other. What was one more? From the quiet rage turning his knuckles white and his eyes impossibly dark, I already knew I was condemned.

"Let me go!" Gurry's spirit cried. "I don't wish to see him anymore! Release me!"

"You are released," I said, heavily. "Go away."

The spirit mist sank through the floorboards and out of sight. I was truly alone with Lincoln now, and I wished I could be anywhere else but there.

"Will my apology be enough?" I mumbled. I couldn't bring myself to look at him.

It was a long time before he spoke. I thought he might walk out, or do the opposite and approach; perhaps shake me. But he simply remained near the door, and I had no sense of what he might be thinking.

"What did you learn?" His voice was quiet, but the steely edge was still there, albeit a little tarnished.

"That he beat you." I dared to glance at him, but his face gave nothing away. "And that you had a reason for killing him."

"And that reason?"

"He didn't say. He claimed he got rid of a distraction to your studies."

His nostrils flared. "A distraction."

"Will you tell me what it was?"

Another long pause, and then, "Not today."

I swallowed. Did that mean he would one day? Did that mean he wasn't throwing me out? "I'm sorry, Mr. Fitzroy. I truly am. I don't expect your forgiveness—"

"Good."

That quietly spoken word was enough to shatter my nerves. Hot tears streamed down my cheeks and my chin wobbled. I dashed away the tears with the back of my hand, but he saw them. He folded his arms over his chest and tucked his hands out of sight.

"Tell me why you did it," he said. "Did she coerce you somehow?"

I nodded but stopped. It wasn't entirely fair to lay all the blame at Lady Harcourt's feet. I had got myself into the situation by betraying Lincoln at the General Registry Office, and I had not refused her request. I could have. I *should* have. "Yes, and no."

He spun round and jerked the door open. "I would have told you what you wanted to know," he said over his shoulder.

"I already asked you," I shot back. "You refused to answer."

"I wasn't ready then. But in time..." He strode out the door and shut it, leaving me alone with my thoughts and misery.

I doubted he would he ever confide in me now. Whatever connection there had been between us was utterly broken, and I wasn't sure it could be mended.

CHAPTER 14

J remained in my rooms for the rest of the day and evening. I couldn't face the others, even though I knew Lincoln wouldn't be among them. Either he'd gone out or he kept to his rooms. At every creak of the floorboards outside, every groan of the settling house, I lifted my head from my pillow and held my breath. But no one came to my door. Perhaps he wasn't going to throw me out, after all.

The longer I dwelled on it, the more I came to realize he wouldn't do that. He wasn't petty. Yet I knew we couldn't go on as we were. I'd crossed a line, and there was no going back. Nothing would be the same. He would never confide in me again, never take me with him to investigate a ministry matter, never simply sit in the library and read alongside me. He might even stop my training. He would treat me as a maid.

I *could* cope with the change between us. I *must*. Lichfield was my home, and I didn't want to leave it, or Seth, Gus and Cook. Or him.

I drifted off to sleep but awoke with a start sometime in the middle of the night. I'd had a dream about the pendant I'd found in his room with the blue eye inscribed on it. That eye had stared back at me in the dream, then winked.

I didn't fall back to sleep, yet I waited until the morning to look through the library books. I did my chores first, making sure the house was perfect, and ate breakfast with Seth, Gus and Cook. They were somber too, and seemed to know that something was amiss. They didn't ask me what had happened, and I didn't offer an explanation. Nor did I ask after Lincoln like I usually did.

I slipped into the library late morning. Lincoln hadn't come down at all, and it seemed that he'd gone out. Even if he walked in on me, it wouldn't matter. Our friendship was in tatters already.

My fingers brushed over the leather spines of the books as I read each one. They were organized by subject matter, with non-fiction occult books near the fireplace. I found one on symbols and flipped to the index. There were several entries for Gypsy, and I checked each page reference until I found the drawings of the blue eye similar to the one on the amulet in Lincoln's drawer.

According to the book, it was a charm to ward off the evil eye, a curse that several cultures believed in, not just gypsies. It was said that witches and evil spirits cursed good people with the evil eye, bringing them bad luck. The amulet with the blue eye defended the wearer from such curses when it was worn close to the body.

If I had any remaining doubts that Lincoln was part gypsy, they were banished. The amulet must have come from his mother.

I returned the book to the shelves and continued with my chores until the early afternoon. Lincoln still hadn't returned when two visitors arrived. Having strangers visit was unusual enough, but the fact that they were two ladies was even more curious. They arrived in a carriage with a footman standing sentinel at the back. He hopped down and opened the door for them. The older lady emerged first. Her gaze took in the house, the garden, and me, standing in the doorway. She wrinkled her nose.

The second lady was much younger, but clearly her relation. Both were beautiful, with high cheekbones, large gray eyes and smooth skin. The older lady wore a green turban that covered much of her hair, while the younger's fair locks were arranged beneath a large brimmed hat trimmed with green ribbon. Both wore striking outfits that hugged their slender frames, although the elder was a more sedate lavender than the girl's vibrant jade.

They looked past me, as if expecting to see a butler hovering nearby. It must seem rather odd to have a maid greet them.

"Is Mr. Fitzroy at home?" the elder woman asked without introducing herself.

"Not at present."

The young woman pouted. "I told you we should have sent a note ahead, Mama."

"When will he return?" the mother asked me.

"I don't know." I stepped aside. "Would you like to wait for him? I'll bring tea and cake into the parlor."

"Please, Mama," the girl begged. "I'd like to see him again."

The mother tilted her head in a nod. "Very well. We will wait. Where is the parlor?"

"Through there." I bobbed a curtsy as both filed past me. "Whom shall I say is calling upon him?"

"Mrs. and Miss Overton," the woman said without turning to me. "We'll stay half an hour, Hettie. No more."

I hurried into the kitchen. "He has guests," I announced to Cook and Seth. Gus wasn't there. "I need tea and cake."

Cook waved his bandaged hand at me. "Can't." He went back to the recipe book open in front of him on the table.

Seth sighed and got up. "Who is it? The general? Does he have an address for Jasper?"

"Not the general. It's Lady Overton and her daughter."

"Lottie and Hettie?" Seth brightened. "Well, that is an intriguing prospect."

"Which one?" Cook asked.

"Definitely the daughter." Seth touched the side of the

kettle on the stove to test its heat, while I fetched cake from the pantry.

"You been servicing 'em?"

"Servicing?" I called out from the pantry. "Does that mean what I think it means?"

"Not the daughter," Seth said. "She's a sweet little thing, but completely ruled by her dragon of a mother, who is even more of a dragon in the bedroom."

"Seth!" I shook my head at him.

He shrugged. "There's domineering and then there's dictatorial. Only one of those is fun, and it's not the one that she is. What are they doing here?"

"They've come to see Mr. Fitzroy."

"About?"

"How should I know?" I lied. If Lady Harcourt had been correct, they were here to see if Lincoln was as interested in Hettie Overton today as he had been at the ball. I didn't think my heart could sink any further, but apparently it could. Hettie Overton was very pretty.

Seth prepared the teapot while I gathered plates and cups. "He'd be bored out of his mind with Hettie," he told me quietly as he placed the teapot on the tray. "The mother is a dragon, but the daughter is a simpering witless girl. And that's putting it kindly."

I shrugged. "There is a lot to be said for simpering witless girls. They tend to do exactly what they're told. Most men like that."

"Not Fitzroy."

I picked up the tray. "Don't be so sure."

I entered the parlor and set the tray down on the table. Mrs. Overton didn't break off their conversation, or so much as pause. Indeed, if she'd not accepted the cup of tea I poured for her, I would have thought she hadn't noticed me at all.

"The sofa will be the first to go," she said.

"Yes, Mama. I quite agree."

It wasn't until Hettie Overton inspected the sofa on which

she sat that I realized they were discussing it, and not their own furniture.

"Everything is at least five years out of date." Mrs. Overton pointed her teacup at a painting of a Paris street scene. "That will be second."

"I wonder what the rest of the house is like," said the daughter.

"Nobody knows. Hardly anyone has been inside Lichfield Towers for years."

"What about Lady Harcourt? They're friends, aren't they?"

Mrs. Overton sniffed. "So I hear," she muttered into her cup.

The girl seemed oblivious to the mother's innuendo. She was too intent on checking out the room as if she were cataloguing its contents. "What do you think of the color scheme?"

"Too drab."

"That's what I thought. I don't mind those chairs, though."

"They don't go with the rest of the room at all."

"That's what I was thinking. They're much too…"

"Ugly."

"Quite, quite ugly." Hettie blinked those big eyes at her mother and sipped her tea.

Seth was right. The girl didn't have a mind of her own. Lincoln wouldn't be interested in her.

I was about to leave the parlor when he walked in. My face colored as his gaze skimmed over me. His thoughts on seeing me there were unclear however. His expression remained bland.

"Mrs. Overton," he said, walking past me and bowing over the mother's hand. "Miss Overton. This is an unexpected pleasure."

A pleasure? He was a fast learner.

"We didn't hear you arrive, Mr. Fitzroy," Mrs. Overton said, smiling.

"I came in via the back door. It's closer to the stables."

"How...interesting. Lichfield's standards are quite lax. We're unused to it." Her tinkling laugh was echoed by her daughter. "A maid greets us, there are no signs of footmen or butler, and now the master of the house tells us he uses the servants' entrance. What are we to think, Mr. Fitzroy?"

"That Lichfield needs a guiding hand to bring it up to standard. As does its master."

I held my breath and walked slowly to the door. This was an exchange I wanted to hear.

"A guiding hand?" Mrs. Overton's voice had softened since Lincoln's arrival. When she'd been talking to her daughter, it had been strong, inflexible. Now, it took on a girlishness that sat awkwardly on her. "Would that be a feminine hand, Mr. Fitzroy?"

"That remains to be seen, Mrs. Overton. Miss Overton, did you enjoy yourself at the ball?"

"Very much," she said in a breathy voice. "I do enjoy balls, don't you?"

"I rarely attend."

"So we've noticed," said Mrs. Overton. "Where did you run off to at the end? Hettie and I looked everywhere for you."

"Then I must apologize. I hope I can make it up to you."

Hettie beamed at him and blinked those big eyes. It made her look even lovelier, if somewhat childlike. Mrs. Overton's smile was less overt. "You can. Come to my dinner party this Friday night."

Lincoln didn't answer straight away. He seemed to be caught, and I wondered if he'd unintentionally backed himself into a corner. It would seem his instincts had failed him on this occasion. If we'd been on better terms, I would have teased him about it later.

He suddenly turned to me, as if he'd just realized I was still there. "That will be all," he said. "You may go."

I bobbed a curtsy and hurried out. I didn't hear his response to Mrs. Overton's invitation.

"Well?" Seth said when I returned to the kitchen. "What happened?"

"I think he plans on getting more servants." I frowned. "Or a wife. Perhaps both."

Cook snorted. "Don't know why he be wantin' more servants *or* a wife. Both be trouble."

"Agreed," Seth said. "Surely the four of us is enough."

"Every gentleman needs a wife," I said quietly.

"True."

"And a wife would want more servants."

"Also true." Seth sighed. "I believe we have our answer. But I can't believe he would be seriously considering Hettie Overton as a candidate. She's not to his taste at all."

"Perhaps we don't know his taste in women."

Cook snorted.

Seth narrowed his gaze at me. "I think we do."

My situation had felt precarious enough last night; now it felt like I had my toes poking over the edge of the cliff. It only remained to be seen whether Lincoln pushed me off or I jumped.

I busied myself in the scullery until the Overtons left. Lincoln didn't come into the kitchen afterward, and I got the impression he was avoiding me. My frayed nerves were stretched so thin that I could no longer bear it. I had to do something, and there was only one thing in my power to do.

With a heavy heart, that wouldn't cease its hammering, I went in search of him. I found him in his rooms, exercising. He opened the door with a towel in hand, wiping away the sweat at his brow. It was the first time I'd seen him sweat during all the times he'd trained, either with me or alone.

I lowered my gaze. "I'm sorry to interrupt." I cleared my throat but the ball of panic that had lodged there wouldn't go away. Part of me couldn't believe I was doing this, but I knew I had to. Our situation was impossible, the tension unbearable. I had to end it.

"Yes?"

I cleared my throat again. "I...I need to talk to you."

"About?"

Hell. He was still furious with me. I'd hoped he would be past it, but I knew in my heart he wouldn't be. He never could be. I'd betrayed him, and he felt it keenly. His reaction helped me realize I'd come to the right decision, but it was no easier to voice it.

"It seems that I can no longer work here," I said to our feet. "Things will never be right between us now, and I can't..." I closed my hands into fists and swallowed past the lump in my throat. "I have to go."

The long pause almost had me meeting his gaze, but then he finally spoke. "You can't," he said gruffly. "You have nowhere to go to." It was hardly a convincing argument to stay. It certainly didn't seem like he *wanted* me to stay.

Any hope I'd held that he would beg me not to go was dashed. It had been a foolish hope anyway. "I have some experience now and should be able to find work in another house as a maid."

"Don't be absurd."

"I'm quite good!" I said hotly.

He blew out a measured breath. "That's not what I meant, and you know it."

A bubble of laughter escaped my throat. It held no humor. "I know no such thing. I can't begin to fathom what you're thinking, Mr. Fitzroy." I stretched my fingers and willed my heart to stop its wild beating. "I will only get another position if you give me a good reference, however. Without it..."

"This is because of yesterday. Because I shouted at you."

"You didn't shout at me." Far from it. I wished he had. Shouting might have got the anger out of his system. "You have every right to feel betrayed, sir, and we both know that a gentleman cannot have his servants betraying him."

"You can't go," he said quietly.

"I have to," I murmured into my chest. "It's for the best, for both of us, and don't try to tell me otherwise. You can never forgive me for what I did."

"You don't know that."

I shook my head and swiped the tear that trickled down my cheek. "Perhaps not, but while I see you every day, I know I can never forgive myself." I swiped my other cheek. "Please place the reference under my door, if you can bring yourself to write a favorable one." I turned and walked quickly down the corridor to my room.

But the flat of his hand against the door prevented me from opening it. He was so close behind me I could hear his ragged breathing, feel the strength of his presence. I closed my eyes, but it didn't shut off the tears, or stop my heart from crashing into my ribs.

"You're right," he said in that maddeningly calm way of his. "We can't go on like this. And we won't. I promise you, all will be well again."

"It can't be. It's not just my summoning of Mr. Gurry...it's everything!" I dared to look at him, to see if he understood my meaning.

If he did, it wasn't clear. His face was closed, the muscles tense as he fought to keep the mask in place. "It's still daylight," he said. "Go outside and get some fresh air. You've been cooped up too long. You'll think more clearly after a walk."

"And if I don't change my mind? If I still want the reference...will you give it to me?"

He drew in a deep breath and let it out slowly. "We'll talk later. Not now. I'm...not in the right frame of mind." He slowly removed his hand from the door.

I didn't enter my room. He was right; I needed to feel the cool air on my face. Perhaps it would blow away the fog that was clouding my head.

I hurried down the stairs and out the front door to avoid the others. The sun shimmered through the trees, but the air had already cooled considerably since I'd opened the door to the Overtons. My hot cheeks needed it.

I walked along the drive and out through the gate, where I could no longer be seen from any of the windows. I needed true privacy from the Lichfield residents, if not from the public.

As I often did when I was troubled, I found myself wandering into the cemetery to my adopted mother's grave. I almost detoured to Gordon's, but I needed the comfort of my mother. I sat on the mat of leaves and leaned back against the headstone.

The twittering of the birds overhead as they settled into their nests chased away any eeriness I often felt when alone in the cemetery. I tried to empty my head and just listen to them, but thoughts of Lincoln and what I would be leaving behind kept returning.

He hadn't seemed like he'd wanted me to leave. Or had he, and I'd just missed the signs? I had hardly looked at him, so it was possible. Yet he hadn't asked me to stay either; not in so many words. He hadn't refused me a reference, hadn't said that Lichfield was my home as much as it was his and that I belonged there.

And when he said we would talk later, how much later? As soon as I got back? Tonight? Tomorrow?

My thoughts went around in circles and did nothing to steady my erratically beating heart. He'd thought a walk would clear my head, but I felt more confused than ever. Earlier, I'd been determined to get a reference and leave Lichfield. Now, I wasn't sure if it was the right decision. It might be...or it could be the biggest mistake of my life.

When the headstone at my back became too cold, I headed out of the cemetery and along Swain's Lane, toward Hampstead Heath. I'd decided to demand he tell me his thoughts on the matter of my staying or going, and leave my decision until after our discussion. I saw no other way.

The sun had sunk behind the horizon by the time I reached the iron gates of Lichfield Towers. They loomed out of the darkness like giant skeletons, but I found them welcoming. I quickened my pace and put my head down into the breeze.

I didn't see the two figures jump out of the shadows until

they were upon me. Acting on impulse, I jabbed my elbow into one man's stomach and smashed my foot into his knee. He cried out as he fell to the ground.

I swung round to attack the second man, but a fist smashed into the side of my face, sending me tumbling into the gate. My cheek burned, but then the pain mercifully faded away as I slipped into blackness.

CHAPTER 15

The room was shrouded in semi-darkness. Coal glowed in the grate, warding off very little of the chill. I shivered. I seemed to be lying on a sofa or bed. My wrists and ankles were tied, and no matter how much I struggled, I couldn't get free of the bonds. My shoulders ached from having my arms wrenched behind me and my cheek felt like it was on fire. I fought back the well of tears banking behind my eyes. Now was not the time to succumb to hopelessness.

I quickly scanned the room then scanned it again. I seemed to be alone.

I sat up. The room swam, but I managed to stay upright A few deep breaths later and I felt almost normal and alert again. The room appeared to be a small office. It contained a filing cabinet, desk and two chairs. I was on a bed, but not the sort used for sleeping on. It was a medical bed found in doctors' surgeries. That meant there must be medical equipment nearby—scalpels and needles and other sharp objects I could use as weapons. My spirits lifted. I could do this. I *would* get out, one way or another.

I hopped off the bed but stumbled to my knees. My legs

felt weak and the rope around my ankles bit into the skin through my stockings. I wasn't wearing any shoes.

Get up, Charlie.

I tried once again to untie the rope, but with my hands behind me, it was impossible. If they had been in front, I might have managed it. Damn, damn and damn!

I got to my feet again and hopped around on my toes as quietly as possible. My progress was painful and slow, but the office was tiny, thank goodness. I tried to open drawers and cupboards, but everything was locked. So was the only door. There had to be some way I could get out, or alert someone that I was trapped in here.

I half shuffled, half hopped to the window and nudged aside the curtain with my chin. The office was on the ground floor! I couldn't believe my luck. It didn't overlook a street, however, but a small garden with other buildings surrounding it. The sun was still sinking behind them and—

Wait. The sun had already set when I'd been taken. I looked again. The clouds were a pinky orange, and dew dampened the patch of grass. It wasn't nighttime, it was morning. I'd been unconscious for hours.

A well of pity and fear opened inside me. There would be no rescue from anyone at Lichfield because they didn't know where to look. No one had seen my abduction. No one had followed us here or I would have been saved already. I was truly on my own.

I drew in a fortifying breath and studied the buildings surrounding the garden. They were not close enough for any occupants to hear my shout. I looked to the ceiling, but if there were more rooms above, I still couldn't be sure if anyone was up there, or if they would hear me. Besides, a shout might bring one of my captors into the room, and that was something I didn't want. I'd recognized Captain Jasper last night, Pete and Jimmy too. This must be where Jasper saw patients.

Another hop around the office brought me no closer to a plan of escape. I needed to get the damned ropes off. Even if I managed to escape the room, I couldn't run anywhere, trussed up like this.

I tried rubbing the rope that bound my wrists against the edge of the desk, but it was hopeless. It didn't even fray. The small rectangular brass plates on the filing cabinet would be better. They acted as both handles to pull open the drawers and holders for the label. Their edges were sharp.

I hopped toward the cabinet, but tripped on the edge of the rug and landed heavily on my side. Pain flared in my cheek again but I bit back a cry.

It didn't matter. My fall had been heard. The door unlocked and swung open. Captain Jasper stood in the doorway and held his lamp higher. If I'd been closer, I could have used the moment it took for his eyes to adjust to tackle him.

But I wouldn't have been able to do more than that with my hands tied behind my back. Particularly if Jimmy and Pete were in the next room.

He spotted me on the floor and came over. "It's Miss Holloway, isn't it?"

"And you're Captain Jasper," I hissed.

He looked surprised that I knew that much. "Are you all right?"

"Do I look all right?"

"I'm very sorry for this, but you shouldn't have fought back. My men were already afraid of you and then when you hit them, they thought you must have been possessed. I tried to assure them that you weren't." He helped me to my feet and waited until I was steady before letting me go. "You're not, are you?"

"What do you want with me?" I snapped.

"We'll get to that in a moment." He set the lamp down on the desk near a stack of papers then sat on the edge. "Are you all right? That bruise on your cheek looks nasty."

"Of course I'm not bloody all right. I am being held against my will. I don't know what you want. My face hurts, and so do my ankles and wrists." I turned and waggled my hands at him. "If you are a gentleman, you would set me free."

"I'll untie you, if you'll listen to my proposal. I don't wish to hurt you. Will you listen?"

He would untie me? It was more than I'd hoped for. I nodded quickly and tried to school my features.

"Sit on the chair and don't attack me," he said. "Jimmy is just outside this door. If anything happens to me, he has my authority to hurt you again."

Jimmy, not Jimmy *and* Pete. I only had two men to get away from, not three. The odds were improving.

I sat quietly while he untied my wrists then remained still as he stepped back out of my reach. He didn't untie my feet, but had no objection when I bent down to do it. The knot was tight and I broke half of my fingernails in the attempt, but I finally got them off. My god, such relief!

"Did you learn to tie knots like that in the army?" I rubbed the raw skin at my ankles then set the rope in my lap.

"I did, as it happens. How much do you know about me, Miss Holloway?"

"Very little. I know you're experimenting on dying men, then testing their bodies after their deaths. I just don't know to what purpose. Or why you've kidnapped me."

"I've kidnapped you because you'll make my experiments so much easier. You can raise the dead, and I wish to speak to the dead. It will solve a host of difficulties I've encountered."

I shook my head. "I don't understand."

"That night at Mr. Lee's establishment, you opened my eyes to a new way of gathering information from my test subjects."

Subjects? Was that what he thought of the men who died after he fed them that liquid?

"I wasn't aware of people like you until then," he went on. "I didn't know it was possible to raise the dead. It wasn't until I got home that I began to consider the applications of your... gift. It could change the way I work and will certainly save a lot of time and effort."

"What work, Captain? What are you doing to those poor men? Killing them?"

"No! Good lord, I'm no murderer. No, I wanted to *save* them."

"That doesn't make sense. Save them how?"

"They were going to die anyway, Miss Holloway. When I found them, they were already close to death. I didn't hurry the process along, I simply watched them as they deteriorated and grew closer to the end."

"Then what was the liquid you fed them?"

"That was supposed to save them. Well, not save them as such, but bring them back to life."

My stomach rolled. Another mad doctor obsessed with bringing back the dead. Why couldn't they leave them be? "The dead don't want to be brought back to life, Captain."

He scoffed. "Of course they do." He pushed his glasses up his nose. "No one wishes to die. I'm trying to develop a serum that brings the dead to life again."

"Is that what you fed them? That liquid was the serum?"

He nodded. "It must be administered *before* death."

"And the blood in the syringe?"

"I extract samples for testing. I need to record the changes to the subjects both before and after death. That's why I kept those four bodies in the butcher's cold room."

"You were testing them too."

He nodded. "I took samples from them periodically to monitor changes to their muscle mass and vital organs. I couldn't bring them back to life yet, but they helped me fine tune the serum."

"And how close are you to developing it?"

He sighed and pushed off from the desk. "Not as close as I would like. It would help if I could speak to the subjects about the changes they experience. That's where you come in." He smiled at me. "You'll raise them for me and I'll interview them and perform tests. We'll start today. Bertram Purley will be buried this morning. It's best to start with a fresh corpse."

I willed him to turn around, to take his eyes off me for a moment. But he did not. "Were you experimenting with this serum in the army?" Keeping him talking was all I could do for now, but biding my time grated on my nerves. I just wanted to get out and go home.

He smiled. "It's where I developed and nurtured the idea."

"Until your superiors discovered what you were doing."

He pushed his glasses up his nose again. "On the contrary. They were quite happy for me to continue. They encouraged me. The application of such a serum has enormous benefit for the army, naturally. Ordinarily, when a soldier dies on the battlefield it means they are a man down. But if he can rise again..." His face lit up, his eyes bright in the lamplight. "It would make the British army a strong force, impossible to defeat."

It certainly would. "None of your superiors objected? How many knew?"

"Only two. But the secret got out." He sighed. "Others learned of it and they didn't see the benefits. The very thought sickened them." His mouth twisted into a mocking smile. "Some people are closed minded, and nothing can convince them of the wonderful possibilities that science and medicine can offer the world. I was dismissed from the army, but I continued my work here, in this office—and at Mr. Lee's and the butcher's too, of course."

"Did you hide the bodies in the cool room to slow down their decay?"

"Very clever, Miss Holloway. That was the intention, but it wasn't cold enough for my purposes. I need to learn what happens to them much, much faster. That's where you come in." The light in his eyes flared again. "Miss Holloway, I haven't been this excited in years. My mind is running wild with possibilities. Perhaps I can study you too, one day."

My chest constricted and my stomach rolled.

"Do you think your master will present a problem?" he asked.

He thought I was going to help him? Just like that? I

opened my mouth to tell him he was wrong, but shut it again. Playing my hand too early would work against me. *Wait, Charlie. Just wait.*

"He might," I said carefully.

"Then you should hand in your notice. I'll rent accommodation for you nearby."

"Where are we?"

"Savile Row."

"That's a nice area. Can you afford to keep me?"

He smiled. "I have funds. My work hasn't been abandoned by everyone. Some still see the benefits."

"Who?" I blurted out.

He shrugged. "Anonymous benefactors." He laughed. "Isn't that always the way?" He grasped my hand and patted it. "You won't regret this, Miss Holloway. I'll pay you a wage too, of course; much better than you're paid as a maid. I trust our arrangement will be to your benefit as well as mine."

I withdrew my hand and forced a smile to my face. "Thank you. You've answered all my questions. Oh, one more. Those two men who work for you..." I effected a shudder. "They frighten me."

"They frighten you?" He laughed again. "My dear Miss Holloway, *you* frighten *them*. Particularly Jimmy. He's terrified you'll set a ghost onto him."

I laughed too. "Shall I assure him that I won't as long as he doesn't hurt me?" I touched my cheek. "Is he just outside?"

"He is, but he's asleep. Let him rest a while longer." He glanced at the window where the birds had begun to wake up and chirp for their breakfast. "It's still early."

"How did you know where to find me last night? From Mr. Lee?" I thought about the boy who'd benefited from Seth's coat and gloves. It saddened me to think he would betray me to this man, but it was understandable. I would have done the same thing when I'd lived in the gutter and a little money meant the difference between living and starving to death.

"One of the groundsmen from Highgate Cemetery, as it happens. Chap with an ugly birthmark on his face. I asked him who had been to Thackery's grave, and he described you. He said you lived in the big house with the iron gates at Hampstead Heath."

I gasped. "How did he know that?"

Jasper shrugged. "Perhaps he followed you home after one of your visits to the cemetery. He said you go frequently."

My fingers tightened around the rope. Had the groundskeeper followed me of his own volition, or on someone else's behalf? Both options filled me with horror. I shuddered again.

"Are you cold?" Jasper asked.

"Yes. Can you build up the fire?"

"Of course. Wait here." He smiled sheepishly. "We removed the fire tools when we brought you in here. Couldn't have you using them as weapons, could we? I am sorry for the harsh treatment, Miss Holloway. We couldn't be certain how you would react when you awoke." He nodded at my cheek. "I'll take a look at that after I see to the fire." He gave me another warm smile, and I almost felt guilty for what I was about to do.

Then I felt the tender bruise on my cheek. I was *not* going to feel guilty for a single thing.

Jasper left the room and returned a moment later with fire irons and coal box. He was still smiling. I smiled back and poked my head out the door.

"He's still asleep," he whispered to me. "Shut the door."

I shut it and couldn't believe the man's naivety. Did he really believe I would just help him? I supposed he thought I was simply Lincoln's employee, easily bought like any other servant.

He knelt by the fire and opened the lid of the coal box.

"It will be nice to be appreciated for what I can do," I said cheerfully as I came up behind him. "And adequately compensated for it too."

"You're not appreciated where you are now, are you?" He scooped out some coal and shoveled it into the grate. "No one ever notices maids. I sympathize, Miss Holloway. No one ever notices the medics on the battlefield, either. It's all about the soldiers and officers. We're expendable but they're not."

I tightened my grip on the rope in both hands and quickly looped it around his neck. I pulled back hard, dragging him against my legs.

Jasper grappled at the rope but I held it so tight that his fingers couldn't get underneath it. He thrashed and tried to call out, but I'd shut off his wind pipe. His face turned red, then purple. His eyes bulged, as he peered up at me, his lips moving in a silent plea.

It was horrible.

I released the rope, but before he could recover, I brought my elbow down on his temple. The blow knocked him out.

I picked up the fire iron and opened the office door. Jimmy's snore was the only sound coming from the reception room. He sat sprawled in a chair, his feet on the desk, his head tipped back and his mouth open. I crept past him to the door that led to the street, but it was locked.

Blast! I searched for a key nearby, but found none. It must be in a drawer or on either Jasper or Jimmy's person.

I couldn't believe I'd got this far only to stumble at the last hurdle. I quietly opened the top drawer of the reception desk, but it mustn't have been quiet enough. Jimmy snorted and woke up. I froze.

"Oi! What're you doing?" He lunged at me, but I jabbed the fire poker into his stomach, not hard, but enough to keep him at bay and make him think I would run it through him if pressed.

"Where's the key to the front door?"

Jasper groaned from the next room. Jimmy glanced toward him, and swallowed heavily "Captain! Captain! You there?"

"He's dead," I told him. "That's the sound of his spirit waking up inside his body."

He licked dry lips. "You're pullin' me leg."

"Am I? Just wait a moment and we'll see, shall we? It takes spirits time to become aware again, but once they are, they're under my control. I'll get him to show you how strong he is now that he's dead." I smiled, injecting it with as much wickedness as I could muster. *Please believe me, you stupid blighter.*

"Don't," he said, licking his lips again. "Don't let him out here. I don't want no trouble."

"Give me the key so I can leave."

Jasper groaned again and called out something unintelligible.

Jimmy crossed himself with a trembling hand. "Take him with you!"

"I have to get out to do that."

"Second drawer." He nodded at the desk.

"You get it, then unlock the door."

I stepped aside and he jerked the second drawer open. The key sat on top of some paperwork. He fished it out and dashed to the door. He fumbled once but managed to insert the key in the lock. I glanced back at the office. I could hear Jasper recovering. If he managed to come out and convince Jimmy that he was alive, I wouldn't stand a chance.

"Hurry!" I whispered.

Jimmy finally unlocked the door and wrenched it open. We jostled to be the first out, and burst through together. I ran one way and he another.

I kept the fire iron with me and fled down lanes and streets that were both familiar and not until I felt I was far enough from the office that I wouldn't be traced.

I slowed to catch my breath and take note of my location. The cold air made my cheek ache even more. Pain shot up from my left foot too and blood dripped onto the pavement. I'd cut it on something sharp.

I held the fire iron tighter and limped out of the lane. I knew this spot. It was near one of my favorite places to relieve gentlemen of their wallets. I was far from Lichfield, but at least I knew the way. I walked on, but the pain in my foot grew worse. The bleeding seemed to have stopped, at least, but I couldn't put all my weight on it. I'd grown soft since moving into Lichfield. I used to be able to walk barefoot for miles in the cold and not feel this wretched.

Few people were awake at such an early hour. Some delivery boys eyed me up and down, and one made a lewd comment about my state, but no one offered me help. I didn't care. I would be home soon.

Home, at Lichfield, with a warm bath and bed waiting for me, and friends to bandage my foot and see to my cheek. Friends who cared for me, not because I was a necromancer, but because they liked me.

Lincoln was among them. At least, I hoped he still considered me a friend. Somehow, that didn't matter as much as being welcomed back. We could rebuild our friendship in time *if* I were to remain at Lichfield.

It took me twice as long to reach Highgate as it would have without a limp. The traffic going in the opposite direction thickened as bank clerks and office workers headed into the city. Several gentlemen asked if I needed assistance, but I politely refused and limped on. It felt like I'd been walking all day, but it had probably only been two hours since setting out from Savile Row.

I finally reached the Lichfield gate and paused at the spot where Jasper had kidnapped me. I drew in a shuddery breath and congratulated myself on getting free and reaching safety.

The pounding of horses' hooves sent my heart racing again. The large beast bore down on me, but I recognized it and didn't try to get out of the way. I suddenly couldn't, anyway. My feet were too sore and my legs felt like lead. Everything ached, from my head to my toes.

The horse pulled to a stop and the rider slid down to land noiselessly on the road. Lincoln stared at me with eyes that were so familiar and yet not at the same time. They swirled with emotion—or was it my vision that swirled?

I could no longer hold myself together. It felt as if every piece of me was unraveling, peeling away, leaving me exposed and vulnerable. I hated that he saw me looking so pathetic, but I couldn't stop my tears. They poured out of me. I dropped the fire iron and covered my face with my hands.

Strong arms cocooned me and pressed me gently against his chest, where I could hear in his erratic heartbeat how worried he'd been.

CHAPTER 16

*L*incoln massaged my neck with one hand, and splayed the fingers of the other across my back. I stayed locked in his arms until my tears dried and his breathing returned to its normal rhythm. I was acutely aware that he hadn't spoken, but his embrace said more than words ever could. He wasn't throwing me out. He *did* care.

His horse moved and the hand at my neck let go to catch the reins. The *clip clop* of hooves on the road grew louder and I looked up.

"Charlie?" Seth jumped down before his horse had come to a complete stop. He beamed at me and opened his arms.

Lincoln let me go and stood aside while Seth scooped me up, lifting me off my feet.

"Bloody hell!" he murmured in my ear. "We were so worried about you."

"Have you both been out looking for me?"

"All night. Gus too. Cook wanted to join us, but someone had to stay here in case you returned." He set me down again and I winced.

Lincoln crouched at my side. He removed his riding gloves and skimmed his hand over the frayed patch of my stockings where the rope had bitten into my ankles. He gently lifted my foot the way one would a horse's hoof. I placed a hand on his shoulder to steady myself, and felt him slump as he peeled away the shredded, bloody mess of my stocking at the sole.

Seth sucked in a breath between his teeth. "Jesus, Charlie. How far have you walked like that?"

"From Savile Row. Captain Jasper has rooms at number nineteen."

"You went to see him? On your own?"

I shook my head. "I went for a walk last night and he abducted me. He had Jimmy and Pete with him. It happened right here on this spot. He wanted to use my necromancy to complete his experiments. You were right," I told Lincoln. "He was expelled from the army for misconduct. He was testing a serum on near-dead men. It was supposed to bring them back to life, but it doesn't work yet."

"Bloody hell." Seth shook his head and glanced at Lincoln as he rose. "Will we ride to Savile Row now, sir? Want me to get the pistols first? Knives would be better. Something that can be attributed to a burglar."

He meant to kill Jasper? Bile rose to my throat. I didn't know why I found the thought abhorrent. Jasper had abducted me, and he didn't deserve mercy. Yet he wasn't a bad man. Strange, yes, and deluded, but not a monster.

I wobbled on my good foot and Lincoln caught me around the waist. Before I knew what was happening, he'd picked me up and planted me in the saddle.

"Ride to the police station," he ordered Seth. "Give them a brief account of the abduction, no more. Have Jasper and his men arrested."

Seth blinked twice, then nodded. "Yes, sir." He mounted and rode off.

"It means the police will come to question you," Lincoln said to me.

"I know."

"You won't have to answer any questions until you feel

ready." He walked the horse along the drive, his gaze straight ahead.

"Lincoln," I said softly.

"Yes?"

"Seth seemed to think that I'd left of my own accord. Is that what you believed too?"

"It seemed the most likely scenario, considering the tension between us lately and that you asked me for a reference just before your disappearance. A reference I refused to give."

"I wouldn't have left without saying goodbye."

"Not...not even after the way I treated you?"

I touched his shoulder and he finally glanced my way. He scanned my face and I smiled gently to reassure him. "You treated me far better than I deserved. I would have thrown me out, if I were you."

"I doubt that." He turned away and we walked on in silence. We were just rounding the side of the house when he spoke again. "They blamed me for your departure." His hand stroked the horse near my leg. "I blamed myself," he added quietly.

I reached out to touch his hair, but drew my hand back when Cook burst upon us from the courtyard.

"Charlie! You came home!" He grinned but it faltered when he saw the state of my feet and cheek. "You had an adventure on your own, eh?"

"Something like that."

"You be making a habit of it. A bad habit," he added with a scowl. "Don't do it again."

I saluted him. "I'll be sure to tell my next kidnappers that you don't approve."

"Kidnappers!"

Lincoln helped me down then once I was steady, let me go. "Take her inside," he said. "Cook her whatever she wants." To me he added, "I'll run you a bath when I come in. Your wounds need cleaning and dressing."

"You don't have to," I said. "I can do it myself."

He walked the horse to the stables without responding and I allowed Cook to help me into the house. I gave him the brief version of what happened as he stood by the stove stirring something that smelled delicious. He didn't complain once about his bandaged thumb.

Gus arrived along with Lincoln, and the brawny fellow drew me into a hug that left me gasping for air. I repeated my story for them both, going into more depth about Jasper's motives for the abduction and how he'd found me. While Cook and Gus inserted their own comments, gasps and growls, Lincoln remained silent. He didn't move a muscle as he stood by the door, his arms crossed and his half-closed eyelids veiling his gaze.

When I'd finished, he suddenly turned.

"Where are you going?" I called out.

"Bathroom."

Cook placed bacon, eggs and soup in front of me all at once. The delicious smells drew my focus away from the door, but not from Lincoln. He'd sounded...odd, like that single word had been torn from his throat.

"Eat," Cook ordered.

"All of it?"

"Every last mouthful."

By the time I finished, Lincoln had returned. "The bath is ready. Can you walk?"

"I'll try." I got to my feet, but the cut one stung awfully, and the other had developed blisters from taking most of my weight on the walk home. "It's not too bad," I lied.

"You can't get all the way up there on your own," Gus protested. He glanced at Lincoln, but Lincoln remained unmoved by the door. With a shake of his head, Gus picked me up. "I'll do it myself," he muttered.

But Lincoln stepped in front of him and held out his arms. Gus handed me over. I felt like a sack of potatoes until Lincoln cradled me close to his body. I could feel his strong heartbeat through his shirt and waistcoat and smell the scents of horse and leather on his skin. I drew in a deep breath and placed my arms around his neck.

He carried me up the stairs, his face in profile as he stared straight ahead. He deposited me in the bathroom then left without a word. I peeled off my clothes and stepped into the bath. The warm water stung my feet at first, but I soon got used to it. I lay there without moving for a long time, thinking about what might have happened if I hadn't been able to get away. Would Lincoln have found me? How long would he have searched? If he thought I'd left of my own volition he might have given up after only a cursory attempt.

The water rippled with my shudder. It didn't bear thinking about. I was home safely, and Jasper would be in jail soon, if he wasn't already.

I cleaned my feet, ensuring the cuts were free of grit, then climbed out of the tub. I dried off but realized I had no clean clothes with me. I wrapped the towel around my body and opened the door.

Lincoln looked up from where he was leaning against the wall opposite and a little down from the bathroom. His gaze heated as it settled on my bare shoulders then moved down to my legs.

"I need clean clothes," I told him as a blush crept up my throat.

His gaze flicked to mine then he quickly turned, presenting me with his back. But not before I saw something I'd never seen before on his face. He looked confused, like he didn't know what to do or say.

I hobbled to my room and quickly dressed before making my way outside again. I didn't get far. Lincoln stood in the corridor, the medical bag in hand. Seth, Gus and Cook stood behind him. When he didn't move, Seth and Gus edged around him. They stood on either side of me, looped their arms behind my back, and carried me to the armchair.

"Sit down," Seth ordered.

I sat, and Lincoln crouched on the floor in front of me. He gently took my foot in his hands and inspected it.

"Did the police arrest Jasper?" I asked Seth.

He nodded and sat on another chair. "He was still in his rooms, dazed from a blow to the head. He sported a rope burn around his throat too, similar to your wrists and ankles. Know anything about that, Charlie?" he asked with a lopsided grin.

"I may. Was he really that dazed?"

"He was. Had a bruise here too." He tapped his temple. "That's quite a punch you must have delivered."

"It was my elbow."

"Ah. Good girl. Elbows are stronger than fists. Clever thinking."

"I wasn't really thinking at all. Not then, and not earlier when I managed to hit Pete. It was instinct."

"Thanks to all that training," Gus said with a decisive nod.

"It be paying off," Cook added.

"Yes." I smiled down at Lincoln, but he wasn't looking at me. "I hope we can resume as soon as possible."

"We can modify training until you're healed," Seth said. "Perhaps some weapons training while you have to stay off your feet."

"Knife throwing," Cook said. "I can show you how from sitting."

"Guns too." Gus rubbed his hands together and blew on the fingers. "I know someone who'll sell me a little muff pistol at a good price."

Seth smacked Gus's shoulder. "The price doesn't matter." He nodded at Lincoln who was now bandaging my foot.

"We can set up targets out back." Cook ran his hand over his shiny head. "One point if she hit a biscuit tin and two for a tea tin."

"If you turn the biscuit tins on their side, they present a narrower target." Seth rubbed his jaw. He hadn't yet shaved, and the pale bristles leant his face a ruggedness it was otherwise missing. "I propose five points for a small tea tin, three points for a biscuit tin on its side and 1 point for when its presented front on."

"You got something smaller than tea?" Gus asked Cook. "We could make that ten points."

Cook nodded thoughtfully. "Tobacco tins be small."

"None of you smoke," I said, laughing.

That didn't seem to concern them. They continued to discuss the best tins for target practice, and how many points each should be worth. They had quite a system arranged by the time Lincoln finished bandaging my foot.

"There are a set of crutches in the attic," he said, rising. "Gus, go fetch them."

Gus obeyed without complaint, and Cook headed out too in search of tins. Seth yawned and sprawled in the chair.

"You've been up all night," I said. "Go get some rest."

"So have you," he said. "*You* should rest."

"I slept most of the night away. I might have been unconscious, but either way I don't feel tired."

"Jesus, Charlie. You were unconscious? We should get a real doctor in to look at her," he said to Lincoln.

"I feel fine," I told them both.

Lincoln nodded at Seth, and Seth rose. "I'll fetch one now."

I sighed as he left. "I feel perfectly all right." I wiggled my foot as best as I could. "Thank you. It doesn't hurt nearly so much."

"Then why did you wince and tense every time I touched it?" Lincoln asked.

"I didn't think you noticed."

"I noticed."

"I suppose you notice everything." I bit my lip, aware of how that sounded. "I...I don't mean your instincts, your gift, I meant—"

He placed a hand to the side of my face. I was so shocked that I stopped talking. "I know what you meant." His thumb stroked my cheek before he lowered his hand and stood.

"Lincoln—Mr. Fitzroy—I need to get something off my chest."

He glanced at the door. Was he looking for an escape route or to see if anyone was nearby? He sat. "Go on."

I clutched the arms of the chair to anchor myself and sucked in a deep breath. "You had every right to be angry with me—"

"That matter is over. We won't speak of it anymore."

"We have to, or things will never be right between us."

"You're wrong. What's between us...it's not that. I don't want you to trouble yourself over it anymore, Charlie. It's not your fault."

I clicked my tongue and stretched my fingers then forced them to be still in my lap. "Let me explain. You don't know all of it." I waited and he nodded at me to go on. "A few days ago, after visiting the orphanages on the other side of the river, I stopped at the General Registry Office. I thought there might be a record of my birth, with Frankenstein listed as the father. I doubted it, but decided that since I was near, I might as well try my luck. While I was there, I realized I could also ask them to check for any records of your birth." I looked down at my fingers, twisted into knots in my lap. "I'm sorry," I whispered. "It was a decision made in a moment, and I regretted it immediately. But I couldn't call the fellow back, so I resolved not to ask him for the information when he returned. Unfortunately, he gave it to me before I could stop him."

"And what did you find out?"

"Nothing. There were no records under your name."

"And about yourself?"

I looked up at him and shrugged. "Also nothing."

"So it was a wasted effort and you tripped the trigger the ministry has placed on my name there."

I gawped at him. "What trigger?"

"The ministry has triggers set up on certain official files, not only within the General Registry Office but in other government offices too. When someone asks to look at them, a particular member of the committee, or myself, is notified. The General Registry Office trigger is set to alert Lady Harcourt. You're fortunate it wasn't Lord Gillingham."

"I don't feel particularly fortunate."

"I imagine not."

As always it was difficult to tell with Lincoln, but he didn't sound angry with me. Perhaps he was too happy to have me back and would never be angry with me again. A girl could hope, couldn't she?

"At least I now know how she convinced you to go through with it," he said.

"You were furious with me when you learned I'd summoned Gurry. Why aren't you angry over this?"

"I wasn't furious. You told me yourself that your investigation at the General Registry Office was hastily decided upon and you regretted it. The summoning was more planned, deliberate. I thought you and Julia had concocted it together. I should have considered the possibility that she'd blackmailed you," he bit off. "It seems so obvious now, but at the time... It was a bad error on my part, and I'm sorry."

"You have nothing to apologize for. You couldn't have known, and it's not entirely Lady Harcourt's fault. I could have refused, but the truth is that I wanted to know why you killed Gurry too."

"Did she ask you the night before?

I nodded.

"I wondered why she came. It seemed odd that she would collect me."

"She was also worried you would change your mind and not go to the ball."

"Was she?" he ground out. He shook his head. "We won't speak of this anymore, Charlie. It's done now."

"It's not. I wish to clear the air."

"It's cleared."

"It's not! Lincoln, you need to know how awful I felt summoning Gurry's spirit. I felt sick. And then when you interrupted us in a fury...I thought you would murder someone."

He flinched. Perhaps that had been a poor choice of words. "I wasn't angry with *you*, Charlie." He rubbed his temple then dug his fingers into his eyes. "I was disappointed. I probably didn't express it very well."

Here was the crux of it. *This* was what I needed to know, although hearing him speak of his disappointment in me was like a blow to the stomach. "You were disappointed because you thought you could trust me," I finished for him.

His hand dropped to the chair arm and he gave a slight nod.

"Lincoln, you *can* trust me." I leaned forward, hoping that would get my point across better. "I won't betray you again. I promise."

He said nothing, just stared down at his hand.

"Lincoln?" I said in a small voice. "I have to know...can you bring yourself to trust me again?"

"I already do."

My lip wobbled. I bit it hard.

"But trust goes both ways," he went on. "And clearly you don't trust me or you would have told me what Julia had threatened to do."

"I almost did. That's why I waited up for you to return from the ball. But you were in a foul temper and I changed my mind."

The muscles around his eyes tightened in another flinch. "Then I deserved what happened. Don't excuse my behavior," he said when I opened my mouth to protest. "That entire evening is one I'd rather forget. I *was* in a foul temper, and unfortunately you were in the firing line at the wrong time. I'm sorry I said the things I did. It was uncalled for."

"Thank you. I forgive you. So...your family wasn't there?"

"One member was, but he knows nothing about my existence. I'm not worthy of his notice, so consequently, he didn't notice me. I don't know why I expected him to."

I bit back my sympathetic response and instead said, "Even though I didn't tell you in advance about Lady Harcourt's request, I want you to know that I do trust you, Lincoln."

His gaze lifted to mine. "Do you? I've betrayed you just as badly in the past."

"That incident was months ago," I said, waving my hand. "I'd already forgotten it." He was referring to the time he'd let me go then set a brute onto me to scare me into staying at Lichfield. It was sometimes difficult to reconcile that incident and the man who'd instigated it with the Lincoln Fitzroy sitting before me.

"No, you haven't," he said quietly. "You still have night-mares about it."

He knew that? "Not only about that man," I assured him. "The nightmares have lessened now, anyway." I shrugged and folded my arms across my chest.

"I was desperate then, Charlie. I didn't know how else to get you to stay. Another man would have known, but not me."

Desperate? For me to stay? Oh. I swallowed and nodded to let him know that I understood. I was too shaken by his honesty to speak. It meant a lot that he would confide in me like this.

"I want you to trust me," he said. "So I'm going to tell you about Gurry."

My eyes widened. "You don't have to."

"I want to. I want you to feel safe here, and that means allaying any fears about me you might still have."

I was about to tell him that I didn't have any fears, but I didn't want him to change his mind and not confide in me so I remained quiet.

"I was eleven when he came to tutor me. We didn't get along particularly well, but that wasn't unusual. My tutors were there to teach me in any way they saw fit."

How could any child learn anything while being beaten? Or fearing a beating?

"When I was twelve, things changed in the general's household. The housekeeper's nephew came to live with us. His parents had died, and he had no one else. He was two years younger than me, but we became friends, of sorts. I'd never had a friend before, never been around other children, so I wasn't easy to get along with. But we did, after a while. The problem was, I was busy with my studies and had little time for him."

"What about after lessons?"

"I studied every day from six in the morning until eight at night for day classes, then the night lessons would begin on those evenings I had them."

"Night classes? What could you possibly learn at night?"

"How to find my way around London in the dark. How to get in through a locked window without waking anyone. How to move about the clubs and dens without being noticed. Among other things."

That was quite an unusual education. I wished I'd had those sorts of lessons. Living on the streets might have been easier at first if I had. "The less I saw of Tim, the harder he tried to get my attention. He was bored and lonely in that house with nothing to do but a few chores. So he would amuse himself by tapping on the windows until my tutors came looking for him, then he'd run off. Or he would place tacks on their chairs, or break their pens and inkwells. He was mischievous, but he did it to get me to laugh."

"He never got caught?"

"Frequently. The tutors would beat him, but never severely. The housekeeper wouldn't let them."

"Did the general know what they were doing to him? And to you?"

He nodded. "It was in the reports they gave him upon his infrequent returns to the city. They'd detail what I'd learned, how well I was doing, how much they needed to discipline me *et cetera*."

"And he didn't try to stop them beating you? Or Tim?"

"The general believes in strong discipline. The more wayward the boy, the harder the beatings should be."

I covered my mouth. "Oh, Lincoln."

He flinched and I bit my lip. It wasn't pity he wanted, it was understanding.

"That's why he liked Gurry so much. His beatings were the hardest. Several months after Tim came to live with us, he took his fun too far. He'd made himself a slingshot and hid outside the window. We'd planned for me to open it during my lesson with Gurry and Tim would fire things at him. I followed through on the plan, and Tim shot a series of small objects at Gurry. Gurry batted some away, but Tim was fast and the rapid fire overwhelmed Gurry. He accidentally swallowed one of the pellets and almost choked. When he recovered, he went looking for Tim. It took all afternoon to find him and catch him, but when he did, he beat him with a cane. Tim was defiant, and refused to apologize. He told Gurry that the object he'd swallowed was a ball of dried horse dung. Gurry was a stickler for hygiene and had a fear of germs. He almost had an apoplexy when Tim told him that. It set him off even more. He beat Tim harder and harder, on his back, his shoulders, and around his head. Gurry went into a frenzy. I tried to pull him off but couldn't. The housekeeper started screaming, but he seemed not to hear her. He kept hitting Tim, even after he collapsed. He was bleeding from the nose and ears, but still Gurry didn't stop. It seemed to go on forever. Finally, he calmed down, but only when Tim was no longer moving."

"Oh God," I whispered into my hand. "He killed Tim. He beat him to death."

"The housekeeper wrote to the general, and the general dismissed Gurry. I never saw him again until almost a year ago in that lane. It all suddenly came back to me, and I couldn't put aside my anger. I'd let Tim down all those years ago. I hadn't been able to save him, but I finally had a chance to see justice served. So I killed Gurry then and there."

I stared at him, stunned by the story and the image of that poor boy at the mercy of Gurry. And poor Lincoln too, living with the memories for so many years. He'd had one friend in his entire life, and that friend had died because he'd been a distraction to Lincoln's studies. It was a lot to bear.

"You didn't fail Tim," I assured him. "You were only a boy

too, when it happened. Don't blame yourself for something only Gurry is responsible for."

He glanced at me, a small crease connecting his brows. "And of my actions in the lane? I was an adult then. I knew what I was doing, and I chose to do it anyway."

I couldn't meet his gaze. While I understood why he'd done it, it still unnerved me to think he could hold onto his revenge for so long then act upon it in a cold, calculating manner. "Was his death swift?"

"Yes."

"Then that's something."

His brows arched.

"I don't blame you, Lincoln. I know the man you are...the man you're trained to be...and I accept that side of you. But it is only one facet of you. There are many others, and together they make up someone I like. Someone I want to get to know better."

I stood to go to him, but he shot to his feet at the same time. He swallowed heavily and placed his hands at his back. He gave me a firm nod, then turned and walked out. Just like that.

I stood there, blinking at the doorway, debating whether to go after him or not. I might have trouble catching him, bandaged up as I was.

"Charlie!" Gus scowled when he saw me standing. "You were supposed to wait until I brought you these." He handed me the crutches. When I continued to stare dumbly at the doorway, he took my hand and placed it on the horizontal bar. "Let me adjust the height for you."

* * *

I SPENT most of the day in the library, reading. The men disappeared at different times to nap, then would return to keep me company. The only one who didn't was Lincoln, and I missed his company terribly. I sent Seth up to his rooms to ask him to join us for a game of cards, but he still didn't come down.

"What's he doing?" I asked.

"Pacing."

"Pacing?"

He nodded as he dealt. "Stop worrying about him, Charlie. He knows his own mind."

He did, and that was partly the problem. His mind was always working, always remembering. What was he thinking now? I would have thought telling me about Gurry would be a weight off his shoulders, but it seemed to have made him more agitated. I was contemplating venturing upstairs to see him when he strode into the library dressed in coat and hat. He handed some letters to Gus.

"Deliver these to the committee members tonight. They're messages informing them of what transpired with Captain Jasper. They'll want to know the outcome, even though it wasn't a ministry matter."

"Can I have a game first?" Gus asked.

Lincoln nodded then walked off without another word, and without even glancing at me.

"Where are you going?" I called after him.

"For a walk." The front door opened and closed.

Gus tapped the cards in front of me. "He'll be all right. He won't get himself kidnapped."

Seth rolled his eyes. "You say the stupidest things sometimes."

"That right? I happen to know stupidest ain't a word."

"Neither is ain't." Seth threw down a card. "Stop dandying about and have your turn."

* * *

GENERAL EASTBROOKE ARRIVED LATE the following morning. I was ensconced in the library once more and heard his arrival.

Lincoln answered the door. It was the first time I'd seen him all day, and I hadn't heard him come home the night before.

They came into the library and the general greeted me with a thin smile. "You're in one piece," he said. "That's the main thing."

I suspected that was all the sympathy I would get. I expected nothing else from a man who allowed his employees to beat children.

"I was going to send this last night when I received your message." He handed Lincoln a piece of paper. "It's a list of disgraced doctors dismissed from the military in the last ten years. Jasper is there." He pointed to the paper. "Unfortunately, I didn't get this in time for it to be of use."

Lincoln folded it and handed it back.

The general pocketed it. "According to his file, he was dismissed for keeping the dead bodies of some of the soldiers and performing tests on them."

I pulled a face. "He'd given them his serum before their deaths and needed to test its effects afterward to see how it performed."

"That what he told you, eh? Sounds like a madman to me."

"He was."

"Lincoln mentioned Jasper wanted to use you to help him."

I nodded. "Hence the kidnapping."

"Well. Glad you got away. How did you manage it?"

"With an elbow to his temple and a little trickery to scare his man."

His grunt held more than a hint of admiration. "Well done. I expect you'll be recovered in no time. Who'll keep house for you until she does?" he asked Lincoln as he walked out of the library again.

"No one," Lincoln said, following. "I don't need anyone else."

He didn't return after the general left. The others came and went, but not Lincoln. Not until Lady Harcourt arrived to see me at around lunch time. At least, I heard her tell him she'd come to see me, but she spoke a long time with him in the entrance hall. I caught most of their exchange since she did all the talking in a shrill voice.

"I don't know where he's gone, and nor does his brother," she said. They were talking about Andrew Buchanan, her stepson. "He left without a word, and he's taken nothing with him. He's gone, Lincoln, and I'm terribly worried."

"He's a grown man. He can fend for himself."

"That's the thing! He can't. He's hopeless. He lurches from one crisis to the next and needs either me or his brother to get him out of them. I'm concerned that he's in over his head."

"Are you?" he drawled. "That's unlike you, Julia, particularly where Andrew is concerned."

I wished I could see her face; it was a long time before she spoke. "I found books on the occult in his rooms. Charms and amulets too."

"You think he's dabbling with forces he doesn't understand?"

"I do." Her voice sounded more like her usual confident one. "I'm going to raise this as a ministry matter since it involves the supernatural."

"We don't know that for sure."

"This is just a courtesy call to you to give you warning," she said.

"I don't need advanced warning."

"Oh, Lincoln, I also came because I *had* to see you."

I pulled myself out of the chair and used my crutches to get to the door and peer round it. She was leaning against Lincoln, her head on his shoulder. He gingerly patted her back as if worried he'd make it worse if he patted too hard.

"I wanted to tell you how sorry I am," she said. "If I'd known how upset you would be over summoning Gurry, I wouldn't have let her do it."

Let me do it! I gritted my teeth and tightened my grip on the crutches to storm out and challenge her, but Lincoln's hand suddenly came up at his side in a "wait" gesture. He knew I was there, listening.

"Don't trouble yourself, Julia," he said. "The matter is closed. We'll speak no more of it." He grasped her shoulders and pushed her gently away.

She dabbed at the corners of her eyes with her gloved finger. "But...I need to know why you killed him. Why not just tell me?"

"Because the people who need to know already know. You do not."

"Lincoln! How can you say that? As your friend, I'm worried about you." When he said nothing, she splayed her hands on his chest. Her eyelids lowered and she tilted her face up to his. "As your lover, I have a—"

"Don't!" He grabbed her wrists before stepping away and letting go.

She blinked back at him, but I was too far to see if her eyes were teary. Her hand fluttered at the black ribbon choker at her throat. "Lincoln?" Her pitiful whisper barely reached me.

"Thank you for stopping by," he said, striding past her to the door.

She straightened her shoulders and her chin rose. I'd begun to feel sorry for her, so I was pleased to see her strength of character return. I did *not* want to sympathize with Lady Harcourt. "I came to see Charlie too. She's had quite an ordeal, and I want to see if she needs anything. Is she in her rooms?"

I shook my head at him, but he didn't lift his eyes and couldn't have seen. Even so, he told her I was not up to receiving callers. "As you said, she's had an ordeal. She needs rest."

"Very well. Tell her I'm thinking of her."

"I will."

She brushed past him and he shut the door before her carriage rolled away. He came over to me in the library doorway. "Apparently Lady Harcourt is thinking of you."

"You didn't tell her that you know she blackmailed me into summoning Gurry?"

He shook his head. "I can if you like."

"No. There's no need. I don't want things to be even more awkward between her and me."

"She's not your enemy, Charlie. She's...unhappy."

"I know. I don't think of her as an enemy, but I'm not sure we can be friends." I laughed at my own ridiculous statement. I was a maid and she a lady. There was no chance of friendship between us anyway. "Do you think there's any cause to worry about her stepson?"

"Possibly. I'll have to investigate now, anyway. She'll present it to the ministry in such a way that they'll feel compelled to find out where he went."

"It's not like we have anything better to do."

"We?"

I smiled. "Yes, we. Now, do you think luncheon will be far away? I'm starving."

* * *

WE RESUMED TRAINING AFTER LUNCH. All of us. Seth arranged a series of firearms on the kitchen table and he and Lincoln went through the particulars of each one while Cook and Gus set up targets outside and a chair for me to sit in. I'd only fired off three bullets, missing all of the tins each time, when a man approached from the side of the house. He wore checked trousers and a brown coat over a black waistcoat. He was a middle aged fellow with brown hair and a graying beard. A uniformed policeman trailed after him.

"Is one of you gentlemen Mr. Lincoln Fitzroy?" the man asked.

Lincoln stepped forward. "I am."

The newcomer introduced himself as Detective Inspector Darby. He didn't introduce his spotty faced constable. "Is this Miss Holloway?"

"Yes," I said with a smile. "You have some questions for me about the abduction?"

"I do, miss, but first, I must inform you that the fellow known as Captain Jasper is dead."

I gasped. Oh God. Had I killed him? "How...?"

"Throat was cut while he was in the cell."

Not me, thank God. Still, what an awful outcome.

"Blimey," Gus muttered. "A cove ain't safe anywhere these days."

"Sometimes those holding cells can get quite full," I said. "And when you put a group of criminals together..." I knew from experience how violent the holding cells could get.

"He was alone, miss," the inspector said.

"Then who killed him?"

"We don't know. It happened in the night. Whoever did it got in and out without anyone seeing him." The inspector shook his head. "It's a mystery."

Seth shifted his weight and I glanced up at him. But he wasn't looking at me. He was staring at Lincoln. Lincoln, however, wasn't looking at anyone. His gaze was fixed on a point on the horizon. His expression was unreadable, his body still.

"What of the two men who worked for him?" I asked. "Did you catch them?"

The inspector shook his head. "They disappeared. I had men stationed at places they frequented, but there'd been no sign of them until this morning. They turned up dead in the river."

"Both of them?" At his nod, I swallowed heavily. "Were their throats cut too?"

"They were. We have no reason to think their deaths are linked to your abduction, miss, but if you have any information that can help us, we'd be most grateful."

I shook my head. "No, nothing. I'm sorry."

"Mind if I ask you some questions about that night?"

"Of course."

They stayed for a mere fifteen minutes then went on their way. The inspector's questions were exactly the ones I expected; he didn't seem to think the deaths of Jasper, Jimmy and Pete had anything to do with us.

He was the only one who thought that.

Lincoln remained at my side while the inspector was there, but left to see him off and didn't return. I continued my target practice, but only for a few more minutes. It had been a lark before, but a dark cloud had descended over our little group and changed the mood.

I got up, and Gus offered to help me inside but I wanted to do it myself. Going up the staircase wasn't easy, and I dispensed with the crutches and hobbled the rest of the way to Lincoln's rooms. I knocked. He opened the door and didn't look at all surprised to see me there.

"You should use the crutches."

"May I come in?"

He hesitated and, if I wasn't mistaken, he was biting on the inside of his lip.

"Lincoln?" If he'd noticed that I'd dispensed with calling him Mr. Fitzroy lately, he didn't point it out.

He held out his hand to me. I took it and he directed me inside to a chair, but I didn't want to sit down. I suspected he would remain standing, and I didn't want to feel at a disadvantage. I leaned on the back of a chair for support and met his gaze. He was watching me.

"You think I did it," he said. "You think I killed them."

There were several things I could have said, but I chose the path that I hoped would encourage him to tell me more. "Why would you?"

"Revenge." His gaze traveled to my bruised cheek. "You know I'm capable of exacting it."

With those few words, he'd put me in the same category as he placed Tim—as a friend worthy of his vengeful form of justice. Despite everything, it was a relief to hear. It meant he truly had forgiven me for my betrayal. I gave him a wobbly smile, but he didn't seem to understand why I was smiling. He frowned.

"I'm mostly unharmed," I told him. "I hardly think what

happened to me warrants such drastic revenge." He said nothing, so I went on. "But you were agitated most of yesterday after we spoke, then you went out last night for a long time. Today, you've been distant. I don't think you killed them, but evidence points that way."

"I didn't."

My hand almost slipped off the chair in relief. If nothing else, it proved I'd harbored a kernel of doubt. "I believe you. So where did you go last night?"

"Nowhere. I walked around for a few hours then came back here."

I frowned. "Why were you just walking?"

"To clear my head and think."

"What were you thinking about?"

He drew in a deep breath, then another, and he stepped closer. He lifted a hand to my swollen cheek but didn't touch it. His eyes turned smoky, warm, and his face lowered. "About whether I should do this."

His mouth met mine. There was nothing tentative about the kiss. It was thorough, confident, yet as gentle as a first kiss ought to be. I'd not expected him to have soft lips. They were usually drawn into a hard, firm line, but now they felt like pillows. They were wonderful. *He* was wonderful. I knew the kiss didn't solve anything between us—if anything, it probably complicated things—but at that moment, I didn't care.

I let go of the chair, buried my hands in his hair, and kissed him back.

LOOK OUT FOR

Beyond The Grave
The third MINISTRY OF CURIOSITIES novel.

Charlie, Lincoln and the other Ministry of Curiosities
employees fight against villains both living and dead in the
search for Lady Harcourt's missing stepson, and in the
process, they uncover twisted family secrets and danger.

To be notified when C.J. has a new release, sign up to her
newsletter via her website:
http://cjarcher.com/contact-cj/newsletter/

GET A FREE SHORT STORY

I wrote a short story featuring Lincoln Fitzroy that is set before THE LAST NECROMANCER. Titled STRANGE HORIZONS, it reveals how he learned where to look for Charlie during a visit to Paris. While the story can be read as a standalone, it contains spoilers from The 1st Freak House Trilogy, so I advise you to read that series first. The best part is, the short story is FREE, but only to my newsletter subscribers. So subscribe now via my website if you haven't already.

ALSO BY C.J. ARCHER

SERIES WITH 2 OR MORE BOOKS

The Emily Chambers Spirit Medium Trilogy

The 1st Freak House Trilogy

The 2nd Freak House Trilogy

The 3rd Freak House Trilogy

The Ministry of Curiosities Series

The Assassins Guild Series

Lord Hawkesbury's Players Series

The Witchblade Chronicles

SINGLE TITLES NOT IN A SERIES

Courting His Countess

Surrender

Redemption

The Mercenary's Price

ABOUT THE AUTHOR

C.J. Archer has loved history and books for as long as she can remember and feels fortunate that she found a way to combine the two. She spent her early childhood in the dramatic beauty of outback Queensland, Australia, but now lives in suburban Melbourne with her husband, two children and a mischievous black & white cat named Coco.

Subscribe to C.J.'s newsletter through her website to be notified when she releases a new book, as well as get access to exclusive content. She loves to hear from readers. You can contact her in one of these ways:

Website: www.cjarcher.com
Email: cjarcher.writes@gmail.com
Facebook: www.facebook.com/CJArcherAuthorPage
Twitter: @cj_archer

Lightning Source UK Ltd.
Milton Keynes UK
UKOW01f1502150218
317952UK00002B/331/P